BEULAH LODGE

BELIAH LOOK

BEULAH LODGE

by
Cathy Dunnell

2021

BEULAH LODGE

ISBN 13: 978-1-63679-007-7

This Trade Paperback Original Is Published By
Bold Strokes Books, Inc.
P.O. Box 249
Valley Falls, NY 12185

First Edition: November 2021

CREDITS
Editor: Barbara Ann Wright
Production Design: Susan Ramundo
Cover Design By Jeanine Henning

Dedication

To my wife, for all her support and encouragement

CHAPTER ONE

The carriage jolted to a halt, and my eyes flew open. For a moment, I thought we had not moved, as the view from the window was exactly the same: rolling banks of featureless moorland under an iron-grey sky. Then the coachman knocked on the door and shouted, "This is Beulah Lodge."

I climbed awkwardly out of the carriage, my limbs stiff and heavy. The coachman gave me his hand as I stepped onto the road. Cold drizzle spattered against my face, and I pulled my cloak tighter about me. The light was beginning to fade, and the sky was low and heavy.

The coachman placed my trunk on the ground.

"Where is the house?" I asked, looking about me.

"Over yonder." He pointed to a track that led up a small hillock and disappeared from view.

I looked at him in dismay. "What about my trunk?"

"Someone from the house can fetch it." He was already hauling himself back up to his box and taking up the reins. "I must get on to town before it gets dark, missus." He touched his cap and without another word, whipped up the horses and rattled away down the road.

I watched him leave and swallowed hard to suppress the tears that were threatening to spill down my cheeks. I had endured a long day of travelling, and for the final few hours of bumping across the moors from Thirsk, I had been alone with nothing but gloomy thoughts to keep me company.

I turned and began walking slowly up the track. The rain blew into my face, and I bent my head, studying my boots as they peeped from beneath my skirts with every step. When I reached the top of the rise, I finally glimpsed Beulah Lodge.

It was a square, grey house nestled in a bowl-shaped dip. The stubby grass and heather surrounding it were punctuated every now and then by grey boulders, and the house itself looked like a great rock that had been discarded by some prehistoric giant. The evening gloaming had thrown the building into shadow, and the barest whisper of white smoke was visible from its chimneys.

I fought down tears once again. In my imagination, I had envisaged lush green lawns in the sunshine and a smiling Aunt Beatrice rushing out to greet me with rosy cheeks and a crisp white apron. I had only met my aunt a handful of times when I was a small child and had no clear memories of her. My mother rarely spoke of her and on the few occasions she did so, it was with a sadness, as if for something that had once been treasured but was now lost.

I dug my fingers into my palm and gave myself a stern talking to. I was being silly. I was tired and cold, that was all. I must present myself to my aunt with a cheerful countenance and gratitude at her kind offer of a home whilst Daniel was away. As had almost become a habit with me over the last few months, I conjured up a vision of our Lord on the Cross, patiently bearing the weight of mankind's sin. Any difficulty seemed tiny when set against his sacrifice. I set my face against the rain and walked doggedly on toward the house.

The wind dropped as the track dipped downward toward Beulah Lodge. There was no gateway or wall surrounding it; the track led straight up to the front door. As I approached the house, I could see ivy creeping up the walls and into the gutters. The front windows were shuttered, and the doorstep was grimy. I pushed the bell but could hear no sound of it ringing within. I pressed my cheek against the peeling paint of the door and tried the bell again but could hear nothing.

I stepped back onto the path and looked about me uncertainly. The beginnings of panic were taking hold in my stomach. Was I at the wrong house? Impossible, I had checked with the coachman at Thirsk. Had Aunt Beatrice died and the house been shut up? I had received no word before I left London, and how could the house grow so unkempt in such a short time?

A sound gradually broke into the tumult of my thoughts. Someone nearby was chopping wood. I could hear the rhythmic thud of an axe against a block. Relief surged through me, and I made my way around the house toward the sound.

The land at the back was sheltered by the hillside sloping away above it, and the rain fell with less ferocity here. It was a working backyard rather than a tended garden. There was a vegetable patch and a chicken coop situated a little way off.

I saw the wood chopper at once, around a hundred yards away, and to my surprise, it was a woman. She was swinging the axe high above her head and bringing it down with a loud thud on the block, splitting the log in two. She threw the two pieces into a wicker basket, looked up, and saw me.

She registered no surprise but simply leaned the axe against the block and watched as I approached.

"Good evening," I said, coming to a halt before her. The girl, who I judged to be several years younger than me, passed her sleeve across her forehead, breathing hard from her efforts. Strands of dark hair were stuck to her face, and her black eyes looked at me with a challenge.

"Who are you?" After hearing nothing but Yorkshire accents for the day, I was taken aback to hear a Cockney voice, exactly like the flower sellers who had shouted on the streets in my father's parish.

"My name is Ruth Mallowes."

The girl's face was blank. "All right. And why are you here?"

"I am here because my aunt invited me here," I said, unable to keep a defensive note from my voice. I had not imagined having to explain myself to a servant.

"Your aunt?"

"Mrs. Beatrice Groves."

The girl scowled. "Oh. I see." She hefted the axe onto her shoulder, the muscles of her forearms flexing. "Best you come in then. Ma'am," she added as an afterthought. She walked toward the back door, and I followed. The back of the house bore more signs of life than the front. The windows were un-shuttered, and a worn flagstone path led through the grass to the door.

The girl pushed it open, and I entered a dingy, cramped scullery, which at least provided some relief from the rain. The girl placed her axe next to a large sink and passed through another door into the kitchen.

The kitchen was a large, low-ceilinged room, one end of which was filled with a range. An older thickset woman with grey hair knelt before it, raking out the embers from the stove. There was a sturdy kitchen table in the middle of the room with several chairs arranged around it. In one of these sat a tall, elderly man smoking a pipe. He regarded me impassively from beneath heavy white brows. I stood by the table, feeling awkward and unsure of who I should address myself to.

The woman called from the range without looking around. "You can't have finished already, my girl. I know it's raining, and the wood will be wet but you know what the—"

"Martha," the girl interrupted. "We have a visitor."

The woman turned and looked at me, her mouth open in surprise. She rose heavily to her feet, wiping ash upon her apron. She gave an awkward, half curtsy. "Beggin' your pardon, miss," she mumbled.

"This here's Mrs. Mallowes," the girl said, her Cockney contrasting markedly with the older woman's broad Yorkshire. "She's been invited here by the mistress."

"Miss Mallowes," I corrected her.

The older woman looked bemused. "I see. I'm Martha, ma'am, the cook. And this here's Eliza. And this is Mr. Tripp." She pointed to the man seated at the table, and he inclined his head. Martha looked about her uneasily. "We didn't know you were coming, ma'am."

"She don't tell us nothing," Eliza said abruptly. "Shall I take you to her?"

"Now? I am hardly in a fit state—"

"You'd best come straightaway," Eliza said. "Mistress will have seen you arrive, and she won't be happy if she don't see you at once."

Martha nodded and passed me a tea towel from the range. "Give yourself a rub dry with that, ma'am," she said kindly.

I rubbed my face and temples with the warm cloth as best I could, uncomfortably aware that they were all watching. I was dizzy from fatigue and wanted nothing more than to sleep, but I could hardly refuse to see Aunt Beatrice.

"My trunk," I said as I handed the tea towel back. "The coachman left it at the top of the track."

"Tripp'll fetch it for you," Eliza said.

Mr. Tripp took his pipe from his mouth. "I'll not take orders from you," he said with such venom that I stared at him in astonishment. Eliza merely rolled her eyes.

"Oh, do go, Tripp," said Martha. "Miss Mallowes needs her trunk, and we can't leave it out in the rain, can we?"

Tripp rose slowly and pulled his cap onto his head. He threw a hate-filled glance at Eliza and stomped out. Martha smiled weakly at me. "Don't pay him any mind, ma'am. If the Angel Gabriel himself came into this kitchen, Tripp would be growling at him."

I did my best to return her smile.

Eliza led the way from the kitchen and along a dimly lit passageway that emerged into the main hallway. I glanced at the front door I had knocked against. Eliza, as if seeing the direction of my gaze, said, "We don't use the front door much."

"So all your visitors are received through the kitchen?" I asked, unable to keep a note of irritation from my voice.

"Don't get visitors," Eliza said over her shoulder, climbing the grand staircase that led up from the hall. We walked a short way along a richly carpeted corridor, and Eliza knocked at a door. A voice sounded from within, and I followed her into the room.

The light from the two large bay windows was fading, lending the room a grey, washed-out look. It was richly appointed: a fine, four-poster bed with a canopy was situated in front of one of the windows with a chaise lounge at its foot. A walnut dressing table with a looking glass stood beside the bed, facing the window.

In the other bay was a large, wing-backed armchair with a small round table next to it. In the armchair sat an old woman dressed in a black dress with a white crocheted day cap upon her head, from which wisps of grey hair emerged. Her hands resting on the arms of the chair were thin and delicate.

I was disappointed that she did not match my imagined rosy-cheeked, bustling matron, but I reprimanded myself. Beatrice had been kind and caring in her letters, and it was unworthy of me to be disappointed by her physical appearance.

"Ma'am," said Eliza softly. Beatrice turned her head and looked at us with sharp blue eyes in a wrinkled face. "This is Miss Mallowes. She has just arrived."

"I know," said Beatrice with a smile. It was not a smile of greeting but rather of satisfaction. She beckoned to me. "Come closer, my dear. Let me look at you."

I approached her chair. She took my hand and peered into my face. I shifted my feet, feeling self-conscious under her scrutiny. "Forgive my appearance, Aunt," I said. "I had to walk through the rain from the main road."

"You are very pretty indeed," Beatrice said, seeming to ignore my explanation. "Is she not, Eliza?"

I turned my head and saw that Eliza's eyes were fixed firmly on the floor. "I couldn't say, ma'am," she mumbled.

Beatrice laughed, making a sound like the wind stirring dried leaves. "Go and make up a room for Miss Mallowes." Eliza hastened away, and Beatrice motioned to a small low stool opposite her chair. "Sit."

"I must thank you, Aunt," I began once I had seated myself, "for your kindness in allowing me—"

She waved a hand impatiently. "We need not waste our time wittering polite nonsense." She gazed at me keenly, leaning forward in her chair. "There is much I want to know. Tell me about your fiancé. What sort of man is he?"

"He is a good man," I said simply. "A kind and generous man who—"

"And from whence came this absurd notion of his for India?" she interrupted. "Did you put the idea into his head?"

I frowned, struggling to reconcile the Aunt Beatrice of my letters with the woman before me. Her letters had been full of kindness and concern for my health. When I had written to tell her of my engagement to Daniel, she had poured out expressions of delight. And when I told her that Daniel would be travelling to India for missionary work, Beatrice had at once written and invited me to stay with her whilst he was away. My heart had leapt at the thought of becoming better acquainted with my aunt, the only relation I had left on my mother's side. Could this woman before me really be the same person who had written those letters?

"No, indeed. I did not know that he was thinking of it until he was near the end of his curacy at Holy Trinity. But I was not surprised. He has always been passionately concerned for the salvation of all men, especially those who have never heard the good news."

"He is wasting his time. They are all damned."

My mouth fell open in astonishment. I forgot myself and said sharply, "You cannot mean that."

She looked amused rather than offended at my outburst. "Does not the Bible state that only one hundred and forty-four thousand shall be saved?" she asked.

"Yes, but our Lord clearly says that whosoever hears his word and believes in him shall have eternal life."

"Belief is a gift from God. If you are not one of the elect, then you will not hear his word."

I was tired to the very marrow of my bones, and my eyes drooped with weariness. The last vestiges of daylight were creeping away, leaving the room in an eerie half-darkness. I closed my eyes for a moment, feeling as if I was in a nightmare. I took a deep breath. "Christ commands his disciples to go and preach the gospel to every creature. When Daniel has established himself at the mission in India, I shall be only too glad to go and join him. If my presence here is unwelcome in the meantime—"

"Hush, hush now. I do not mean to vex you," she said in a more conciliatory tone. "You are tired after your journey. Go to your room now and sleep. We will talk further in the morning." Her face was in shadow, and I could not see her expression. I wanted nothing more than to sink into bed, so I rose to my feet and bid her good night.

"Send Eliza to me," she called as I passed from her room.

I stood in the passageway and was just thinking that I did not know where my room was when I saw the flickering light of a candle coming from a chamber a few doors down on the opposite side of the passage.

Eliza was placing a warming pan under the covers of the bed as I entered. It was a handsome bed with a fine wooden frame and a thick rug beneath. I was relieved to see my trunk placed beside it. "Shall I unpack your things for you, ma'am?" Eliza asked.

"No, thank you. I will do it myself." Sleep was all I needed, just sleep. Everything would be different and better in the morning.

"Will there be anything else?"

"No, thank you. Oh wait," I said as she turned to go. "Your mistress wants you."

She grimaced with displeasure. I turned to begin to unpack my things and then realised Eliza was still lingering awkwardly by the door.

"What is it?" I asked wearily.

"I hope she weren't too awful to you, ma'am?"

"It was a private conversation," I said sternly.

Eliza held up her hands in a placating gesture. "All right. Don't go flying off the handle. I was only asking."

"Your mistress wants you," I repeated. To my intense relief, she curtsied and withdrew, closing the door behind her. I lay down on the bed, still in my clothes, and sank at once into a deep sleep.

CHAPTER TWO

I awoke the next morning to the sound of chopping wood. I sat up stiffly and took a moment to remember where I was. The sun was shining through the curtains, lending the room a cheerful aspect that worked to dispel the gloom from the night before.

I rose and washed with the pitcher of water on the dressing table. I changed my dress and combed and re-pinned my hair. I then unpacked the rest of my trunk, laying my things out carefully. I placed my Bible by my bedside and then stood at the window and watched Eliza chopping wood. There was something soothing about the regularity of her movements in the morning sunshine, her arms raising the axe and bringing it down upon the block. Things always seemed better in the morning, I thought. Today I would speak again with Beatrice. In the clear light of day, the conversation would progress differently. I would be polite and pleasant, and she would be warm and kind.

I descended the large staircase and noted an open door across the hall that was clearly the dining room. It was empty, but the table was laid with one place with eggs, rolls, and marmalade set out before it. A musty smell pervaded the room, making me suspect it wasn't regularly used. I was very hungry so I sat and had a hearty breakfast. The room looked out over the front of the house, and I watched the hills change colour as clouds moved across the sun.

I heard footsteps approaching, and Martha entered, carrying a tray of tea things. She started when saw me, causing the cups and saucers to rattle.

"Beg your pardon, ma'am," she exclaimed. "I didn't realise you had risen." She set the tray on the table and poured out a cup of tea for me.

I thanked her as I took the cup and said, "Has your mistress breakfasted already?"

"Mrs. Groves always takes breakfast in her room, ma'am. All her meals in fact. Eliza takes them to her on a tray."

"Indeed?"

"Yes, ma'am. Mrs. Groves is practically an invalid."

"I am sorry to hear that. What ails her?"

Martha busied herself with straightening the tablecloth and said, "I would say it's her nerves, ma'am. Not that I know anything about medical matters."

"I see. So, all this"—I gestured to the laid table—"is purely for my benefit?"

"You are our guest, ma'am," said Martha with a shy smile. "We so rarely have guests these days. And you are one of the family too."

"Have you been with the family long?"

"Why, I have been in service at Beulah Lodge for nigh on thirty years, ma'am. Ever since my dear husband died." I looked at her in surprise. She was middle-aged but not yet elderly and must have been widowed young. "You know, ma'am," Martha continued, "I remember when you and your mother came to stay all those years ago."

"Indeed? Was I a good child?" I asked with a smile.

"Oh, you were a dear little thing with your golden curls." The crinkles at the corners of her grey eyes deepened as she smiled. "You would run up and down these corridors with your dolls. It was wonderful to hear a child's voice in this house."

"I don't remember that visit at all," I said. "And I don't think my mother ever came again."

Martha's smile faded, and she sighed. "Yes. Mr. Groves died shortly afterward, and Mrs. Groves and her sister were estranged. Mrs. Groves became estranged from everyone, really."

"And she wished to stay in Beulah Lodge once she was widowed?"

"Yes." Martha paused and glanced around the faded dining room.

"It seems a lonely place," I ventured.

"It is, ma'am. Which is why there are only three servants now. Mr. Tripp has been in service here since he were a lad, since Mr. Groves were a lad too. His father served the old Mr. Groves. Tripp is the steward of the estate, though most of it has been sold off now. But there are still a few tenants, and Mr. Tripp collects the rents and deals with that side of things. Mrs. Groves, for all her strange ways, has been a fair mistress to me. When she first came here as young Mr. Groves's wife, she was a bonny thing."

I tried hard to imagine a young and bonny Beatrice and failed. "And Eliza?" I asked.

"Oh, she came to us only a few years ago. From London." Martha dropped her gaze and picked up the tray. "Will there be anything else, ma'am?"

"Is there a parlour where I may sit and write a letter?"

"The parlour hasn't been used in a long while. The library is the next room down, ma'am. That would be better. It gets more light in the mornings." She smiled and carried the rattling tray from the room.

I felt fortified by my breakfast and Martha's kindly good humour. I wandered from the dining room and back out into the main hall. I pushed open the next door along and entered the library. It had the same musty smell of the dining room, and dust particles danced in the light from the windows. There was a thick carpet beneath my feet, and three walls of the room were covered in heavy mahogany shelves, filled with books. A large desk was situated by the window, a thick film of dust covering it.

My heart leapt at the sight of all the books, for reading was my life's great pleasure. The prospect of a few months at Beulah Lodge now seemed much more enticing.

Daniel had teased me that now I was soon to be a married woman, I must lay down my books and take up my needle instead. I walked carefully around the room, scanning the titles. My initial enthusiasm waned upon discovering that many of the books were weighty religious volumes. I was, however, pleased to discover a copy of St. Augustine's *Confessions*. I sat at the desk with the book, happy that I should have the chance to finish it.

It was my reading of *Confessions* that had prompted Daniel's comment about taking up my needle, and my copy of the work had vanished from our small bookshelf shortly afterward. As I opened the pages, I felt a pang of guilt. There was no doubt in my mind that Daniel had removed the book because he'd felt I should not read it.

Was it right to read it now, simply because he was absent? I pushed the book aside.

There was some faded writing paper in the top drawer of the desk with "Beulah Lodge" embossed at the top. I retrieved a pen and a bottle of ink from the other drawer and began my letter:

Dearest Daniel,

I arrived safely at Beulah Lodge last night after a gruelling journey. I find it to be a most charming place, and Aunt Beatrice has been kindness itself...

I stopped and laid my pen down. I was writing lies. I screwed the letter tightly into a ball, angry at myself. I was not a person who told untruths. Why did I feel the need to write a fairy tale to my fiancé? *Because it will be easier,* a voice whispered. *Because Daniel will not like to hear of your complaints. He is engaged in difficult and dangerous work on God's behalf. Are you really going to worry him with your petty difficulties?* I tried again:

Dearest Daniel,

I arrived safely at Beulah Lodge last night after a gruelling journey. My aunt has provided everything I could need, and I am eager to make a closer acquaintance with her.

Nothing there was a lie. I was interrupted by a knock at the door. "Come in."

Eliza entered the room. "Mistress is asking to see you, ma'am."

"Of course." I folded my letter and placed it into my pocket. I took up Augustine's *Confessions* and replaced it on the shelf. "Mrs. Grove has a fine collection of books," I remarked.

Eliza shrugged. Really, her manner bordered on insolence, I thought as I followed her up the stairs to Aunt Beatrice's room.

Beatrice was sitting in the same chair by the window with the low stool placed before it. The only thing different was the brilliant daylight that bathed the room, doing much to banish its eerie aspect from the night before. Beatrice looked at me as I approached, and I saw the same malignant gleam in her eye. That had not been a dream.

"You look refreshed, my dear," she remarked as I sat before her. "Like a daffodil revived by the sun. A very pleasing sight. Is it not, Eliza?" Eliza stared straight ahead and said nothing. This seemed to irritate Beatrice, and she snapped, "Fetch us some tea." Eliza left the room, and Beatrice fixed her keen blue eyes on mine.

"You slept well?" she asked.

"Yes, thank you." I was determined that this conversation should be a pleasant one, and I resolved to say nothing to antagonise or contradict her. I was a guest in her house, after all.

"You will forgive me if I do not join you for meals. I take all my meals in this room."

"I understand. You are ill?"

"I am merely old. A condition for which there is no cure." She gave me another of her keen glances. "You are my only family. When I heard you were engaged, I wanted to know what sort of man might one day be master of Beulah Lodge." I looked out at the view of the moors and tried to picture Daniel here. "But I expect he would sell it to fund his foolhardy mission to the heathen, eh?"

"I cannot say."

"I was disappointed to discover that you were so eager to repeat the mistakes of your mother."

"What mistakes are those?" I asked blandly, determined not to rise to the bait.

"In hitching yourself to a penniless clergyman. Yet you go further than she and are determined to hitch yourself to one with delusions of missionary glory."

I said nothing, and Beatrice's eyes glittered coldly at me.

"As you are a guest in my house," she said, "you will do me the courtesy of answering my questions. Your father died not so long ago?"

"Yes. He died almost a year ago exactly."

"I did not care for him. I thought Clara was a fool to marry him."

"My father was the best man I have ever known," I said, fighting to keep my voice steady.

"And when did Clara die, exactly? It is so long ago that I forget."

"Eighteen fifty-seven. The day before Shrove Tuesday. I remember because the first thing I thought of when I heard was that mother and the baby would miss their pancakes." I looked away as I said this, still finding the memory painful after all these years.

"How old were you when she died?"

"Six."

"And an only child. I wonder that your father never remarried."

"I wondered myself when I was older. But he always said that he had God for his master and me for his mistress, and there was no room for anyone else." I smiled, but Beatrice's face remained stony.

"When your father died, did you inherit money or property from him?"

I bristled at being questioned in such a manner but kept my voice and my gaze steady. "There was a small amount of money."

"But you are not a wealthy woman?"

"By no means."

"So. Your fiancé does not intend to marry you for your money," she said with a hoarse chuckle. She leant back in her chair and looked me up and down. "Does he hope you will make a good missionary's wife?"

"I hope to be a good wife to him, whatever our circumstances."

She snorted again. "Out in India? With the heat, the disease, the natives plotting to kill you?"

"I am bound to go wherever my husband goes," I said.

"Humph." Beatrice looked out the window, her gaze resting on the barren moors. "My husband married me when I was still a girl and brought me here. I had lived all my life in Kent, the garden of England, and then I came here." Her eyes were unfocused as she stared at the moors. "He used to say that you could see the face of God on these moors. And that it was a cold, unforgiving face."

I felt a chill run through me.

"I have spent nigh on forty years in this place," Beatrice continued. "My husband died seventeen years ago. And I have been alone since then. Mistress of an empty house."

"You did not wish to return to Kent?"

"Unmarried daughters are a burden upon their fathers, widowed daughters even more so. Why would I give up being mistress of my own house to live under the rule of another man? Would a freed slave willingly place his wrists back into the shackles?"

"But have you not been lonely, Aunt?"

"I have found I desire company less and less as the years passed. And besides, I still have my servants." She gave a sudden bark of laughter, as if at some private joke.

"They are certainly very loyal to you," I said, feeling nettled on their behalf that their years of service were not acknowledged.

"Tripp is like a dog that is kicked but will always return cringing to its master. Martha is as lumpen and stupid as one of those boulders out there. And Eliza…" She tailed off as Eliza entered the room with the tea things and began setting them out on the low table.

Beatrice smiled at her, her thin lips stretching over yellowing teeth. "I brought Eliza here from London. Before I grew so feeble, I used to visit the city every year to see my solicitors on Chancery Lane." Eliza finished laying the tea things and stood with the empty tray, her face an expressionless mask. "Miss Mallowes knows the East End," she said to the girl. Eliza's eyes flicked briefly to me, then continued to stare ahead of her.

"Will that be all, madam?" she asked.

"I found Eliza in Covent Garden," Beatrice continued. "Plying her trade." Eliza's hands tightened around the tea tray. I looked from her to Beatrice, sensing something terrible in the atmosphere between them. "Tell Miss Mallowes your story," she said, her eyes fixed on Eliza's face.

"That is not necessary," I said hastily.

"Ah, you see? It is not fit for the ears of a lady."

"Will that be all, madam?" Eliza asked again.

Beatrice's eyes narrowed. I stood abruptly. "I think I will leave you now, Aunt," I said. They both looked at me in surprise.

"We have not finished our conversation," Beatrice snapped.

I looked down at her wizened face, twisted with anger, and I knew that my impressions of the previous night were not a product of tiredness or a nightmare. I felt a calmness settle over me. Beatrice might be vicious and cruel, but I was not one of her servants to be trodden under her heel. "We can continue it later," I said. I turned to Eliza. "I have a letter that needs to be posted. Perhaps you will take it into the nearest village for me?"

Eliza nodded, still staring at me. I turned and walked from the room, hearing Beatrice call after me, "You will answer more of my questions tomorrow."

Eliza followed me out. She closed the door behind her, and we looked at each other in the dim light of the hallway. "You'd best gimme this letter of yours, then," Eliza said abruptly.

"Actually, I think I would prefer to walk into the village myself. I could do with stretching my legs."

"Suit yourself." Eliza walked past me down the stairs. Really, if it had not been for Beatrice's unkindness toward her, I would have felt obliged to speak to the girl sharply about her manners.

I returned to the library and finished my letter to Daniel. I ended with bland assurances of my well-being and enquiries after his own health. I hoped that it would be waiting for him when he reached the mission station.

The village was four miles away and the walk there and back took up most of the day. It was a relief to escape the oppressive atmosphere of Beulah Lodge and to breathe in the fresh country air. Coldkirk was a small village that contained a pub, a church, and a general store that doubled as a post office. The lady who kept the post office was agog with curiosity about me, even more so when I revealed I was staying at Beulah Lodge.

She leaned forward over the counter. "I hear there's all sorts that goes on at that house," she whispered.

"There is only Mrs. Groves and three servants who live there."

"But I hear she has taken in…" She paused and looked around her tiny shop dramatically. "A *fallen woman*."

I blinked. She could only mean Eliza, who had recently come from London and about whom Beatrice had dropped so many nasty hints.

"The Bible teaches that we are all fallen, does it not?" I said, brusquely.

The woman flinched as if I had struck her. "Indeed," she said hastily as she took my letter. I felt my face flush with anger as I left the post office. I had met many so-called fallen women whilst supporting my father's work in his parish and had seen first-hand the grinding poverty of their lives. I could not condemn Eliza, nor anyone, for doing whatever they could to escape from it.

Dusk was falling as I approached the house again. I went in through the back door and into the kitchen. Martha was standing at the range, stirring a pan of broth. "Is Nancy still off lay?" she asked without turning around.

"Who is Nancy?" I asked, smiling.

"Oh, ma'am, forgive me. I thought it were Eliza with the eggs. Nancy is one of our hens. She hasn't been herself these last few days. Oh, but you must be wanting your supper. It's almost ready. I can bring it up to you in the dining room." The kitchen was pleasantly warm after the chill of the evening air, and the copper pans gleamed welcomingly on their hooks.

I thought of the dusty, still dining room, and my heart sank. "Might I not eat my supper here?" I asked.

Martha looked appalled. "Oh no, ma'am, that wouldn't be right at all. You cannot take your meals with the servants. Mistress wouldn't hear of it." I did not press the point but went up to my room to change.

I ate Martha's delicious broth on my own in the dining room, watching the moors gradually settle under a blanket of darkness. After supper, I took myself to the library and settled into an easy chair with my Bible. When the light from the lamp became too faint to read by, I made my way upstairs to my bedchamber, hearing the creaks of the house settling around me.

As I knelt beside my bed in preparation to say my prayers, I reflected on my earlier encounter with Beatrice. I had been undeniably rude, and there was nothing to stop her from commanding me to leave her house. How would I explain that to Daniel? I pictured the conversation with him where I explained what had happened, and I could see very clearly his face falling, his head shaking in disappointment. He would upbraid me for my impulsiveness, for the way I let my heart rule my head. Since we had become engaged, all my qualities that had previously delighted him now seemed to be a source of anguish to him.

I shifted on my knees, trying to banish such unwelcome thoughts and focused my mind on my prayers, asking God to keep Daniel safe and to grant me the patience and strength to treat Beatrice with kindness.

Chapter Three

The next morning proceeded almost exactly as the one before, right down to the sound of Eliza chopping wood. I once again stood at my window whilst I combed my hair, watching the steady rise and fall of her arms. There was another solitary breakfast in the dining room, and then I sat again in the library, trying to focus on my daily Bible. But I couldn't settle to it. My mind turned over the possibilities of what Beatrice would do. I formulated endless scenarios where I would either beg Beatrice for forgiveness or haughtily hold my ground. I could not predict how Beatrice would react to any of the encounters my fevered mind conjured up, and so I paced restlessly around the room until there came a soft knock at the door, and Eliza entered.

"Miss Mallowes? Mistress wants to see you."

I took a deep breath, trying to steady my nerves. "How is she?"

"She is her usual self," said Eliza dismissively. And then she must have read my face for she added more gently, "Don't fret, ma'am. It'll be all right."

"Will it? Will it indeed?"

Eliza gave a kind of half shrug. "Course it will. Everything always comes right in the end, don't it?" She did not sound very convinced, and so the sentiment did nothing to assuage my nerves.

She led me upstairs, and I entered Beatrice's chamber. Beatrice was sitting in the same chair by the window. Only her different dress gave any indication that she had moved from the spot. Her face was unreadable as I took my seat before her, the same cold, malevolent expression in her eyes.

I was half forming an apology, but she barked at me before I could speak. "You would do well to remember your position, young lady. You are in *my* house."

I moistened my lips and said carefully, "I do remember, Aunt. I apologise if I have caused you offence."

"What would your fiancé say if I were to tell him of how you have behaved?"

"He would say that I had not acted in a manner that befits a future clergyman's wife." I could not suppress the bitterness in my voice, and Beatrice smirked.

She leant back in her chair and looked at me. "Will he make you a good husband?"

"He is a good man," I said.

"Did your father approve of him?"

"Yes. He was anxious for the match."

"All fathers are anxious for their daughters to marry. To marry anyone. After all, no father would want to risk their daughters ending up like poor Eliza."

I turned my head, having quite forgotten that Eliza was still in the room. She was making Beatrice's bed and did not look up from her task.

Beatrice snapped, "Be gone with you. I have things to discuss with Miss Mallowes." Eliza left the room, Beatrice's eyes following her. "That girl is the most ungrateful wretch I have ever known," Beatrice spat after Eliza had gone. "If it were not for me, she would still be earning her living on her back." I pushed down the anger that flared within me and said nothing. "I get nothing but insolence and surliness from her." She looked at me sternly. "You see what comes of trying to help the reprobate. Daniel will be wasting his time in India."

I changed the subject. "Were you fond of London, Aunt?"

"It is a den of sin and vice. Which is why so many lawyers are based there." She gave a shout of laughter, and I smiled politely. "I used to amuse myself by having my coachman drive through some of the more colourful parts of the East End. The sights I saw...my husband would have turned in his grave."

"Life is hard in the East End," I said. "My father moved to a London parish precisely because he was concerned with the suffering of the poor. He worked tirelessly to help them."

"Then he too wasted his time."

"Did Christ also waste his time amongst the poor?" I said, nettled despite my best intentions.

Beatrice smiled as if pleased to have provoked a reaction. "Only those whom God has ordained will be saved."

I pressed my lips together. I could feel myself getting angry, and I was wary of crossing Beatrice again. To my great relief, Beatrice herself changed the subject. "Will Daniel send for you in due course?"

"Yes. He wishes to establish himself at the mission, and when the time is right, he will write for me to join him."

"And then your fair skin shall be burnt to a crisp," she said, shaking her head in mock sadness.

"I am not concerned about my looks," I said.

She threw back her head and cackled. "Oh, you are delightfully naïve, my dear. A woman's looks are all the value she possesses in the eyes of this sinful world…just ask Eliza."

"The values of the world do not concern me."

"Then, you will do very well as a missionary's wife." She waved her hand. "Go now. I am tired. But you will come back tomorrow morning at the same time." She turned her face to the window to emphasise that our interview was at an end. I curtsied and bade her good morning, relieved to have been released.

I went back the next morning and every morning that followed. We would converse for about half an hour. Our conversation settled into a pattern: she would harangue me about religion, Daniel, and the uselessness of her servants. She only seemed satisfied when she had provoked some sort of response from me, and then she would dismiss me. From then on, I had the day to myself. These meetings with Beatrice left me alternately angry and drained, and the thought of the long months stretching ahead of me at Beulah Lodge filled me with gloom.

On Sundays, I would rise and breakfast early and then walk into the village with Martha to attend worship at the tiny village church of St. Rumbold's. The vicar was a Reverend Glossop, who mumbled his way through the service with almost unseemly haste, and the organist was reliably a beat behind the congregation during the hymns.

Martha smiled apologetically as we walked back to the house after my first visit. "Reverend Glossop ain't the most...charismatic of preachers, but he does his best."

"I am sure he does." We walked on for a few minutes, and then I said, "Does Reverend Glossop ever visit your mistress?"

"Oh no, ma'am. Mrs. Groves won't have him in the house. Mr. Groves had no truck with the Church of England, you see. He preferred to lead the household in prayer himself every Sunday."

"I get the impression that Mr. Groves was a very pious man."

"He took his religion very seriously." After a few moments, Martha said, "Reverend Glossop is a kind man, and to my mind, that makes up for any deficit in his other qualities."

I smiled. "I quite agree. Kindness should be the dominant quality in a man of God."

"I expect your father was a kind man, ma'am?"

"Indeed he was."

There was a brief silence, and then Martha said, "Mr. Groves was very clear that this life is nothing but a vale of tears, and he didn't think it was worth bothering with. He used to say how much he looked forward to death so that he could enter the world to come." I shivered. Martha nodded grimly. "Aye, I was glad when Mrs. Groves did not continue the Sunday lessons and let me go to St. Rumbold's. I hoped it was a sign of better days ahead but...it was not to be."

"Do Mr. Tripp and Eliza ever accompany you to church?"

"Tripp knows the mistress's opinions, and he wouldn't go against her in anything. And Eliza is always saying that she has no truck with religion. So I am quite glad, ma'am, to have a companion."

"I can imagine it must be lonely sometimes."

"Oh, I do all right. Tripp ain't so bad really, and since Eliza came, I have had someone else to talk to. And," she added, "I am blessed with my son and his family. I know there's many who ain't so fortunate."

"And I too am glad to have a church companion."

She turned a shy smile on me, and I responded with a warm smile of my own.

❖

After I had been a week at Beulah Lodge, a letter arrived from Daniel. He told me he had docked in Cochin and would be travelling south to the mission in Travancore. He asked after my health and that of Beatrice and bade me treat her with all possible respect and kindness. I should ensure that I was kept sufficiently occupied at Beulah Lodge so that my mind did not fall into idle and unprofitable thoughts. I should further my skill with a needle, as a missionary's wife would have great need of it, and he had observed that there was much room for improvement. He was keen to begin the work of spreading the good news and eagerly awaited the time when he should have me at his side as his helpmate. He remained my affectionate fiancé, etc.

I put the letter down on the desk and gazed out the library window, watching a blackbird hop across the path. Emotions were pressing at the edge of my consciousness, and I focused hard on the bird, trying to keep them at bay. Irritation and disappointment seeped through, and I pushed the letter away. Was that really what I had to look forward to? Not even to be regarded as an equal to Daniel in his work but only valued for my domestic skills?

I got up and went down to the kitchen. Martha was rolling dough on the table and looked up as I passed. I went out the back door and stood in the yard, already feeling better now I was free of the house. The spring air was crisp without being cold, the sky a brilliant blue. The moors seemed to be rejoicing at the advent of spring, the grass bursting into life and daffodils dotting the slopes.

I strode through the yard, following the rough path that led from the house and into a paddock where the henhouses were. The hens were scratching about happily in the grass, and I saw Eliza crouched next to one. As I walked by, I could hear her speaking softly, but she stopped when she saw me.

She sprang to her feet. "I'm collecting the eggs, ma'am," she said defensively. "I was just seeing to Nancy cos she ain't been herself lately."

"All right. You needn't worry. I am not checking up on you."

"Well, what do you want, then?" She seemed to think better of it at once, cleared her throat, and said, "Begging your pardon, ma'am. I mean, did you need something?"

I ignored her rudeness and said evenly, "No, I am merely on my way for a walk across the moors. It is a beautiful morning after all."

Eliza glanced at the sky as if she hadn't noticed it before. I made to walk on when a thought seemed to strike, and Eliza said, "If you keep to the left as you go up and walk on for about half an hour, you'll come to a tor. You might see a plover nesting in the heather at this time of year."

I looked at her in surprise. "A plover? How would I know one if I saw it?"

"It's got golden speckled feathers on its back. And it makes a kind of sad call. Like this." She pursed her lips and whistled a low clear note.

"That does sound rather melancholy." I did not add that it matched my mood precisely.

"Martha said her mum told her that it was cos they used to nest in trees, but then the moorland came and swallowed all the trees, and the plovers is always mourning for them. But I think they're just mourning the passing of the day cos they always call more at dusk, you see. And when you see twilight on the moors, you'll see what I mean. The light leeches slowly away like colour fading from a beautiful dress. It's a sight worth seeing." She smiled, and the effect was startling. The usual surliness of her expression was banished as the smile reached her eyes and made them sparkle. She was very pretty.

"It certainly sounds it," I said, taken aback. "And I will keep my eyes and ears peeled for plovers."

Eliza seemed to sense something of my discomfort for her face at once closed and resumed its usual expression. She gave me a curt nod before turning back to the henhouse.

I set off on the route she had suggested. I drew deep breaths of the sharp air into my lungs, imagining them clearing out the dust of Beulah Lodge.

As I tramped across the moors, I allowed the feelings I had been keeping at bay to wash over me. Daniel's letter had infuriated me. He had addressed me as if I were an unruly child who needed a firm hand to be kept out of mischief. He had known me before he asked for my hand in marriage. He was a regular visitor to our house, he had sat in the parlour with my father, and we had talked of theology, history, and politics. How was it that he could now ask me to focus my energies on needlework?

But beneath my indignation was a cold, creeping dread. I had now given Daniel my promise to be his wife, and I could not break my word. Daniel had been so supportive when Papa had died, it would be as if I were breaking a promise to my father, somehow. And without Daniel, there was no one with whom I could share memories of Papa.

The track took a steeper course, and I kept my pace up, feeling a release in being breathless. I reached the brow of the hill and stood amongst the brown, stubby branches of the heather, looking out over the moors. I could see the spire of St. Rumbold's poking up amidst the rolling green and brown landscape. The clouds moved across the sun, making shadows flicker across the banks of heather.

My attention was caught by movement in the undergrowth. A small bird darted over the ground and stopped around ten feet away, looking in my direction. I knew at once that this must be the plover Eliza had spoken of. The golden flecks on its back were lit up by the sun as it moved from behind the clouds. I smiled at it, and it cocked its head and then flew away over the heather. Another cloud moved over the sun, robbing the moors of their momentary beauty.

Why had I agreed to marry Daniel? Because my father had wanted me to. Because he was ill, and I knew that he worried about what would happen to me after he had gone. Because Daniel was a dutiful and decent man. I knew myself enough to know that I did not love him, not in the way that I had read about in books, but I liked and respected him, and that had seemed sufficient. And besides, the deep, passionate love that I had read of rarely seemed to bring people happiness.

I sat down on a rock, tucking my legs beneath me. I folded my arms in my lap and waited whilst my breathing returned to normal. I was not some naive, unworldly heroine in a gothic novel who had been forced into marriage. I was long past the age when most girls married, and my father was not the sort of man who would have forced me into anything. I had given my promise to Daniel willingly. I must be happy with the lot I had chosen. I would practice my needlework… but I would also continue to read. That way, I could fulfil my duty to Daniel and also to God. For God had graced me with an eager and enquiring mind, and it would not do to squander his gifts.

I stood and brushed down my skirts. The walk had done me good, and I felt as if I had reached a resolution within myself. I picked my way carefully down the track and back in the direction of Beulah Lodge.

Chapter Four

I tried very hard to stick to my resolution. Over the next few days, I applied myself to my needlework and made sure to be as polite as possible to Beatrice at our morning interviews, biting my tongue when she needled me about theology.

When I was not practising with my needle, I read only the Bible and placed the copy of St. Augustine's *Confessions* back on the shelf so I would not be tempted. When the confines of the house became intolerable, I took walks across the moors and gradually became familiar with the tracks and paths that crisscrossed the landscape.

And yet, it was not enough. My mind and body seemed to chafe against the idleness. And it was idleness compared to what I was used to. My father's house had been a busy one, with parishioners and petitioners calling at all hours throughout the day. I acted as my father's secretary: I wrote letters for him, managed his appointments, and would even assist him with composing his weekly sermon. This last provided a fount of happy memories, of sitting in Papa's study with the battered family Bible open upon my knee, searching out references for him as we discussed the readings for that week, and my father expounded his ideas for the sermon.

Once Daniel was appointed as curate, he took over this duty, but my father would still dictate the sermon for me to write and would always ask for my opinion and amend his text based upon my comments.

I was also in charge of the Sunday school, and I would accompany my father on his visits amongst the parish to the sick, the elderly, and anyone who was in need. My days in the rectory were long, and

I frequently fell into bed exhausted but with the assurance that my energies had been spent in furthering the mission of Christ in our own little patch of the world.

But now, at the day's end at Beulah Lodge, I would climb into bed and spend long hours staring at the ceiling and waiting for sleep to come. My mind churned with fears and anxieties about the future, about what my life with Daniel would be like in a place so far removed from everything I knew. Although I was loath to admit it, Beatrice's constant wheedling was beginning to take its toll. I began to doubt the value of our missionary work in India, wondering if we were not just as needed at home as abroad but knowing that my saying so to Daniel would not change his mind.

Sleep would finally overtake me, but I would awake early with the dawn, feeling tense and unrefreshed.

I needed meaningful occupation. If I could not find something to occupy my mind, then I could at the very least ensure I did labour that would leave me physically exhausted at the end of the day.

The sound of the wood chopping had become a regular attendant to my early rising, and one morning, as I stood at my washbasin and observed Eliza swinging her axe, I resolved that this would be a good way to begin my regime of physical labour.

I dressed swiftly and wrapped a shawl around my shoulders to guard against the morning chill. I walked out through the kitchen where Martha was busy lighting the fire in the range.

"Good morning, Martha," I said cheerfully as I passed through the scullery and out into the yard.

Eliza was bringing the axe down with a thud as I approached, splitting a log in two. She threw the pieces into the basket and only then looked up and saw me. Her face was pink from the exertion, her hair coming loose from its bun. Upon catching sight of me, she looked at first astonished and then alarmed.

"What's the matter?" she asked.

"Nothing is the matter. I thought I would help you with chopping the wood."

Her eyes narrowed. "You what?"

"Well, I am always awake at this hour, and I do not like to be idle."

"I don't need no help." Eliza's face was stony, and she pointedly took another log from the basket and split it in two with one fierce blow.

I stood for a moment, irresolute in the face of her unexpected opposition. I could insist. I was, after all, a guest in the house, and she could not disobey a direct instruction from me. But that would create nothing but bad feeling.

I cast a glance around the yard and said, "Perhaps I could collect the eggs, then?"

"No. You'll get your dress all dirty, and then Martha and the mistress will go blaming me for allowing it." She spoke to me dismissively, as if I was a small child annoying her with my foolish requests. I felt my face redden, and I turned away.

I could not bear the thought of going back to my room and simply waiting until breakfast should be served. So I walked over to the henhouse, deliberately ignoring Eliza's gaze as I passed.

The hens were pecking about in the dried earth in front of their coop, clucking gently to each other. I squatted on my haunches and smiled as they eyed me with a mixture of hope and trepidation. Nancy trotted over, looking particularly regal as the early morning sun made her black feathers appear to glow.

"Hello, Nancy," I said softly. "You don't mind if I sit here a while, do you?"

Nancy clucked from somewhere deep in her throat and cocked her head before pecking at the ground around my skirts. The cooing of the hens was deeply soothing. I felt tears threaten, and I scrubbed my eyes angrily with the back of my hand, annoyed with myself for my lack of fortitude. It was beyond ridiculous to cry because of a sharp word from a servant.

At that moment, I heard footsteps and looked up. Eliza was standing nearby with a basket. She looked at me with a mixture of concern tinged with suspicion. "You ain't crying, are you?"

I stood so I would not have to awkwardly gaze up at her. "No," I said brusquely. "I am not given to tears at the drop of a hat."

Eliza shuffled her feet and gave a kind of cough before saying, "I s'pose if you held the basket, I could pass the eggs out from the coop. That way, you wouldn't get your dress dirty."

"I don't care a fig about whether my dress gets dirty," I said. "I am not one of those useless women who thinks of nothing but their looks. And I am more than capable of explaining myself to Beatrice, Martha, and whoever else may think it their business."

My rising voice had caused the hens to look at me nervously, and I was sure I detected a smile quirk at the corners of Eliza's mouth. "I do not doubt it, ma'am," she said seriously. She handed me the basket and ducked her head into the henhouse. She passed the eggs to me one by one, and I placed them smooth and warm under the cloth.

When all the eggs had been collected, Eliza backed out and closed the wooden front of the coop. "Nancy's still off lay."

"Is she ill?"

Eliza frowned and looked thoughtfully down at Nancy, who was jabbing her beak into the soil. "She don't seem to be. She ain't broody or nothing."

"Perhaps she just doesn't feel like laying any eggs?"

"Maybe. But then we all have to do what we don't feel like doing." She wagged her finger at Nancy to emphasise her point. Nancy unearthed a worm and devoured it with a cluck of triumph.

I smiled and said, "Perhaps Nancy would rather eat worms than lay eggs."

"And I would rather eat cake than clean the range," Eliza said, "but we all got our duties to do."

"At least you don't have laying eggs as part of your duties," I said, pleased that I was able to joke with her.

Eliza looked at me as if she wasn't sure if I was being serious. But then a broad grin spread across her features, and it was impossible not to smile back at her.

I felt emboldened by my success, and the next morning, after waking early yet again, I simply appeared in the yard as Eliza prepared to chop the wood. She opened her mouth to protest.

"It would be quicker if I lifted the logs onto the block, wouldn't it?" I said, pointing to the pile of logs.

"I'm sure it ain't right for you to be hefting wood about," Eliza said. "What with you being a lady and all."

"Nonsense, I am not a duchess. My father was a poor clergyman." I bent and lifted one of the logs onto the block. It was heavier than I had anticipated, and I stumbled, almost dropping it onto my toe. Eliza snorted with suppressed laughter.

After a brief struggle, I deposited it onto the block. "There. Now you can chop it."

Eliza sighed resignedly and lifted the axe above her head. I turned aside as she brought it down with tremendous force. As she shifted the axe off the block, I threw the pieces into the basket and then lifted another log into position.

We worked together in silence, establishing a rhythm as we went. Eliza's face tensed as she raised the axe, and her breath came out in a rush as it smacked down upon the log. The sleeves of her dress were rolled up, and I watched the muscles of her forearms tense and relax with each blow. There was a pleasing, rhythmic quality to the vibrations of her flesh when the axe fell, and I blinked and looked away when I realised how intently I had been staring.

When we finally reached the bottom of the pile of logs, she leaned on the axe, her bosom rising and falling as she caught her breath again. Her dark eyes were bright, and her face lost its wary, suspicious expression as she looked with satisfaction on the pile of wood in the basket. "Not bad, eh?" she said.

"Not bad at all. I told you it would be quicker."

Eliza smiled, and I was struck again by how pretty she appeared. I heard footsteps behind me and turned to see Mr. Tripp walking past. He stopped a little way off, his heavy white brows drawn together in a scowl.

He pointed a gnarled finger at Eliza. "You should be getting on with your work and not pestering the missus."

"She is doing no harm, Mr. Tripp," I replied. "I offered to help."

Tripp's small eyes met mine. "Mistress would not approve."

"Then she may voice her disapproval directly to me," I said. We gazed at each other until Tripp harrumphed and moved on. He threw a venomous look at Eliza as he passed. "Why is he so unpleasant to you?" I asked when he had gone inside the house.

Eliza bent and hefted the basket of logs to carry back into the house. "He ain't never liked me. Not since I first came here. He don't like where I'm from and what I was." She spoke with affected carelessness, but I looked at her seriously.

"I don't see how it is any of his business."

"S'pose it ain't, really. But it's also cos he was sweet on the mistress once...still is."

"Tripp?" My mouth dropped open in astonishment.

Eliza nodded. "So Martha says. He didn't like it when Bea— Mrs. Groves—brought me up here."

I barely heard what she said as I was so distracted by the thought of a gruff, surly Tripp paying court to Beatrice. I pictured him standing under her window, singing a serenade and holding a rose, and I laughed so loudly that the hens clucked in alarm. "I'm sorry," I said. "It's just that I am trying to imagine him as a pining lover and..." I dissolved into laughter again.

It must have been contagious for Eliza chuckled too, her face relaxing again into girlish prettiness.

"It is hard to imagine him writing her poems and asking her to dance." I wiped my eyes and felt a great release. It was the first time I had laughed in months.

❖

I could tell as soon as I entered Beatrice's room later that morning that she was displeased with me. She dismissed Eliza at once, and as soon as I had sat before her, she snapped, "Do you make a habit of hobnobbing with the servants?" I blinked. "I saw you, laughing as if you were a couple of giddy schoolgirls."

"I am glad that you are not solely confined to this room, Aunt," I said. Her window faced the front of the house, so the only way she could have seen us would have been from a chamber on the other side.

"Do not attempt to change the subject. This is my house, and I know everything that takes place here."

"Mr. Tripp said that you would not approve," I said. I battled to keep my tone light. I was determined that my good mood would not be so soon deflated, but the thought of Beatrice observing my interactions with Eliza made my skin prickle uncomfortably.

"Tripp?" she barked.

"Yes, he warned us of your likely displeasure." Her eyes narrowed. "He is a very loyal servant." I met her gaze evenly.

Beatrice finally sat back in her chair with a grunt. "He is a fool. But…he is very fond of me." She gave what was clearly meant to be a coquettish smile, which looked more like a grimace. "I was very pretty once, like you. Tripp was only a boy when I came to this house. He used to tramp back and forth to the village several times a day to get me what I fancied." She appeared lost in the past, and for a moment, I pitied her, growing old alone in this great house. But then she seemed to remember where she was, and the malevolence returned to her expression. "But you should not forget what that girl is. She is not fit company for you, a future missionary's wife."

"But she was fit company for you, Aunt," I said gently. "After all, you brought her here."

"In a misguided act of charity that I bitterly regret. She has brought me nothing but trouble."

I dearly wanted to know what trouble she could possibly mean, as I had never seen Eliza be anything but compliant in Beatrice's presence. But I did not wish to push my luck, and so I steered the conversation to the safer waters of Daniel's mission to India and listened patiently whilst Beatrice listed for the umpteenth time all the reasons why the venture was doomed to failure.

I helped Eliza chop the wood the next morning and every subsequent morning. We would sometimes talk as we worked, about the moors and the hens, and gradually, the suspicious, wary look on Eliza's face disappeared. Sometimes we would say hardly anything to each other but simply work our way through the pile of logs. It was an easy, companiable silence, and I was grateful to Eliza for how she seemingly knew when I preferred to be quiet.

Once I had finished the chopping and had my breakfast, I tried very hard to stick to my resolution to either practice my needlework or read the Bible. But my resolve was worn away with the tedium of the sewing, and my eyes frequently strayed to the titles on the library shelves.

Eventually, one morning, I took down St. Augustine's *Confessions* again. I salved my conscience by vowing that I would spend precisely the same amount of time with my needle that afternoon as I did in perusing Augustine and other works from the shelves.

After reading for a while, I wrote a long and carefully worded letter to my fiancé describing the house, the moors, and my conversations with Beatrice. I wrote a great deal about my hopes for our future together and for the success of the mission. At no point did I express any disquiet. It was a letter full of hope and sunshine, the sort of letter Daniel wanted to read. I placed it in my pocket and threw my shawl around my shoulders.

I walked from the library into the kitchen. Martha was rolling out pastry on the table whilst Eliza cut out small pie casings from the dough and placed them onto a tray. They both looked up as I entered and smiled. They had grown accustomed to my comings and goings through the kitchen, and Martha no longer looked quite so scandalised by my presence. This, in turn, made me feel more as if I were among friends rather than strangers.

"I am going to the village to post a letter," I said.

"Eliza or Tripp can take that for you, ma'am," said Martha, wiping her floury hands on her apron.

"No need. I will enjoy the walk."

"I meant to say to you, ma'am, there's a shortcut you can take across the moors," Eliza said. "It's much quicker than going by the lane."

"Easy to get lost, though," said Martha.

"I can show Miss Mallowes the way."

"Yes, please do. I should be glad of the company," I said. Martha looked doubtful.

"I can get some more of that thread you wanted. Save you waiting for Tripp to go on Thursday," Eliza said. Martha still looked unsure. Eliza bumped her playfully on the shoulder. "Oh, go on. You'll be glad to be rid of me. I can tell you're dying to rearrange my pie cases." She grinned, and her smile was so infectious that Martha could not help but smile back.

"Oh, all right then. But mind you don't go leading Miss Mallowes into a bog." Eliza pulled off her apron with gusto and reached for her shawl which was draped on the back of a chair. "And make sure you get the right thread. None of that cheap rubbish that snaps as soon as you look at it." She dug into her apron pocket and handed Eliza a few pennies.

"Cheerio," Eliza called as she went through the back door. I smiled at Martha and followed her. I felt slightly giddy with excitement, as if I had been let out of school early.

It was a fine day for a walk. The spring was ripening slowly into summer, and although there was still a chill in the air, the sky was perfectly blue and clear.

We set off on a rough sort of path that led up the ridge from behind the henhouse. There was a steep climb to begin with until we reached the top and could look down on Beulah Lodge.

We paused to catch our breath, and Eliza swept her arm out and said, "We circle 'round the house then cut straight across to the village."

I looked out at the barren landscape. Although I had become familiar with the main tracks and paths that led from the house, I had not yet ventured in the direction Eliza was indicating. "How do you guard against getting lost? There are no landmarks to guide you."

"Course there are. You just have to look close enough. See that rock down there?" She pointed to one of the large, moss-covered boulders that scattered the moors. "Looks a bit like St. Paul's cathedral, don't it?"

I peered at it. "If you say so."

"And that hillock over there," Eliza continued, "is like the Tower." Her face was rosy from the climb, and her dark eyes bright with pleasure. She was hatless, and the breeze stirred the dark strands of hair at her temple. I found it hard to credit that I had believed her to be so surly and insolent when I had first met her.

"Do you miss London?" I asked.

"Sometimes I do, and sometimes I don't."

"It must get lonely here."

Eliza carried on walking, and I fell into step beside her. "It does. But it could get lonely in London too," she said. "You could be on a street teeming with people and still not have a friend in the world."

"It must have been...difficult," I said, wanting to allow her to speak of her past if she wished without placing pressure upon her to do so.

"Yes," she said simply. "But at least I could buy food and lodgings most days. There was some folk under the arches who hadn't slept within walls for years."

"The arches?"

"Hungerford Bridge. Used to kip under the arches there sometimes if I didn't have the money for a doss house."

I looked at her, appalled. "But that can't have been safe. Especially for a young girl."

"It weren't. Had to keep your wits about you. And a sturdy pen knife too." I sensed her stealing a glance at me before she said, "Mistress said you knew the East End."

"My father was rector of Holy Trinity in Poplar. He was most concerned with the suffering of...of girls in your situation and worked with many of the church missions there." Eliza merely grunted. We walked on for a few minutes in silence before I said, "Did you ever encounter people from the church?"

"We used to see 'em sometimes. You could get a bowl of soup, provided you let them read the Bible at you."

"Which part did they read?"

"I dunno. Some part about hell and sin, usually. We had to say we was sinners before they'd give us the bloody soup." She shot me a glance and mumbled, "Begging your pardon, ma'am."

I waved my hand. "I have heard much worse."

"I never thought that much of those church folk. But I met a Quaker lady once. She told me I had a spark of the divine in me." Eliza smiled sadly. "I liked hearing that."

"I believe that too," I said. "There is something of God in everyone."

"That why you're going to be a missionary?"

"Yes," I said, feeling that thoughts of my future life in India were clouding over this moment.

"It'll be terrible hot out there, won't it?"

"Yes, I expect so."

"Won't you get all burnt?" Eliza looked at me with genuine concern.

"I may do, I suppose."

"That would be a crying shame. You have such lovely fair skin."

I blinked at her, startled, and she blushed and looked at her feet. It took a moment for me to collect myself and respond. "Fair skin will be of no use to me in India." I was aiming for light-hearted, but it came out heavier and sadder than I'd intended. We walked on in silence.

It was indeed a much quicker route to Coldkirk and decidedly more scenic than the winding country lane. We picked our way carefully down the ridge to descend into the village, Eliza nimbly hopping down the rough, rocky slopes. I had to focus all my attention on my feet to avoid falling, and my knees were aching by the time I caught up with her.

We had come into the village on the other side to the main approach. The houses here had gardens that ran up the slopes into the moorland and rough mud paths led between them. Eliza led the way onto the lane that ran through the village. Several women working in the gardens stopped what they were doing to watch us pass. Once on the main lane, we walked into the centre of the village, and again, I noticed people staring.

"Why are they looking at us like that?" I whispered to Eliza as a matronly woman carrying a bundle of washing turned her head to watch.

"Some of them won't have seen you before," she replied. "They ain't all a churchgoing lot here. And they're staring because you're with me. I'm famous 'round here." She grinned at a passing old woman who turned away with a disgusted look on her face.

"Who are they to cast stones?" I demanded indignantly. I stared defiantly back at anyone who met my eye.

The woman in the post office pressed her lips together as I handed over my letter with Eliza standing beside me.

"I suppose you must know Eliza, who is maidservant at Beulah Lodge?" I enquired innocently.

The woman did not look up but muttered, "Yes, I know." She stated the price for the letter, but I did not hand over the coins until she met my eye.

We made one further stop for Martha's thread and then took the route back the way we had come.

"Let's be gone from here," I said. "The moors are friendlier than this place."

We climbed back up the slopes, Eliza again seeming to leap up them whilst I laboured behind. As I approached the top, Eliza leaned down and offered her hand. I grasped it, and she hauled me up with surprising strength. We stood on the ridge for a moment, catching our breath. The climb had been hot work, and I took my hat off, feeling relief as the breeze ruffled my hair. It felt good to be up in the wind again, away from the stuffy small-mindedness of the village.

Eliza looked at me and smiled.

"What is it?" I asked, feeling shy.

"The natives in India ain't got a chance, have they?"

"What do you mean?"

"If you go at them like you just did down there, they'll all be Christian in a week." We both laughed.

I looked back down at the village and shook my head. "And they say London is a cruel place."

"I know. I never got half so many filthy looks in the big smoke." We walked back along the ridge together. I was curious to know more of Eliza's life in London and hoped that she might trust me enough to tell me.

"Did you always live in London?" I asked.

"Born and bred. My grandfather was from the country, though, came to the Isle of Dogs to work on the docks."

"And your parents?"

"My mother was in service for a while. Then she met my father and lost her place. She sold watercress for a while when we was little."

I remembered the watercress sellers that would walk up and down the streets of Poplar and knew how precarious a trade it was. "And what of your father?"

"Dunno. Mum said he was a sailor. She said his name weren't worth remembering."

"You said 'we.' Do you have brothers and sisters?"

"Just an older brother. Frederick. He was with me till Mum died." I was about to commiserate, knowing what the loss of a mother felt like, but she waved her hand to forestall me. "Don't need to say you're sorry. It was typhus what got her, and she didn't put up much of a fight. I think she was glad to be out of it, to be honest. Me and Fred was in the workhouse for a bit after she died, and then he scarpered after that."

"He left you?"

Eliza nodded. "Didn't want to be stuck with a little sister to look after, did he?" Despite her casual, off-hand way of talking, the thought of her as a young girl being left to fend for herself in London made my heart ache for her.

"What happened to him?"

"Dunno. I reckon he's either dead or in gaol. He had a terrible temper on him."

"What did you do once he'd left you?"

"Oh, this and that. Sold matches for a bit, got some odd jobs in Covent Garden. And then…well." She pulled a long stalk of grass up as she walked and swung it by her side in an exaggerated attempt at nonchalance.

"You do not have to talk about it."

"It ain't a nice story." We walked on in silence for a moment before she said, "It seemed easy at first. An easy way to earn a living. But then, it got worse and worse. And I soon realised that there wasn't any way out of it." Her mouth set into a hard line, and she looked older than her years. She had experienced more suffering in her short life than I likely ever would, and I clenched my fist at the unfairness of it.

"I'm so sorry, Eliza," I said.

She looked at me in astonishment. "What on earth you saying sorry for?"

"That you have suffered so much when there are so many born into comfort and idleness."

"Mistress always says that this life is a vale of tears, full of sorrow and suffering. Some'll get their heavenly reward, and some'll get eternal damnation. And I know which one she thinks I'm getting."

"You mustn't believe a word of her nonsense," I said vehemently.

A smile twitched at the corners of Eliza's mouth. "Nonsense, is it?"

"I have met many like Beatrice. They would seek to confine the greatness of God's love within their own, narrow limits. God's love is boundless and freely given, and they cannot accept it because they would prefer that it was not so."

"God don't love sinners, though, does he?"

I stopped and gazed at her, appalled. "Of course he does. Surely, some of these church folk you met must have told you of how Christ came to save all sinners?"

Eliza gave a hard, bitter laugh. "We got told we was the worst sinners of all because we led good Christian men astray. That's what the church lot told us. But I never saw them telling the gents not to sin. And they was never to be found when one of us girls got beaten or cut or forced. They just told us to pray for forgiveness." I could see her jaw clenching. "It was all words," she said, "and not even kind words at that."

I looked out at the moors, and we were both silent watching the shadows lengthening. The wind had picked up and whistled softly around us.

After a moment, Eliza said, "I weren't having a pop at you, ma'am. I know you're a good sort of church folk, what with your missionary work and all."

I felt a stab of shame, thinking of all my doubts and fears about India. "We are none of us perfect."

"Well, I'm glad you came to Beulah Lodge." She seemed to have surprised herself with her own words for her eyes dropped.

I felt my face flush with pleasure. "And I am glad too," I said.

The afternoon was easing into evening by the time we returned to Beulah Lodge. As we made our way past the hen house, Eliza stopped to look in on Nancy. "I do believe she's looking better," she said, squatting next to where Nancy was pecking about in the dirt. "She looks perkier than before, don't you think?"

I put my head on one side and studied Nancy intently. "She looks very much like a chicken," I said. "As she did before."

"Don't pay her any mind, Nancy. She don't know you like I do." Nancy clucked inquiringly and looked at me. I was enjoying the playfulness of our conversation. It came as a blessed relief in contrast to my tense encounters with Beatrice.

I made a solemn curtsy to Nancy. "I should be honoured to become better acquainted with you, madam."

"Ah, we've heard that before, ain't we, girls?" The hens seemed to cluck in agreement as Eliza bolted the door of the henhouse. She grinned at me, her teeth showing white in the fading light. "You gotta work hard to win Nancy's affection. She don't just give it out like penny sweets."

"I will woo her with slices of Martha's pie and invite her to take a turn with me about the yard."

Eliza sucked her teeth. "I wouldn't go straight in with the pie if I were you. You need to build up to that. Maybe start with a bit of ribbon."

"Or a nice juicy worm?"

"Now, she is most partial to a worm."

We continued in this vein as we walked back to the house, laughing and joking, and I had to resist the urge to link arms with her as if we were two schoolgirls.

The evening passed in much the same way as any other. After taking dinner alone in the dining room, I went again to the library to continue my reading of Augustine. I did not do any needlework, telling myself that the light was too poor. I became so absorbed that I was startled when I heard the clock strike ten. I closed my book for the night and ascended the staircase to my room.

As I approached my door, I heard a disturbance coming from the direction of Beatrice's chamber. I could discern a raised voice, almost a scream, and then a loud thump that made me jump. I hastened toward Beatrice's room with my candle. As I approached, I saw Eliza standing outside the door with one hand held against her head and the other unsteadily clutching a candle.

"Eliza?"

She looked up, and I saw with horror that there was blood trickling down one side of her face. I went to her at once, opening my mouth to ask what had happened. "Shh," Eliza hissed and led me away from Beatrice's door. "Not so loud."

I drew her aside into my room and closed the door behind me. "Sit down," I said, indicating the chair at my dressing table.

"I'm all right."

"You are not. Sit down at once."

Eliza lowered herself into the chair and set her candle on my dressing table. I pulled up another chair and looked closely at her face by the light of my oil lamp. There was a large gash on the left side of her forehead, just below her hairline, and it was bleeding profusely. I wet a flannel in my water jug and pressed it to the wound. Eliza winced, sucking her breath in between her teeth.

"What happened?" I asked.

"Nothing."

"Your head did not begin to bleed by itself." Eliza winced again and said nothing. "You are not leaving this room until you tell me," I said.

She huffed like a sulky child. "The mistress just…"

"Your mistress what?" I asked as I dabbed at the gash.

"She threw her letter opener at me."

My hand froze. "She did what?" I said it calmly, but I could feel outrage boiling inside me.

"She chucked her letter opener at me. You know the one, that great, clunky brass…what are you doing?"

I was on my feet, fury coursing through me. "I will not have it," I said. "I…I will not." I was so angry that I could barely speak.

"No, no," Eliza said, clutching my arm. "You must not make a scene."

"I will make fifty thousand scenes."

"It's all right, really."

"It is not all right!" My own voice was rising as I tried to shake Eliza's hand and make for the door.

"Do you want me to lose my place?" There was a note of panic in her voice that finally made me pause.

I looked at her, pale and bloodstained in the dim light, and saw the fear writ large across her face. I took a deep breath and made myself sit again. "Very well. But you must tell me exactly what happened."

Eliza pressed the flannel to her wound and closed her eyes. "She was in a temper cos...cos she saw us from the window."

"When?"

"When we came back from our trip to the village."

"And what of it?" I asked, a cold feeling of dread seeping into me. Surely Beatrice would not seek to extinguish all joy from my existence at Beulah Lodge?

"She didn't like it, did she? Didn't think it was proper." Eliza took the flannel from her head and looked at the blood smeared across it.

I took the cloth from her and leaned forward to press it to her forehead. "But even if she did think my familiarity with a servant to be improper, that can hardly give her cause to throw a paper knife at you."

"She don't even need a cause half the time."

"You mean, she has done this before?"

"Not with the paper knife, that's new. She threw her teacup at me once, but her aim weren't so good. Maybe she's been practising since then."

"I cannot believe you can joke about this."

"What do you suggest I do?" she asked tightly.

I bit my lip as shame welled within me. She was right. What could she do? Beatrice could dismiss her instantly, and Eliza would have nowhere to go. "Does she do this to Martha and Tripp?"

Eliza shrugged and stared into the flickering flame of the lamp, the shadows playing across her face. "Dunno. I ain't ever asked them. But she don't hate them like she hates me."

"Why should she hate you? It was she who brought you here from London, was it not?"

I had laid my other hand along Eliza's jaw to steady her head as I pressed the flannel to the gash in her forehead. Eliza met my gaze, and I realised I was so close that I could see the individual lashes framing her dark eyes. I felt her breath momentarily on my face and an inexorable force bid me draw closer to her.

I drew back, confused. Eliza also abruptly seemed to recall where she was. She moved her head back and said with an artificial breeziness, "I have been a disappointment to her is all. Don't blacken the grates as well as I should." She stood abruptly. "It's stopped bleeding now. Thank you."

"Eliza—"

"I'll leave you to go to bed now, ma'am. You must be tired. Will you be wanting anything else before you retire?" She met my eye calmly, clearly determined that the usual mistress and servant relations should be restored.

"No," I said, quietly. "I do not require anything. But Eliza, Mrs. Groves's treatment of you is wrong. Very wrong."

"Yes, ma'am," she said without expression, and it felt as if a door that had been half-ajar between us had now been slammed shut.

CHAPTER FIVE

It took me a long time to get to sleep that night. I was not unworldly. I was aware that some masters and mistresses struck their servants. And I had seen plenty of instances of cruelty and injustice through my work with my father in his East End parish.

But I had never witnessed such cruelty first-hand, and I had never felt as powerless as I did now. That was what enraged me so, that such injustice could be committed before me, and there was nothing I could do to prevent it. I could remonstrate with Beatrice, but it would have no effect. I could not offer any protection to Eliza for I too was dependant on Beatrice's goodwill for my continued accommodation in her house. I was sure that if I gave her reason, she would take a particular delight in casting me out.

I turned over restlessly. I could not fathom why Beatrice should despise Eliza so. She must have liked the girl to begin with to want to try to save her from her life in London. What had happened to those charitable instincts now? Admittedly, I could not imagine Beatrice being charitable to anyone, but for what other reason would she take Eliza into her household?

I had no answer to these questions and awoke in the grey light of dawn feeling exhausted and uneasy.

I heard the sound of wood chopping and pulled aside the curtain and looked out. Eliza looked as if she too had passed a restless night. The gash was clearly visible, ugly and red against her skin. I let the curtain fall back with a sigh. I did not go down to offer my usual assistance. I felt nervous at the thought of seeing Eliza again but could not explain to myself why this should be so. I fussed with my toilet, which seemed to take three times as long as usual.

I picked at my breakfast and then retired to the library to await my summons from Beatrice. I fiddled with my needlework but had made no progress by the time Eliza knocked at the door.

"Mrs. Groves is ready for you, ma'am." Her face, like her voice, was devoid of expression.

"Thank you, Eliza," I said, rising. "Does your head trouble you this morning?"

"Not too much. Thank you for your kindness last night."

"You are welcome. I am only sorry that I cannot do more to help you."

"You don't need to be sorry. Ain't your lookout, is it?" she said as she turned to lead me from the room.

Eliza knocked on Beatrice's door and entered at the barked command from within. I took my usual place, and Eliza withdrew.

Beatrice was gazing moodily out the window and did not acknowledge my presence. As the silence deepened, I felt some of the anger from the night before rising up in me. I kept a firm hold of it until she finally turned her watery eyes to me. "Are you always so familiar with servants?"

"I do not see familiarity with servants as being improper," I said slowly. "But if I have displeased you, then I am heartily sorry."

"I do not care to see *my* servants being distracted from their work by idle chitchat."

"I do not believe I have ever disrupted their work."

"Oh, so when Eliza was giggling with you yesterday, that was her working, was it?"

"It was a few moments of innocent merriment, Aunt."

"Innocent?" She spat the word as though it was a burr in her mouth. "There is nothing innocent about that girl. Do not forget what she is."

"What she was."

"The filth of sin will never be washed from her. It is only discipline and chastisement that keeps her base nature in check."

"Was that why you threw the paper knife at her?"

Beatrice blinked, and I could see that I had surprised her. "How I discipline my servants is no concern of yours. You are a guest in my house. Or had you forgotten that?"

"No, Aunt, you remind me of it frequently," I said. "But being a guest does not preclude my duty as a Christian. You were wrong to have thrown a paper knife at Eliza."

"The girl is a whore," Beatrice said shrilly. "A common, street-corner tart."

"That does not excuse your behaviour!" My voice rose to match hers, and we both stared furiously at each other for a moment. My hands shook with the effort of keeping my anger under control. I could not allow the incident to pass unremarked, but I was also painfully aware of how completely dependent I was on Beatrice's goodwill.

Then Beatrice turned away from me to look out at the moors. "You are a fool, taken in by a pretty face and a quick tongue. But you will realise soon enough what she is. As I did."

I rose from my chair. "I will bid you good morning if you have no further need of me."

Beatrice eyed me distastefully. "I never had need for you." She waved her hand in dismissal. "You may go. But I'll thank you to cease your familiarity with my servants."

I was about to reply when there was a knock at the door, and Mr. Tripp entered, bearing the morning's post. He silently handed a letter to Beatrice with Daniel's handwriting on the front.

Beatrice looked at the postmark and cackled with glee. "Your intended has written to me. How very kind of him. Let us see how the missionary work progresses, eh?"

I stood and watched her read it, with Tripp standing behind me like a sentinel. I studied Beatrice's face, trying to deduce what was in Daniel's letter by her expression.

Beatrice chuckled, her yellowing cap shaking on her head. "Oh, he does very nicely. The heat is somewhat oppressive, and the flies are troublesome, but he rejoices in being able to take up his cross and follow his Lord." She skipped over a page or two and then said, "He thanks me for my kindness in providing you with a home whilst he prepares a place for you. He hopes that I have come to know you better and to appreciate your many fine qualities." She laughed out

loud. "Why, so we have. Is that not right, Tripp? We have never known anyone to chop wood so nicely."

"The lady shouldn't be choppin' wood, ma'am. Tain't her place." He looked at me sideways from under his heavy brows.

"Quite right, Tripp, but then it should be your task to chop the wood, should it not? It is only because you are such a broken-down ragdoll that Eliza has to do it."

Tripp's face drooped as if all the flesh had been sucked out of it. His look at Beatrice was almost pleading as he began, "Please, ma'am, tain't my—"

Beatrice waved her hand in the now familiar gesture of dismissal. "Enough. Be gone, both of you. I have letters to read."

I left the room with Tripp following. Tripp turned to close the door after us. "Mrs. Groves can be…sharp. On occasion," I ventured.

Tripp looked at me, his face set and stony. "She is a fine and fair mistress."

"You know her far better than I do."

"I been in service with the family since I were a boy," Tripp replied proudly.

"So, you knew Mr. Groves well?" We began walking back down the stairs together. I deliberately took my time in the hope that I would be able to eke out further details.

"Yes, ma'am. He were a fine gentleman and the last of his line." He shook his head sadly. "There won't be no more Groves at Beulah Lodge."

"There were no children?"

"No. The Lord did not see fit to bless them in that way." Tripp was scowling again, and on following his gaze, I could see why.

Eliza had entered the hall from the kitchen, carrying a mop and bucket. She caught sight of us and called out cheerfully, "Good morning to you Mr. Tripp."

"Get on with your work, girl." he barked as he entered the passage to the kitchen.

"It *is* a beautiful day, ain't it?" Eliza called after him. She shook her head as she dunked the mop into the soapy water.

I paused in the dim, draughty hallway. Eliza glanced up and then slopped the mop onto the floor. The wound on her forehead still

looked angry and sore. I cleared my throat and said, "I am sorry I was not there to help with the wood this morning. I did not sleep well."

Eliza made a noncommittal noise and did not look up from her work. I considered simply walking on and leaving her to it, but I felt compelled to try to dispel any awkwardness from the previous night. "I meant to say, I saw your plover on the moors a few days ago."

Eliza looked up. Her face was alight with interest. "Oh yes? Where was it?"

"Err…on the way to the big rock," I said.

Eliza cocked an eyebrow at me. "Ah, I see. I know exactly where you mean."

"I fear I cannot be any more precise," I said, smiling. "But I recognised the bird from your description."

Eliza sloshed a fresh mop full of water over the hall tiles. "That's good. I hope we'll see more of them as the summer goes on."

"Is the plover your favourite bird?" I asked.

Eliza leaned on the mop whilst she pondered this. "I think the lark is," she said finally. "Cos of its song." And then she pursed her lips and whistled a long, lilting tune that seemed to come from somewhere far away from the dingy hall.

"That is quite beautiful," I said.

"The real thing is even better," she assured me.

"And a sound you would never hear in London."

"No. Though I used to like hearing the pigeons cooing of a morning. I always felt like pigeons was my kindred spirits, them being dirty little street urchins like me."

It pained me to hear her speak of herself in this way and I said, "You are nothing like a pigeon." Eliza looked at me quizzically, and I wished I had found a better form of words. I changed the subject. "Where does this love of ornithology come from?"

"You what?"

"Why do you love birds so much?"

"I dunno really. I only started paying attention to them when I came here. I think it's cos they were all new to me. I felt like I'd seen everything in London. There was nothing that could surprise me anymore. But then I arrive here and everywhere I look, I'm seeing things I ain't never seen before. And good things too, not just seeing a different type of dead meat getting pulled from the Thames."

"Do you keep notes on what you see?"

A flush of colour stole up her throat. "Nah," she said, in that studiously casual way of hers. "Can't hardly write my own name let alone notes on anything."

I felt my own face flame at my tactlessness. I had clumsily tried to rebuff her assertions about being a street urchin, and now I had made her feel embarrassed about her background.

"Well," I said, wanting to make up for my blunder, "you have certainly made me pay more attention on my walks." I sensed that she was not used to receiving compliments for she coloured again and mumbled something about how she had better be getting a shift on.

CHAPTER SIX

Much as I enjoyed my early morning wood chopping with Eliza, the days continued to pass at a leaden pace, and my restlessness was unabated.

Sundays offered a respite from the usual routine. Martha and I would set off after breakfast to Coldkirk, with Martha leaving Eliza strict instructions on what Mrs. Groves was to be given for lunch. Tripp was nowhere to be seen on Sundays, but I gathered from Martha's embarrassment and Eliza's wide grin when I asked that he passed the Sabbath in the Red Lion.

We walked down the lane to the village, Martha being adamant that the shortcut over the moors was unsafe.

"Like as not, you'd turn your ankle on a boulder, ma'am," she declared.

She asked me how I found life at Beulah Lodge, and I said carefully, "It is a quieter life than what I have been used to in London."

Martha nodded sympathetically. "I can imagine, ma'am. After all that hustle and bustle, we must seem quite dull."

"Not dull exactly," I said, "but I am unused to having so little with which to occupy my time."

Martha asked me about my life in London, and I took great pleasure in talking about Papa and the work we did together in his parish. Martha was a sympathetic listener, and when I came to speak of my father's death and my voice began to shake, she laid her hand on my arm as we walked and said, "What a terrible loss, ma'am. To his whole parish but to you most of all."

I merely nodded, not trusting myself to speak, and by that time, we had arrived at St. Rumbold's.

I found the familiar words of the liturgy a comfort, as I always did, and as the congregation's strains of "We Plough the Fields" faded, Reverend Glossop ascended into the stone pulpit to deliver his sermon.

His text was the parable of the talents from Matthew's gospel, and he urged us to consider what the Lord had given us. For some, it would be much, for others, less, but the Lord had vouchsafed all of us with talents, with treasure.

"God is our Lord and Master," Mr. Glossop declared sternly. "And as the gospel clearly states, we shall all be called to give an account of ourselves. What have we done with the gifts that the Lord has given us? How shall we answer Him on that fearful day of reckoning? Consider, my brothers and sisters, what the Lord has blessed you with and consider how you shall make use of those blessings to glorify and magnify His name!"

After the service, we shook hands with Reverend Glossop and then turned our steps homeward. We walked in silence along the lane for a few minutes until Martha asked me what I had thought of the sermon.

"It was thought-provoking," I said, and indeed I had been reflecting on Reverend Glossop's words. God had blessed me with much, but I felt I was squandering and wasting time at Beulah Lodge, not doing good for anyone.

"Aye, it was," Martha said. "He is a good man, is Mr. Glossop. He never fails to ask after the mistress's health, and he is always most concerned for our souls. I know it pains him that it is only me from the lodge as goes to church regular. But I have tried," she said with a sigh. "Tripp takes after the mistress in all things, including religion. He thinks like her, that Anglicanism is the same as devil worship. But at least he reads his Bible still. When Eliza first arrived, I suggested we read the Bible together of a Sunday, but the poor girl cannot read a word. And I have not the wit to teach her."

I stopped in the middle of the lane so abruptly that Martha had walked on a few paces before she realised and turned back.

"Of course," I said. "What a sluggard I am not to have thought of it before!"

"Ma'am?"

"I can teach Eliza to read." Martha looked doubtful. "I have done it before," I said. "I used to give lessons after Sunday school to a few of my father's parishioners who wanted to learn."

"Why, ma'am, that would be…" Martha's hopeful expression halted. "I mean…if the mistress agrees, that is."

"She will not object," I said with a confidence I did not entirely feel, but I was determined that my excellent idea would not be deflated.

We walked onward, my heart lightened now that I had hit on a practical way to be of service.

"Yes, ma'am," Martha said thoughtfully after a few minutes. "I think that would be a very good thing. Eliza is a bright girl. Why, she knew next to nothing about birds and flowers and suchlike, yet now she knows more about 'em than I do. And her sketches are quite remarkable."

"Sketches?"

"She was always asking me the names of birds she'd seen, and I told her she should draw them for me, and then I would be better able to recognise them. I think she has a real eye for it."

"Has she had any schooling that you know of?"

"No, ma'am. Mind you, I don't claim to know everything about what her life was like before she came here. She don't like to talk about it much, understandably. When she first arrived, she barely spoke. I think the poor girl was terrified. She hadn't never been out of London before, never been in service. And here she was in a great big house with no friends or family nearby."

"Mr. Tripp does not find her presence congenial, I believe?"

"No, indeed. He is always saying he doesn't know what the mistress was thinking."

"It does seem a surprising act of charity. From one who doesn't routinely engage in charitable concerns." I was being very careful with words so as not to give offence by seeming to criticise Beatrice, but Martha nodded vigorously in agreement.

"It was. I have never known the mistress to be the slightest bit concerned about the poor. I mean," she said hastily, "I mean that—"

"That it was a surprise when she returned from London with Eliza in tow," I spared her.

"Exactly. And I don't know what she wanted from the girl. After a few days, she said to me, 'Martha, make her a housemaid,' and that was the last time she ever spoke on the matter. And I know she is dreadful fierce with Eliza. One can't help but hear…and see." Martha shook her head, the grey curls bobbing from beneath her old-fashioned bonnet. "My own belief is that the mistress simply took a fancy to her and then grew tired of her, like she did with other things when she were younger. She once had a craze for French cuisine and was insisting that Mrs. Hawkes, that was the old cook before me, should be making onion soup and fancy pastries, and I don't know what else. Mrs. Hawkes would slam the pots about and say that one Eccles cake was worth a dozen éclairs any day." Martha laughed, a warm, hearty sound that chimed in with the birdsong from the hedges.

"But the craze for French cooking did not last?"

"No, thank goodness. And neither did her enthusiasm for Russian novels or formal gardens or spiritualism. They were harmless enough, I suppose, but it is a different matter when it is people that one picks up and tosses aside. Just ask poor Mr. Tripp."

I nodded, thinking that Beatrice's treatment of Eliza was finally beginning to make some sense.

"Mr. Groves was always very indulgent of her whims. The only thing he was severe about was his religion. When he died, Mrs. Groves didn't have so many of her fancies anymore."

"It must have been a great change for the household after his death."

"Aye. He was a hard man, Mr. Groves, but he were fair. Since he died, Mrs. Groves has become more like him…but not so much in regard to his good qualities."

"Did you never think of leaving Beulah Lodge?"

Martha sighed heavily. "I was widowed when my sons were still children. I needed a position, and I was lucky that Mr. Groves took me on. I couldn't afford to be choosy, not even when Mrs. Groves grew to be so…difficult. There's always mouths to feed."

I nodded sympathetically and moved the conversation on to more general talk of the village and its scandals, which occupied us very happily until we came back to the house. Martha's kindly good sense had cheered me greatly, and my affection for her grew.

CHAPTER SEVEN

Now that I had a clear purpose and plan before me, I was determined to put it into action. And so, the next morning, as I placed logs on the block for Eliza I said, "I shall teach you to read, Eliza."

The axe split the log in two, and Eliza stared at me. "You'll what?" she said, slightly breathless from her exertions.

"I shall teach you to read. I used to teach some of my father's parishioners, so I will be perfectly able to do it."

Eliza pulled the axe from the block. "No doubt. But there's no point you wasting your time, ma'am."

"It would not be a waste of my time."

"It would be a waste of mine, then."

I laid another log and waited for her to split it before saying, "But should you not like to be able to read?"

"Oh yes, ma'am," she said, lightly. "Just as I would like to be able to juggle."

"Being able to read and write would be a more useful skill."

"Would it? People pay to see jugglers." She split the last of the logs with tremendous force, grunting with the effort. I let the matter drop for the time being, but I was not going to be deterred. I felt that I had to do some good whilst I was at Beulah Lodge and, having seen how Beatrice had treated her, I was anxious to help Eliza most of all.

My interview with Beatrice later that morning proceeded along the usual lines. As it was a Monday, she asked me to summarise Reverend Glossop's sermon for her, and then she spent a happy quarter of an hour holding forth on its and the reverend's many failings.

"He may not be the most skilled orator, but I believe he means well," I said. "He asked after your health."

Beatrice snorted derisively. "He has been trying to ingratiate himself with this family for years. My husband held him in contempt, as he did all Anglicans."

"You never attended St. Rumbold's?"

"My husband took charge of the religious instruction of the household," said Beatrice with a touch of pride in her voice. I remembered Martha's comments on Mr. Groves' religious instruction and suppressed a smile.

"It is admirable that he was concerned with the education of his servants."

"He knew that sin is the most virulent of diseases, especially amongst servants."

"My own belief is that ignorance is the dance partner of sin. Education and self-improvement bring their own rewards in virtue and good living."

"Education is wasted on the lower classes. It merely gives them the idea that they are better than they are."

I felt the now-familiar spark of indignation but I kept my tone steady and said, "But say, for example, if all people could read, then they could read the word of God for themselves."

"And what a calamity that would be. The only thing the papists had right was in not allowing every Tom, Dick, and Harry to read the Bible. Do you seriously expect a plough boy or milkmaid to be able to discern the mysteries contained in God's word?"

"I do not think it is so mysterious," I ventured.

"'He hath put down the mighty from their seats and exalted those of low degree,'" Beatrice quoted. "If all the lowly villains in the country read those words, then we would end up like the French with their bloody revolution."

"But—"

"The Word must be guarded by men of learning and right theology. They may then expound it to those who have not the ability to understand."

I was silent. I had been hoping to somehow gradually build up to the idea of my teaching Eliza to read. I tried desperately to think of other arguments I could make, but Beatrice dismissed me before I could say more.

I returned to the library later that afternoon, after my customary walk on the moors after lunch. When I opened the door, I found Eliza already in the room, running a feather duster along the spines of the books.

"I won't be much longer, ma'am," she said as I entered.

"Don't hurry on my account," I said, seating myself in an armchair and reaching down to retrieve the sampler I had been half-heartedly embroidering. "I am glad you are here. I saw a bird on my walk I wanted to ask you about."

Eliza's eyes brightened with interest.

"It was somewhat small," I said, "with a speckled colouring, rather like a thrush."

"Was it perhaps…a thrush?"

"No," I said, smiling. "I can at least recognise common garden birds. It had a high-pitched kind of song, and then it swooped down very suddenly."

Eliza nodded at the paper on the desk. "Could you try and draw it, ma'am?"

I moved to sit at the desk and drew a sheet of paper and a pencil toward me. I spent the next few minutes frowning over the paper as I did my best to render an accurate picture of what I had seen. Eliza came and looked over my shoulder as I finished.

"There," I said doubtfully. I had managed to sketch a basic bird-like outline, but it could equally have been either a sparrow or an eagle.

I felt rather than saw Eliza suppress a laugh. She slid the paper over to her and, taking the pencil from my hand, sketched an astonishingly accurate picture of the bird I had seen. "Was it perhaps this that you saw?"

"Yes," I said, "yes, that is it exactly."

"A pipit. They are sweet little things. That swoop they do is how you recognise 'em."

I held up the paper with our two drawings on it. "I mean, I think it should have been perfectly obvious from my rendition." The sight of my childlike scribble next to hers was too comical, and we both laughed.

"You know," I said, as Eliza was still grinning, "I am determined that I shall teach you to read."

Eliza waved her duster dismissively. "It would be a waste of your time, ma'am. I am too old to learn now."

"Nonsense. What are you, two and twenty?"

"Don't know for sure. But about that."

"I have taught people twice your age. It is never too late."

"Mistress would never approve."

"Mrs. Groves has not forbidden it." I told myself that this was perfectly true, even if I had not directly asked for permission.

Eliza turned back to dusting the bookshelves. "But what good would reading do me? I got no need for books."

"It would give you options. There would be different sorts of work you could do if you could read and write. I imagine you don't want to be at Beulah Lodge forever?"

"Hmm. That's true." Eliza paused in her dusting and looked at me almost shyly. "You…you really like reading, don't you, ma'am?"

"I do. Eliza, I cannot tell you what delight there is to be had in reading. For you may go anywhere in the world when you read, to any time and any place. Even when I have been at my most unhappy, I have found comfort and joy in being taken elsewhere. Your mind and your heart may be led down paths you never would have suspected, and your imagination can soar into such heights, like a great eagle taking flight. It is like sunlight bursting in upon a darkened room." I could sense myself getting carried away by my own rhetoric and forced myself to stop.

Eliza was staring at me with an expression I had not seen before and which made my face grow hot. I shifted my gaze to the floor and said awkwardly, "As I say. I think there are countless advantages to being able to read."

Eliza was silent for a while, still staring at me in that unsettling way. Finally, she nodded. "All right," she said rather gruffly. "If you insist. We shall have to do it in the afternoon, though. After I've given the mistress her lunch and cleared it away. That's the only time I'd have. And then only if Martha don't want me for nothing."

"That would do very well," I said, my heart rejoicing within me.

Chapter Eight

And so, a new routine began to slowly establish itself. After lunch, I would spend some time in the library with Eliza, teaching her letters. We never had any longer than an hour, but Eliza proved herself to be an able pupil.

My teaching materials were somewhat limited. There were pencils and plenty of paper, but the dense theological tomes were hardly suitable for someone just learning to read. I had used primers and chapbooks at the Sunday school, and I recreated these from memory as best I could.

I found a useful starting exercise was for me to write the letter and a word beginning with that letter and for Eliza to sketch a corresponding picture. It wasn't long before we had the fully illustrated alphabet with charming drawings of animals and plants for every letter.

Eliza mastered the alphabet quickly, and I then moved to writing out simple sentences and passages to illustrate the various letter sounds. I derived great enjoyment from penning nonsense about "chuntering chaffinches" and "shy shags."

Indeed, Eliza's learning progressed at such a rate that I found that my time was increasingly occupied in preparing materials for the next stage of her lessons. I felt an enormous sense of relief at finally having found an occupation that engaged me and felt as though a dark cloud had been lifted from my shoulders.

I slept easier than I had done in months and woke feeling refreshed and enthused for the day ahead. Even my interviews with Beatrice could not dampen my spirits, for I had adopted a new resolution to be as patient and kind to her as I could.

Beatrice seemed to find my kindness rather irritating. She could not get the reaction she wanted from me and so tended to dismiss me after a mere half hour. This left me with plenty of time to prepare my lessons and spend the requisite hour on my needlework. This was something I forced myself to do to salve my conscience and assure myself that I was preparing to be a good wife to Daniel. I would watch the clock like a hawk, and when my designated hour was up, I would go for a walk.

The moors were alive to me now as a place of beauty. Their apparent bleakness had vanished as my own contentment had grown. The moors might take on a more sombre hue on grey, overcast days, but the undercurrent of despair that I had felt when I first arrived at Beulah Lodge had gone.

My daily routine of wood chopping and lessons with Eliza had led to an easy familiarity developing between us. The early surliness of her manner toward me had entirely disappeared, and we conversed amicably about what we had seen on the moors and our shared knowledge and memories of London. Indeed, spending time in her company became one of the few pleasures that life at Beulah Lodge afforded me.

My relations with Martha too also grew warmer, to the extent that she tolerated and even seemed to enjoy my presence in her kitchen. I would occasionally take my needlework down and talk with her as I laboured to embroider handkerchiefs or hem skirts.

Although I had made firm friends of Eliza and Martha, Mr. Tripp remained a gloomy and foreboding presence in the house. I saw him but rarely and usually when he was either entering or leaving the kitchen. He would incline his head solemnly to acknowledge my presence but did not engage in conversation with me, despite my best attempts.

Tripp's notional responsibility was for the management of the estate. "The estate," so far as I could gather, consisted of around two hundred acres, much of which was used for grazing sheep. The tenants of the estate numbered no more than fifty souls and were spread out in cottages and hamlets to the south around Coldkirk and to the west toward Hawnby. This flatter land toward the river supported a few small fields of potatoes but not much else.

Travelling around all these far-flung tenants seemed to take up the majority of Tripp's time. He possessed an aged cob named Prospero for this purpose, who was kept in a stable at the side of the house, and no one aside from Tripp was permitted any contact with the horse. Indeed, I would not have known of Prospero's existence had I not had occasion to see Tripp a few times trotting down the lane toward the village. He patted the horse's neck affectionately as he rode along, which was the only sign of fondness I had seen him display to any living thing.

It was on an enforced visit to the stable that I discovered that this was also where Tripp kept the accounts for the estate.

There was an ancient chandelier hanging from the ceiling of my room which looked as if it had not been used in years. Cobwebs hung about it like ghostly bunting. I had paid it no mind until that morning when I had happened to glance up and saw several large cracks radiating out from its centre, gradually fading as they stretched toward the wall.

The chandelier hung partially over the end of my bed, and I had no desire to have my legs crushed in the night. After consulting with Martha, I had discovered that general handyman was another of Tripp's roles, and so I had gone to seek him out, despite Martha's dire warnings that Tripp would not take kindly to being disturbed in the stable. I had retorted that I would not take kindly to losing a leg to a chandelier and had promptly made my way around the side of the house.

The stable had clearly once been home to several horses but was now in a sad state of disrepair. One half of it had completely collapsed into ruin. The remaining half still had a roof, although it was fighting a losing battle with the thick tendrils of ivy that had taken root in the ruined half. The iron guttering around the roof was rusty, and the tracks of water could clearly be seen against the grey bricks of the wall as it had trickled down onto the broken slabs of what had once been the stable yard.

I ducked my head into the half stable that was still standing and was greeted by a snort from Prospero. Despite the pervasive smell of damp timber, Prospero's end of the stable was dry and in reasonably good repair. The horse had a roomy stall with a generous allowance of hay, but he whinnied hopefully at me and pushed his nose toward me.

"I have nothing for you, I'm afraid," I said to him. "I gave my last piece of biscuit to Nancy."

"He always be askin' for what he ain't permitted." I turned and saw Tripp sitting at the other end of the stable, nearest the ruined half. He was seated on a wooden plank balanced between two barrels. His pipe was in his mouth, and he had a large book open on the bench beside him.

Although it was broad daylight, it was dim in the stable, and I wondered that he could see well enough to read.

"I'm sorry to disturb your reading," I said.

Tripp snorted. "I ain't reading, not your sort of reading anyway."

"My sort of reading?" I asked, widening my eyes in mock surprise.

Tripp got to his feet slowly, his knees clicking. "I mean the sort of reading that young ladies of leisure do. Novels and suchlike." He practically spat the word out.

"I can recommend the works of Mr. Trollope if you have a care to try a novel."

Mr. Tripp grunted. "Can I be of service to you, ma'am?" I suppressed a smile.

"Yes. The chandelier in my room has some rather alarming cracks surrounding it. I wondered if you might be able to take a look and let me know if I should live in fear of it falling down upon my head. Or at least my legs."

"All those chandeliers fall down eventually. Roof leaks, see, and some of that gets into the timbers, and then they can't take the weight of the chandeliers no more."

"Is there anything that can be done?"

"A new roof is what's needed, but Mistress would never agree to the expense. And that's assuming there was the money for it," he said, casting a glance back at where his book was lying upon his makeshift bench.

Now that my eyes had grown accustomed to the gloom, I noticed a pile of similar looking books were piled in the corner behind Tripp's bench, the bottom layer almost entirely covered with dust.

"Do you do all your accounts work in here?" I asked.

"Aye."

"But the light is so poor."

"Aye, it is."

"And you have no proper table," I said, looking around the cramped stable.

"Aye, right enough," Tripp agreed.

"Surely, there must be a room in the main house that you could use?" I looked at his hunched frame and could imagine his discomfort.

"Ain't no space in my chamber. And the kitchen is always full of Martha and *that girl*."

"But of all the rooms in Beulah Lodge, there must—"

"Mistress wouldn't like it," Tripp said firmly.

I had to clench my jaw to prevent an exasperated sound escaping me. "Did she expressly forbid it?"

"She once said that she despised the very sight of account books and columns of figures."

"When did she say this?"

Tripp made a noncommittal noise, as if it mattered not when the pronouncement had been made because once made, its effect was everlasting.

"Perhaps you would be so good as to look at the chandelier in my chamber, and I will speak to Mrs. Groves about whether you could perhaps make use of the library for the storage of your account books."

"Mistress won't never agree to it," Tripp barked.

"Maybe she won't," I said breezily. "But no harm can come from me asking."

When I raised the question of the account books with Beatrice the next day, she stared at me as if I were speaking Greek to her. "The account books? Tripp takes care of all that."

"Yes, but he does so in the stable. That is hardly a suitable place. There is no light in there, there is no desk and the damp—"

"What of it?" Beatrice snapped irritably.

"I thought perhaps it would be better if he had the use of the library. I only use the library for a short while in the morning and after lunch, so Tripp would not be disturbing me. And if the account books are rotted by damp, you know, that will cause you no end of trouble in the future if bailiffs or creditors should come—"

Beatrice waved her hand as if she could not bear to hear any more about it. "Yes, yes, very well. He may store his blasted account books in there if he wishes. God knows, I have no wish to know by exactly how much he is cheating me."

"Mr. Tripp does not seem to live an extravagant lifestyle," I said, trying not to sound as exasperated as I felt.

"But what about that wretched nag of his? Eating up no end of money in feed and shoes and whatnot."

"But you must have kept horses in the past."

"We kept our own coach and pair, and that was sufficient. My husband did not approve of hunting and kept no horses for that purpose."

"Were you fond of riding, Aunt?" I was curious about what her life was like when she had been a young wife.

"I did not spend my time engaged in frivolous pursuits," she snapped.

"So where did Prospero come from?" She frowned at me. "Mr. Tripp's horse."

"How should I know? Probably some clapped-out farm nag, I imagine."

We moved on to our usual discussion of the rightness of Beatrice's theology, but I was pleased that I had managed to secure one more minor improvement in the life of Beulah Lodge and its inhabitants.

❖

I was not so naive as to expect gratitude from Mr. Tripp, but he surprised me by grimacing in a way that I believe was meant to approximate a smile when I told him that Mrs. Groves had consented for the account books to be moved into the library. I felt as triumphant as Wellington after Waterloo.

I had been sitting at the kitchen table with my needlework, chatting with Martha when he had come in, and I'd told him the good news.

"That will be better, ma'am," he said.

"Oh yes," Martha agreed. "It will save your eyes, Tripp, let alone the books. He can't see so well these days," she said to me.

"Nothing wrong with my eyes, woman."

Martha winked at me and disappeared into the larder to fetch the cutlets for supper.

"Shall we move the books now?" I asked, getting to my feet.

"There are a lot of them," said Tripp hesitatingly.

Eliza entered the kitchen at that moment from the hallway passage, bearing the tray from Beatrice's room. As she set it on the kitchen table, I said, "Eliza can help us."

"Help you with what?" Eliza asked, eyeing Tripp suspiciously.

"We are moving the account books from the stable to the library," I explained. "A far more sensible location for them, wouldn't you agree?"

"Less chance of Prospero eating them, I s'pose."

"Exactly. Come on, then, let's see if we can't all do it in one go."

"You needn't be lifting them, ma'am," Tripp said as he followed me out into the yard. "The girl and I can manage them."

"You couldn't manage more than a page," Eliza muttered. Tripp snapped at her to speak up, and at the same time, I caught her eye. She coughed and said more loudly, "I said how many pages?"

"I got all the books going back to the time Mr. Groves bought the estate."

"And when was that?" I asked.

"Oh, back when the old king was still on the throne." My heart sank.

When we got to the stable, I realised the enormity of what Tripp meant. Under an old horse blanket in the corner were piles of account books, each one covering a period of three years. Tripp rummaged amongst them, passing them back to myself and Eliza who stacked them in piles on the floor, away from a curious Prospero.

The farther Tripp went into the pile, the worse condition the books were in. All of them were thick with dust and many of them had clearly been happy homes for various insects and mould. Tripp remembered there was a wheelbarrow and went off to fetch it.

Eliza and I looked at the mouldering pile of ledgers. I took one of the more recent ones and flicked through its pages. Spidery columns of figures and notes covered the page, and I frowned, trying to make sense of it.

Eliza nudged me and whispered, "He's coming back. Don't let him catch you looking at them." I replaced it hurriedly.

The operation of transporting the books into the house was rendered straightforward by the wheelbarrow, but they still had to be carried up the stairs from the kitchen, Tripp being adamant that the front door could not possibly be used for such a menial task and that the mistress wouldn't like it.

I did not want to endanger my victory by pushing too hard so I did not argue with him. Eliza and Tripp carried handfuls of books up and down the stairs, and I arranged them by date on one of the empty shelves in the library.

When the last one had been slotted into place, we all stood back and admired our handiwork. I thought the tatty row of books looked rather lost and sad amongst the luxuriously bound theological volumes, but Tripp seemed satisfied.

"They look better there," he announced. I agreed, and there was a silence. I looked again at Eliza.

"Yes, they do," she said. And then, after a moment, "The wheelbarrow was a good idea. Would've taken us hours without that."

Tripp looked at her suspiciously, as if searching for the barb in her comment. Seeing Eliza's blandly pleasant expression, he grunted and said that the wheelbarrow had been made by young Thomas, an under-gardener who had worked at the house many years ago.

"Was he also here when the old king was still on the throne?" Eliza asked. Her tone was gently mocking, and I was about to interrupt when I saw a strange, smiling grimace cross Tripp's face.

"No. Thomas left us to go fight in the Crimea. Died out by the Black Sea or the White Sea, can't remember which. His mother told me so."

"Probably better for him that way," Eliza said. "Knew a few fellers who'd fought out there. All had bits missing, either in their bodies or in their heads, if you know what I mean."

"Aye…lads never come back from a war better than they was before."

It was the first normal exchange I had ever heard between Eliza and Tripp, and I was relieved that it was not laced with the usual sarcasm and contempt. They also seemed to sense this, for Tripp coughed awkwardly and mumbled something about how he really ought to be getting on.

He took the wheelbarrow and wheeled it back out in to the hall, and presently, we heard it bumping down the steps to the kitchen.

Eliza and I remained, still staring at the row of neatly arranged account books.

"Well," I said after a few moments silence. "I think we could say that you and Mr. Tripp are positively friends now."

"Let's not get carried away, ma'am," Eliza said.

"But that wasn't so hard, was it?"

"I dunno. I find cleaning the range easier."

"Practice is all it takes," I said. "If you practice saying one nice thing to Mr. Tripp every day, before you know it, it will simply be a habit that you hardly notice anymore."

Eliza's lips twitched as she curtsied to me and said, "If you say so, ma'am."

And so, we again transitioned to a new routine at Beulah Lodge. Several times a week, Mr. Tripp would stump up to the library and frown over his accounts. At first, he leapt up if I entered the library and made as if to go, but I was eventually able to assure him that his presence was not disturbing to me.

Then I would sit with my needle or my book whilst Tripp's pen scratched in the ledgers. The accounts seemed to be a trial to Mr. Tripp, for I frequently heard him sucking his teeth, blowing out his cheeks, or making great sighing noises. I wanted to ask him if I could help in any way, but I sensed he would not take kindly to my offering assistance.

But one overcast morning, I observed him squinting hard against the weak light from the window. I took my lamp from the small table next to me and brought it over to his desk.

"Here, Mr. Tripp," I said, setting it down at his elbow. "Perhaps this may give you extra light to ease your eyes."

He grunted his thanks, and I took a quick glance at the page of the account book he was working on. It was a jumble of figures in one column with Tripp's spidery handwriting all over it. He saw where I was looking, and his eyes narrowed suspiciously.

"I have some experience with bookkeeping and figures," I explained. "I managed the accounts for my father's church, mainly to do with the distribution of collection money to the poor and suchlike."

He eyed me carefully, as if I was an unknown horse whose measure he had not yet taken. I waited patiently. He finally seemed to make a decision and ran his finger down the page until it stopped at an entry. He cleared his throat.

"It's Curran, you see, ma'am," he said.

"Curran?"

"Down at Whistler's Fell. He says he has already paid his rent this quarter, and I say he hasn't. He gave me part of it last month, but he still owes at least a guinea."

I said carefully, "Perhaps a second pair of eyes may be of use in this case?"

Tripp nodded, and I drew up a chair beside him.

"Have you a record of his previous payment?"

"Aye, here." He pointed to the figures scrawled on the page. I studied it for a moment. I could clearly see the figure of three pounds and ten shillings recorded under the "Received" column, with an X placed next to it.

"That is Curran's mark?"

"Yes, ma'am. I always make them sign when they give the rent."

"And how much is the rent each quarter?"

"Five pounds."

"So Curran owes a further one and ten this quarter?" I phrased it as a question and looked to Tripp for confirmation.

He twisted his cap unhappily and said, "That's what I say, ma'am. Only Curran says he gave me two extra boxes of taters over what he owes, and that should count against the rent."

I took a seat at this point and waved Mr. Tripp into the other chair. I drew pencil and paper toward me. "Very well," I began. "And what is the value of a box of potatoes?"

We worked through the problem together in this way until we had finally established that Curran's potatoes had been recorded in the accounts book and that if Mr. Tripp was feeling generous, he could deduct ten shillings from the rent that Curran owed.

"But that would still mean he owes a pound," I said, finishing off my sums.

Mr. Tripp leaned over my shoulder and nodded. "Aye, that seems right, ma'am." He pointed at some of my calculations. "And what is this here?"

"This? It is merely the way I do long multiplication. I find it prevents me getting muddled along the way. Here, let me show you. Say we wish to multiply five boxes of potatoes at two and six each..."

I showed Mr. Tripp my method, and he frowned and then nodded. I went through another example and another, until I could sense that he was getting the hang of it. Then I suggested that he attempt one himself. Tripp licked the end of the pencil and worked through the sum, slowly but correctly. I felt immense satisfaction at this and was just suggesting that he should try another, more complex calculation when the door opened, and Eliza entered.

She was visibly startled to see Tripp there but quickly recovered herself. "Mistress is ready for you, ma'am."

I rose and said to Mr. Tripp, "I think you should do a few more, whilst it is fresh in your mind. If you have any difficulties, I can help you later today."

Tripp nodded absently, still frowning at the paper before him. I left him to it and followed Eliza up the stairs to Beatrice.

The interview with Beatrice passed as usual, and when I returned to the library after lunch, the account book and the papers with the sums had been cleared away.

I took out all the exercise books and papers for Eliza's lesson. She arrived promptly, removing her apron as she entered and draping it over the back of the armchair. I felt a pleasing sense of anticipation, as I did before all our lessons. I enjoyed teaching her and was filled with pride at her progress in her reading and writing.

We went straight into our work, reading through some basic Bible passages that I had carefully selected for the words they used. We made good progress and were coming to the natural end of our session when Eliza said, "Was you helping Mr. Tripp with his sums?"

"Yes. I was showing him a way of doing long multiplication which is easier and less prone to errors. He bears a weighty responsibility, looking after all the accounts of the estate."

"I s'pose so. I ain't never really enquired too much into what he did. He just has a go at me and Martha if we get through the carbolic too quick."

"I suspect he has not had much of an apprenticeship in how to manage the books."

"Is it that hard?"

"It requires constant attention to keep track of what income is coming in and the expenses going out. I cannot imagine how he ever managed it from that damp stable."

"Not anymore, eh? Thanks to you."

"It is a small enough thing, but I hope it will make a difference."

"Teaching me to read, helping Tripp with the books, and going with Martha to church. The mistress is the only project you got left now."

"You are not a project," I said and saw a flush come to her cheeks. "And anyway," I said, "I think my aunt may be beyond me. Although, she cannot have always been as she is now. Something must have made her this way." I looked at Eliza expectantly, inviting her thoughts.

Eliza picked at the edge of the paper and said, "I s'pose so. Martha always says she was a nice girl when she first came here."

"I wonder what Mr. Groves was like as a husband."

"It don't sound like he were a barrel of laughs."

"No," I agreed. "The only impression I have of him is as a stern, rather unyielding man. I have tried to get my aunt to talk further about him but with no success."

Eliza doodled absently on the side of our exercise, sketching out various bird-like shapes. "She once told me that Mr. Groves had chosen her as a wife because she was so young, and he knew she could be bent to his will."

I looked at her in surprise. I could not imagine Beatrice vouchsafing such a confidence, particularly not to Eliza, whom she always seemed to treat with contempt.

Eliza seemed to read my thoughts in my face for she said, "Like you say, the mistress weren't always as she is now. She was very kind to me when I first knew her."

"Kind?" I repeated, and Eliza gave a wry smile.

"I know. You'd never think it, but she was. I was in a bad way when I met her. I'd just got kicked out my lodgings and was down to my last few pennies. I was having a row with a punter when Beatrice drove by in her carriage."

"What sort of a row?"

"Oh, the usual dispute one has with tradesmen," Eliza said, affecting an airy, upper-class voice. "We simply could not agree on a price." I looked away and then felt angry with myself for doing so. "Anyway, it was all getting a bit heated, and this bloke had hold of me." She must have seen my shock and waved her hand. "Just grabbing my wrists is all I mean. So I was trying to pull away, and then a Hansom draws up, and this old bird leans out and asks if I require assistance." Eliza smiled and shook her head. "The bloke was all flustered and trying to say nothing was happening. I called him... well, I called him exactly what he was. And that seemed to amuse Beatrice, so then she told me to please get into her cab so's she could speak with me."

"And you did?"

"She seemed a safer option than the feller that didn't want to pay."

"And then what happened?"

Eliza began to shade some of her bird doodles with the side of her pencil lead. "She started talking to me," she said, not looking up from her work. "Asking me all about myself, about my life. So I just told her. Told her everything. I'd had a bit of gin, you see, to keep the cold out, so I was more forthcoming than usual. Told her stuff I probably shouldn't have. But to me, she just seemed like a sweet, kindly old lady."

"And where did you go in her cab?"

"Back to her hotel. Some fancy place in the Strand. She got some filthy looks for going in there with me, but she didn't care. I sat in her rooms, and she ordered champagne. Champagne." Eliza looked up at me incredulously. "Can you imagine that?"

"No. I definitely cannot imagine Beatrice drinking champagne."

"Oh, she didn't drink any. Least, not that I remember. But it was all starting to get a bit fuzzy by then. I remember her saying nice things to me, though. Holding my hand and telling me I was a pearl cast before swine. I think she might have stroked my hair," she said, frowning.

I stared at her, speechless with amazement. I could not conceive of Beatrice making such gestures of tenderness, and that she should do so to Eliza was simply baffling. In all my time at Beulah Lodge, I had only ever heard Beatrice speak unkindly to the girl. At best, she was barely civil. Thinking of Beatrice's gnarled and veiny hands stroking Eliza's dark hair gave me a sick, knotted feeling in the pit of my stomach.

"I must have left at some point," Eliza went on. "I remember walking down Fleet Street and catching a few hours kip in a doorway. It was so cold, 'specially after that nice hotel room. Beatrice must have invited me to return at some point cos I went back there the next evening. I could see that they didn't want to let me in, but she must have given them instructions cos they showed me to her rooms. And she was getting ready to leave. All her boxes were out, and the chambermaid was packing everything away. And she says she's departing today and going back to her great house in Yorkshire and that she could offer me a position in her household, but I would need to come with her today. I didn't know what to think. And she told me to decide quickly because she would be taking a cab to Euston within the hour.

"I hadn't ever been outside London before. Furthest I'd ever been was Greenwich. So I said I had to think about it, and I went and walked over Waterloo Bridge. I told myself that by the time I had made it back across, I would have made my mind up. I didn't know any other life 'cept London, but what did I really have? No family, no real friends, and probably not much chance of still being alive ten years from now. So by the time I came back across the bridge, it seemed obvious. I went back to the hotel and told Beatrice I accepted her offer."

"Was she pleased?" I wanted Beatrice to have been pleased, to have recognised what a huge choice this had been for Eliza.

"I think so. She smiled and told me I would be very happy at Beulah Lodge." Eliza looked around the dusty library. "And I suppose it ain't been all bad."

"But did something happen with Beatrice? How did she go from being so kind to you to being as she is now?"

Eliza looked at her doodles. "I dunno," she muttered. "I think she just got bored of me. Or maybe she wanted me to be eternally grateful, and I've been too moody for her liking." I felt there was more that Eliza was not telling me, but I did not push.

"You know," I said, "once you can read and write, you have many more options open to you. You needn't stay at Beulah Lodge forever."

"But where would I go?"

"You could go into service at another house. Or find work as a paid companion."

"Mistress wouldn't give me a reference."

"Perhaps not but I could."

"You?" she asked in astonishment, looking up from her doodling.

"Why not? I think you blacken the grates wonderfully. And your wood chopping is second to none."

I smiled at her, and she looked at me for a long moment.

"You are…so kind," she said finally. I began to protest, but she carried on, "I seen lots of people be apparently kind, but then it turns out they're after something else entirely. Like the church folk who made us confess ourselves to be sinners before they'd give us soup. Or Beatrice who was so kind at the beginning." She swallowed hard. "She was so kind to me that I couldn't quite believe it. I thought p'raps God had sent her, that he had finally listened to me. I think I thought she was an angel or something."

She attempted a smile that faded quickly from her face as tears sprung to her eyes. She looked away as if embarrassed, and I leant forward and put my hand on hers.

"You deserve kindness," I said softly. "I wish I could go back for you and undo all the cruelties that you have suffered."

She did not reply but turned her face back toward me. Her dark eyes glistened with the unshed tears. It was like looking into two dark wells, I thought, and having no idea how deep they were.

Without being fully aware of it, I had drawn closer to her, so that now her face was only inches away from my own. I could see the fine, dark hair of her eyebrows and the individual lashes that framed her eyes. I smelt woodsmoke and polish and found myself leaning ever closer toward her, drawn in by her scent.

Eliza leaned toward me at the same moment and pressed her lips against mine. They felt impossibly soft, and I returned the kiss without thinking. My eyes closed involuntarily, and I felt a warm, quickening sensation course through my body. Eliza's lips parted, and I was overwhelmed with the sensation of her mouth opening against mine like a hollow opening up in the dark, wet earth.

I pulled back sharply, suddenly aware of what I was doing. We looked at each other as if for the first time. Eliza was looking at me with the guarded expression that had been so usual in our first interactions.

I said quickly, "I'm sorry. That was my fault. I...I don't know what came over me. Forgive me."

"There is nothing to forgive," Eliza said. "*I* kissed *you*."

I stood up and moved to the other side of the desk. "Either way, I should not have allowed that to happen."

Eliza put her head on one side and regarded me. "It was only a kiss," she said.

I blinked, astonished by her calm manner. "It was a mistake," I said firmly. I saw a fleeting expression of something like hurt cross Eliza's face, and then she too rose to her feet.

"Thank you for the lesson, ma'am. I must be getting on with my work now."

"Of course." We both avoided looking at each other as Eliza curtsied and withdrew. I sat and looked out at the moors. My insides were churning, and I castigated myself over and over for my foolishness. But I could not prevent my fingers rising to my mouth to touch the point where Eliza's lips had pressed against my own.

CHAPTER NINE

The rest of the day, I could not concentrate or settle to anything. I walked restlessly over the moors, turning what had happened in the library over in my head. I ate hardly any dinner and retired early, but sleep eluded me. I tossed and turned as I went over and over it, thinking of what I should have done and what I was to do now.

When the grey light of dawn finally began to seep through the curtains, I gazed at the ceiling of my room and equally unflinchingly at myself.

I had to take full responsibility for what had happened. Eliza was a servant and I her superior. I should not have allowed a friendliness to develop into…and here my thoughts failed me. I had no words for what had occurred. Eliza had kissed me on the mouth. Daniel had done the same, but he was my fiancé, and that was his right. Eliza had no right to do such a thing. And yet, as I compelled myself to examine my heart with a steely gaze, I could not help but admit that Eliza's brief kiss had felt far more pleasant than any of Daniel's. His kisses had been scratchy, and on several occasions, he had forced his tongue into my mouth such that it was all I could do not to push him away. And his kisses had never induced such a feeling in me. As I recalled the feel of Eliza's soft lips against my own, I felt a recurrence of that warm, urgent sensation, and I quickly rose and doused my face in cold water from my basin.

I could not think of it anymore. As I dressed, I resolved to put the incident from my mind and go on with my day as usual. And then, I heard the familiar sound of an axe.

I went to the window and looked at Eliza chopping the wood. She looked better than I felt, and as she stooped to put another log on the block, I saw her glance up at my window. I stepped back swiftly.

I dithered until it was time for breakfast and then descended to the dining room. Martha served me my meal, and then as usual, I repaired to the library. I fidgeted with my sewing, pricking my finger repeatedly until I flung the work from me in frustration. I contented myself with gazing out the window until the knock on the door came, and Eliza entered.

She looked exactly the same as usual, and this vexed me. It was as if I expected her outward appearance to reflect the turmoil that I was feeling inside.

"Mistress is ready for you, ma'am."

I got to my feet and saw Eliza hesitate by the door. "What is it?"

"You won't mention to the mistress…about me planting one on you?"

"Good heavens, no." I said, vehemently. "I would not speak of it to anyone. As I hope you will not," I added.

Eliza shrugged with studied nonchalance. "Like I said, it were nothing to speak of." She looked at me keenly as she said this, but I did not meet her eye.

"Let us not keep Mrs. Groves waiting," I said.

Aunt Beatrice may have had her failings, but there was no denying her acute observational skills. "You look tired," she said as I seated myself before her.

"Yes. I had a restless night."

"Fetch some tea for Miss Mallowes," Beatrice barked at Eliza.

"That is very kind, thank you."

"I would not have you fall asleep in front of me," Beatrice said as Eliza curtsied and withdrew.

"Daniel favours coffee in the morning, especially if he has not slept well," I remarked.

"I have never enjoyed coffee. And you should get used to sleepless nights. The nights in India will be hot, and when you have a baby, you will be kept awake all night. Unless you can find an ayah to assist you."

Her tone was neutral, but I felt as if someone had thrown a bucket of cold water into my face. "A baby?" I repeated.

"Yes," said Beatrice impatiently. "They are small, squalling things completely incapable of rational thought."

"Yes I…I simply had not…had not thought—"

Beatrice made an exasperated noise. "They are a normal product of a marriage, are they not?"

I did not reply. Of course, the notion of children had crossed my mind, but since Daniel had announced his intention of being a missionary, the thought of children had been subsumed by this larger change. But we would be missionaries for many years, and so I would be bringing up my children in India.

My children. The thought of this suddenly made me dizzy, and I put a hand to my forehead. At that moment, Eliza entered bearing a cup of tea. She handed it to me and looked at me with concern.

"Are you all right, ma'am?"

"She is perfectly all right," Beatrice snapped. "Leave us." Eliza withdrew, glancing back anxiously at me as she did so.

I sipped the strong, sweet tea and began to feel a little better.

Beatrice looked at me appraisingly, a smile playing at the edges of her mouth. "You will delight in having a brood of children running about your skirts. As all women do, apparently."

I looked at her and asked, "Would you have liked children, Aunt?"

As if she had been expecting the question, Beatrice leaned back in her chair and stared thoughtfully out the window. "It was not part of God's plan," she replied blandly. "But I do not think I would have liked them. They appear to cause a lot of noise and mess for very little reward."

"Did Mr. Groves feel the same?"

She looked at me sharply, and for a moment, I was sure that she was about to snap at me. But something changed her mind, and she replied in a normal voice, "He naturally wished for sons. Even more because he was the last of his own line. As you are the last of mine."

"You had a brother, I believe? My father could not tell me much about him."

"That is because there is little to speak of. A dithering, foolish little man. Oh, everyone always spoke of how kind he was, but kindness is nothing more than a weakness that others will exploit. It was no surprise that he died so young. He was too weak-willed for this world."

I was silent, thinking that no one could accuse Daniel of possessing a weak will. Was he a kind man? He had been kind to me when my father had died. I cast my mind back to all the times I had seen him with my father's parishioners, and I recalled that his manner had always been courteous but tinged with a faint impatience, as if he could not comprehend why these people did not simply will themselves out of whatever predicament they were in.

My mind began to wander along the pathways of the past, and I suppressed a yawn. Beatrice grunted and said, "You may go now. Perhaps you should try to recoup some of the sleep you have lost. You are even poorer company than usual in this state."

I mumbled my thanks to her and retired back to my room, where I took her advice and lay down on my bed. I was asleep within minutes.

❖

I awoke feeling disorientated, and it took me a good minute or two to remember where I was. It seemed as if I had forgotten everything because the remembrance of the scene in the library with Eliza came rushing back to me, and I felt hot all over.

I got up and splashed water on my face. I felt groggy, as if my head had been stuffed full of cotton wool. A glance at the clock told me that I had slept for a few hours and that it was almost noon.

I decided that a walk would do me good. On my way out through the kitchen, I told Martha that I would not require any luncheon.

I set off in the direction of the track up to the moors, almost without thinking. And then I stopped and turned and walked around the front of the house and down the lane to the village. I wanted to put the incident with Eliza out of my head, and I knew that if I walked upon the moors, I would not be able to look upon any bird or flower without thinking of her.

As I walked down the lane, I ran through what had happened for the umpteenth time. Eliza seemed supremely unconcerned by it. "It were nothing." Was it nothing? Was my reaction out of proportion?

I had never been kissed by anyone but Daniel. Perhaps it was common for people to kiss each other and to not think anything of it. Eliza had acknowledged that it had been her kissing me, and she clearly did not want Beatrice to ever hear of it. So perhaps it was simply a silly mistake that we would both forget about in due course, a misunderstanding arising from the affection that had grown between us. I did not wish there to be awkwardness so it would be best if I simply acted as if nothing had happened...which was essentially true.

I observed a figure on horseback coming down the lane toward me, and as I drew closer, I saw that it was Mr. Tripp on Prospero. I greeted him warmly, relieved to find someone to talk with to distract me from my thoughts.

Mr. Tripp dismounted and held Prospero's reins with one hand as he touched his cap. "Good morning, ma'am. On your way into the village?"

"Yes. Well, not really. I am merely taking a walk and decided to come in this direction. You are heading back to Beulah Lodge?"

Mr. Tripp nodded, and I fell into step beside him, happy to return the way I had come. I asked whether he had been out on estate business, and Tripp explained that he had been visiting one of the farms that lay out in the direction of Thirlby.

"I tries to get round all the farms least once a month. This one's a cattle farm mostly, though their herd ain't nowhere near what it was. Time was they'd be sending carts up to the Lodge regular with milk and butter and whatnot." He shook his head sadly. "Old Bill Simpson is saying that his son is likely to try his luck in Canada when Bill dies. They say it's an easier living out there."

"And what will happen to the farm then?"

"We'll try and lease it, but tain't easy to find tenants these days. The land ain't so good, and so we have to drop the rents each time."

"Could you not just sell the farm?" I asked.

Tripp looked horrified by the suggestion. "We can't afford to sell up much more. Mistress wouldn't hear of it." I wondered if this was another of those issues where Mr. Tripp assumed on Beatrice's refusal without ever having asked her. But then I could not imagine how he would broach the subject of estate management with her.

"How many people lived at Beulah Lodge when Mr. Groves was alive?"

"Oh, there was a full complement of servants, ma'am. A housekeeper, cook, housemaids, and a few footmen. And the grooms and gardeners. I should say around twenty including the master and mistress."

"And what happened to them all?"

"After Mr. Groves died, the mistress didn't have no stomach for managing the estate. We lost some tenants, couldn't find new ones, and had to sell off bits of the land. We let more and more of the servants go as an economy, and because the mistress…has her ways. So here we are," he finished, glumly.

I looked at his profile as he walked along beside me. His shoulders were stooped as though weighed down with a burden. I felt sorry for him and wondered if Beatrice had ever given him a word of thanks for the responsibility he shouldered alone.

"What would attract tenants to a farm?" I asked, trying to be helpful.

Tripp blew out his cheeks. "A good portion of land, enough to support a family. A rent that's not too high and a landlord that is fair. Problem is that most of our tenancy holdings are small and on bad land."

"Could the boundaries of the farms not be redrawn?" Tripp frowned, bringing his heavy eyebrows together. "Perhaps if you had some tenancies falling vacant at the same time, they could be combined into a larger holding?"

"I s'pose," he said slowly, "but that would need a solicitor and all sorts of legal gubbins."

"Your mistress has spoken of her solicitors being in London. They must have some overview of all the estate holdings."

"I suppose they would." We walked on for a few minutes in silence, and then Tripp said, "Perhaps, ma'am, you might mention to the mistress that it would be useful to have a copy of the holdings of the estate with all the boundaries marked."

"You do not have such a document?" I asked incredulously. Tripp shook his head. I pressed my lips together to conceal my frustration.

We talked more of the problems of managing the estate, and by the time I had parted from Mr. Tripp at the stables, my mind was absorbed with his difficulties. My early impression of Tripp had undergone a transformation. Beneath his outwardly grumpy, spiky exterior I could now perceive the heavy weight of responsibilities that he had borne alone.

I spent the afternoon working on a skirt that I was attempting. As I worked, I turned over the problems of the estate in my mind, searching for solutions and for ways I could act to improve things. I had no knowledge of the intricacies of estate management, but I was convinced that I could learn enough to be able to assist Mr. Tripp. I felt a sense of responsibility as Beatrice's niece. If she would not take any action to safeguard the livelihoods of her servants and tenants, then it fell to me to do so.

My annoyance with Beatrice grew as I concluded that many of the problems Mr. Tripp grappled with could have been resolved with a limited intervention, or at least interest, on Beatrice's part. Tripp did not bring the problems of the estate to her because she was dismissive of them, and so the problems festered. I was not sure whether I would have any better luck in persuading her, but I was determined to try. From everything that Tripp had told me, the tenants of the estate seemed to be struggling, and if I had it in my power to improve their lot even slightly, then I had to attempt it.

Eliza served me at suppertime, and her appearance reminded me that my thoughts had for once been otherwise occupied. She was polite yet distant, and the only flicker in her mask came when I apologised for missing her lesson.

"I lay down for what I intended to be a brief nap and slept for several hours."

Eliza lifted my dessert plate from the table and said, "That's quite all right, ma'am. I wasn't sure if you wanted to continue with them anyway."

I glanced up at her and saw that the line of her jaw had hardened. "But of course, I do. I said I would teach you to read, and I shall." I almost added, "no matter what happens" but bit the words off at the last minute.

Eliza nodded, and that was the end of our conversation. I felt a sharp sting of pain at how formal and cold it had been compared to the easy friendliness we had shared.

I lay in bed that night and thought with relief that the incident with Eliza could now be safely consigned to the past under a heading of "unfortunate accidents." Exactly like the time I had boasted to my friend Esther that I could ice skate better than she could. I had strapped on my skates and had set off across the rink with total confidence only to come a cropper a minute later. I had hit the ice with such force that I had a lump the size of a plum on my forehead. And Esther had stood on the sides doubled up with laughter as concerned ladies and gentleman had swarmed around me.

I smiled to myself as I turned over. It had taken years for me to be able to think of that incident without burning with humiliation, but now I could smile about it. And with that comforting thought, I fell asleep.

CHAPTER TEN

I was jolted into consciousness by something. It was still night, and I sat up, looking into the darkness for whatever it was that had awoken me.

I could see nothing and sat for a few moments, hearing only my own breathing. And then I heard the sound of an angry raised voice coming from somewhere nearby.

I reached for the matches on my bedside table and fumbled with them in the dark as I heard the raised voice again and knew that I was not imagining it. It seemed to take an age until I finally managed to light a match. I leaned over to my bedside table and lit the candle.

The floorboards of my room creaked as I stood, and the cold draughts washed over my feet. I grasped my candle firmly and opened the door of my chamber, fear making my heart thud painfully against my ribs.

The noises at once became more distinct. I could hear what sounded like Beatrice's voice, harsh and angry. I could not discern any other voice, and I stood irresolute for a moment, wondering whether I should do anything or simply return to bed.

But I reasoned that I was Beatrice's closest neighbour. My chamber was closer than the servants' quarters on the next floor, and so it was reasonable that I should investigate to see if she had need of anything.

I padded softly along the corridor toward Beatrice's room. As I drew closer, I could see that the door was slightly ajar, with a small sliver of candlelight spilling out onto the carpet. I paused and heard again Beatrice's raised voice.

"You know that I could simply dismiss you at any time I wished? And then what would you do? Eh? You'd have to go back to the filth from whence you came."

For a moment, I thought that Beatrice was talking to herself, perhaps having some kind of waking dream, but then I heard another voice answer her, so quietly that I could barely make the words out. "Yes, ma'am."

I had only just registered that it was Eliza's voice when Beatrice unleashed another string of invective. "Yes ma'am, no ma'am. Is that all you can say? You had a prettier turn of phrase when I could offer something you wanted." There was no reply, and I heard a loud thump, and Beatrice practically shrieked, "Well? Answer me."

"I will get your milk for you, ma'am, and then I think you ought to try to sleep."

"You will not leave this room unless I tell you to. Now come here. I wish you to rearrange my pillows."

I heard the sound of footsteps and a rustling of bed clothes. And then Beatrice's voice came again, softer but somehow more chilling than her anger. "What would you have charged if I had asked?"

I felt a wave of cold sickness pass over me. Eliza's voice had the brash tone that was now familiar to me but with a tightened edge to it. "One bob for a knee trembler. Two and six for all the way. But we charged extra if we didn't like the look of you."

The sound of the slap almost jolted me from my feet, and I heard Eliza's sharp intake of breath.

"Get out." Beatrice hissed. "You whore!"

There was a creak of floorboards, and then Eliza came into the corridor, carrying a candle and closing the door behind her. She was dressed in her nightclothes with a shawl over the top, and her hair was loose about her shoulders.

She turned and took a few steps toward me before seemingly registering my presence and stopping where she stood. We looked at each other for a moment by the light of our candles. Eliza's cheek was red from the slap, and she looked at me open-mouthed with surprise.

"I heard raised voices," I whispered. "I came to see if all was well."

"Yes, thank you," Eliza replied, also in a whisper. "The mistress wants a glass of milk is all, to help her back to sleep."

"Ah, I see."

The soft glow of my candle fell on Eliza's face. Her hair gleamed in the light. I had never seen it outside of the usual bun at the nape of her neck, and the sight of it cascading around her face and shoulders seemed suddenly indecent. I tried to stop staring at it but found instead that my eyes lingered on her neck, white and smooth in the candlelight.

My face grew hot, and I prayed that it was dark enough for Eliza not to notice.

"She should be all right once she has her milk," Eliza whispered. You can go back to bed now, ma'am." I realised that I had been standing there staring at her for a while and that Eliza would need to come past me to get to the kitchen.

"Yes," I said, rousing myself. "I shall do just that." I turned and walked back the way I had come. Eliza followed a pace or so behind, and as I reached my door, I turned and wished her good night as she walked on.

She passed so close that strands of her hair trailed against my bare forearms, and I hardly heard her answering good night.

My dreams that night were charged and restless. In them, I felt again the sudden cold sickness that had gripped me when Beatrice had asked Eliza that question. But then the dream changed so that the spiteful, leering figure of Beatrice changed into the figure of Eliza in her night dress. Except that she was different somehow. She looked at me with a bold and knowing glance, as if she saw exactly into the heart of me. And I was still afraid, but it was a different kind of fear, tinged with something else.

I awoke bathed in sweat and feeling the tension reverberating through my bones. I took several deep breaths and lay still, looking up at the cracks in the ceiling where the now absent chandelier had been.

The dream was already fading fast, but the image of Eliza with her crown of hair and white skin was still vivid in my mind.

I rose and began the familiar cycle of the day, but my mind returned again and again to that vision of Eliza. I did all I could that morning to shake it. I tried to focus on my Bible reading and took out the account books, working my way down the column of figures in an attempt to decipher the complex arrangements of the estate over the last few years.

But it was hopeless. My mind would drift again to Eliza, and every time it did, a strange kind of heated tension seemed to take possession of me, and I had to get up and circle the room restlessly.

It only grew worse as the day wore on and the time for Eliza's lesson approached. I could hardly eat any luncheon. My stomach felt as if it were tied into a knot, and by the time Eliza's knock on the library door sounded a little while later, I was coiled tighter than a spring.

Beatrice had not summoned me that morning, and so I had not seen Eliza since the previous night. When she opened the door, I was shocked by how like her usual self she looked. Her hair was confined into its bun, and everything about her looked just as usual. But I could not look at her with anything like my normal equilibrium. My eyes seemed to burn over her, and so I moved them away, looking instead at the shelves behind her.

She came and took her customary place beside me, and we began the lesson. Eliza read through the various passages that I had copied out for her and then began to write out short sentences. I watched her forming the letters slowly and carefully with her pencil, her brows drawn together in concentration. Her face was in profile to me, and the sunlight coming through the window picked out threads of gold in her hair. Her lips parted slightly, and the tip of her tongue protruded as she focused ever more closely on curving her pencil around the letters.

She looked up from her work at me, and I felt the jolt of her eyes meeting mine.

I looked at the page where she had written, "The red hat is on the black dog."

"Good," I said, relieved that my voice was steadier than I had expected. "What you have written is legible…and so it passes the basic test of writing." I smiled at her, and she returned my smile with a flush that spread up her neck.

"I still find the g's difficult."

"It is all a matter of practice. Anything can be achieved with enough practice." I drew a fresh sheet of paper in front of her. "Why don't you try writing out a line of g's?"

She took up her pencil and wrote a few g's. After observing her for a while, I leaned forward and said, "Try starting from the top of the letter, going around and down. Like this." I took the pencil from her and drew a g.

I was now even closer to her and felt the proximity almost as if it were a physical pain. All my senses were heightened. I could smell the woodsmoke from her hair and hear her steady breathing. But above all this, I was aware of her arm lying close to my own. They were not quite touching, but I could feel the presence of her flesh near to mine as if I were standing next to a roaring fire.

I drew a few more of the letters while she watched and then handed the pencil back to her. Eliza copied my letters and nodded. "That is easier. Thank you."

I sat back in my chair and felt the distance between us as both a relief and an ache.

"Perhaps that is sufficient for today," I said.

She looked at me with her eyes slightly narrowed, as if she was trying to see what my true intent was. But it was only a fleeting glance, and then her face resumed its usual, politely distant expression.

"Very good, ma'am," she said, rising from her place. She moved past me, and I caught her scent as she passed. As the door closed behind her, I sat down heavily into the armchair as the tension ebbed from me.

I walked across the moors that afternoon, walking faster than I needed to so that the exertion would distract me from the thoughts that churned unceasingly in my mind. I could not fathom what had happened, how I had gone from finding Eliza impertinent to now finding her so unsettling that I could barely be in the same room with her.

I have never been afraid of examining my own feelings, my own sins, with unflinching scrutiny. My father was fond of saying that we could not know God if we did not lay our full selves before Him. As I pushed relentlessly forward through the bracken and heather, I acknowledged to myself that I had always found Eliza's physical appearance pleasing somehow. I liked her dark eyes and her pale skin and the way her face softened and transformed when she smiled. That enjoyment had always been there, but surely it did not necessarily follow that…and then I would remember the feeling of Eliza's lips on mine, and I could not continue the train of thought.

I could not coolly file away what had happened as an "unfortunate accident." Eliza would not have done such a thing out of the blue. One did not kiss another person without some form of invitation. Perhaps I had somehow given an invitation without being aware of it. If that was the case, then I had to be clear to Eliza that whatever she thought of me was mistaken. I was not the sort of woman who…and here again my thoughts failed me. I did not know what kind of woman kissed another woman in such a way. Oh, I had heard whispers. Snatches of gossip caught in queues at the market, where I heard girls being called Toms or from women in the pew behind me at church speaking in hushed tones about followers of Sappho.

I had a theoretical understanding of what they referred to, but I had given it as much thought as I would give to the customs of some remote South American tribe: something exotic and dangerous sounding but completely detached from my own experience. Until now.

I sat on a low tor and looked at the sun beginning its descent toward the horizon. I had somehow become embroiled in the kind of thing that the market women and the respectable women in pews both found salaciously alarming. I shook my head, amazed at my own stupidity. I had been so lonely and anxious for friendship that I had allowed this situation to develop. I had not heeded God's words to Cain, that sin lies constantly at the door, desiring and yearning.

I stood with a steely resolve. I would not allow sin to master me. I would master *it*. The words resounded through my head as I tramped determinedly back down toward the house.

I entered through the back door and came into the kitchen. There was a delicious smell of meat and herbs wafting through the room. I paused to take my shawl off and looked around for Martha, but she was not there. I stepped over to the range and saw Eliza huddled in the corner of the high-backed bench that was placed alongside it. Her chin was nodding against her chest as she slept.

I watched her for a moment, watched the steady rise and fall of her chest and the smoothness of her face in repose. I felt an almost overwhelming urge to touch her cheek and reminded myself sternly that I had to conquer my urges. As I turned to go, my heel scraped on the tiled floor, and Eliza stirred and opened her eyes.

She saw me and looked confused. "Miss Mallowes? What is it?" Her voice was thick with sleep.

"Nothing. I have just come back from a walk."

Eliza looked over at the range, and a sudden panic gripped her. "Bugger, the stew!" She leapt up and stirred the pot on the range with a ladle, her face creased with anxiety. After several moments of peering at it she straightened up. "Thank Christ for that. Martha would've had my head if I'd let it burn." She flushed. "'Scuse my language, ma'am."

"Where is Martha?" I asked.

Eliza sat back on the bench and rubbed her eyes. "She is having one of her afternoon rests. I told her I would watch the dinner for her."

"And Tripp?"

"He is posting some letters for the mistress. He'll probably stay for a jar or two in the Red Lion." She took out a tobacco pouch and began rolling herself a cigarette, balancing the paper deftly between her fingers.

"Well," I said, preparing to take my leave, "I must continue with my needlework. Poorly tailored skirts don't make themselves."

Eliza nodded, still bent over her task. I was amazed at her placidness, her apparent unconcern when I could think of nothing else.

"I wonder that you can be so calm," I said.

"'Bout what?" Eliza asked, without looking up.

"Oh, Eliza!" I burst out in frustration. "You are perfectly aware of what I mean." She looked up at me then, and her face told me that she did indeed know. She paused while she finished rolling her cigarette, and then she patted the bench beside her.

"Here," she said. "Come and take the weight off. Looks like you've been out for a good old tramp." I looked at my boots, which were coated with mud. And then I looked at the spot beside Eliza. My better judgement told me to simply leave, that spending any time alone in Eliza's company was dangerous. But I did not heed my better judgement and sat next to her.

She perched the cigarette between her lips and took a book of matches from her pocket. She struck one and lit the cigarette, inhaling deeply. Then she held it out to me. "Like some?" she asked. "I find it helps when you're trying to have a think about something."

I looked at the cigarette for a long moment. Almost everyone I could think of in my life would be horrified at the idea of a lady smoking: my father, Beatrice, and most certainly Daniel. I took it from Eliza's fingers.

"You breathe it in to your mouth and then into your chest," Eliza said.

I did as she said and coughed violently as the acrid smoke hit my lungs. My eyes were watering as I passed it back to a laughing Eliza. "That is…truly foul," I said when I had regained my breath.

"Yes," Eliza admitted, looking at the glowing tip before taking a deep drag. She blew the smoke out in front of her in a long sigh. "But it gets to be very soothing. Was one of the few pleasures me and the other girls had."

She tapped the ash from the cigarette into the grate of the range and settled back into the bench. I looked at her profile, at the smooth lines of her cheek and jaw. I thought about what her life must have been like in London, and my own fretting over what had occurred between us seemed petty and unimportant.

"Eliza," I began slowly, "I cannot be as calm as you about what happened."

"You talking about when I kissed you?" Eliza blew smoke out languidly.

"Yes," I said, my face growing hot. "I should not have allowed it to happen. It was very wrong and…and I hope you can understand."

Eliza looked at me thoughtfully for a moment and then said, "All right. I know it was a bit, what's the word? Impulsive. I didn't mean to upset you. I only did it cos…well. Why do people usually kiss each other?"

I could not even begin to contemplate the answer to this question so I said hurriedly, "Just so long as you understand that it was a mistake and must never happen again."

"Don't matter either way. Soon enough, you'll be in India, and I'll still be stuck here."

We were silent for a moment as the pot simmered on the range. The kitchen was darkening as the afternoon drew in, the low light from the range casting an orange glow across the floor.

"Yes," I said. "That is very true." It had been a while since I had thought about where my future lay.

I was aware of Eliza's eyes on me as she asked, "Are you looking forward to your new life?" She said it gently, and when I looked up at her, her eyes were full of kindness. I felt a sudden lump in my throat as I realised that I had missed kindness since Papa had died.

"I don't want to go," I said, the words coming out in a sudden rush. "To India. I don't want to go."

"Why not?"

"I, I don't…" I struggled to put the feeling into words. "I can't explain it. It's as if, as if my inner self—"

"Is it about being a missionary? Do you think God don't want you to go?"

"I do not know what God wants from me. Before, when I prayed, I used to feel His presence surround me, like I was standing beneath a vast willow tree. But since my engagement, I cannot find Him." I had voiced something that I had not even fully expressed to myself and felt as if a weight had been removed from my chest.

"And your fiancé?" Eliza asked.

"He is a good man."

She didn't reply immediately but took another drag of her almost extinguished cigarette. "I've met a lot of good men. Most of the blokes who came to see us girls on the streets was good men. Fine upstanding gentlemen. That's what the world thought of them. But how a man is in public and how he is in private…" She shook her head. "They was never good to us." She stubbed out her cigarette on the side of the range.

"Yes," I whispered. "I fear that Daniel…does not respect me. He wishes me always to be something I am not."

"And that's why you don't want to go to India?"

I nodded miserably, fighting the tears that were pricking at my eyes.

"So tell him you don't want to go."

I shook my head. "I have given him my promise to be his wife and to go wherever he goes. I cannot go back on that."

Eliza took my hand in her own. Her grip was firm. "Well, you ain't there yet. You're still here, aren't you?"

"Yes," I said. "I'm still here." I looked at her face, knowing that at some point in the future, I would be in India with Daniel and would be remembering her face and how it looked at this moment. My eyes dropped to her lips, which parted slightly.

One day, I thought, I will be far away from here, and I will be unhappy. The certainty of my future misery made the present seem of no account. I leaned forward and pressed my lips tentatively against Eliza's.

She kissed me back, her lips moving against mine as her hand came up and rested against the side of my face. I felt the tip of her tongue caress my lips, and it prompted a wave of longing that coursed through my entire body.

I put my hand up to her face and then into her hair, pulling strands of it loose from her bun. I felt a curious mania overtake me, as if I wanted to devour her, to absorb her into myself. I wrapped my arms around her and pulled her tight against me. As her tongue moved deeper into my mouth, I felt her bosom press against my own. The sensation caused a hot wave of fire to flare up to my eyes.

I shuddered, and Eliza broke the kiss to ask, breathlessly, "Are you all right?"

Her words brought me back to earth, and I saw myself as if I was an observer of the scene: in a passionate embrace with a maidservant. I pulled back and moved farther along the bench, putting distance between us. We were both breathing heavily, and Eliza's face was flushed, her eyes bright.

"Are you all right?" she asked again.

I leaned my head into my hands, my body still singing with sensations that I could not explain. "What am I doing?" I whispered. "What in God's name am I doing?" Eliza said nothing, and I closed my eyes and breathed deeply, trying to ignore the intense need that seemed to cry out unbidden from my being. I did not know myself. My body seemed to have been taken over by a force I could not control. Was I possessed? I thought of the pigs in the gospel story being driven over the cliff, and fear gripped my heart in a cold, hard vise.

I opened my eyes to find Eliza looking at me. Her hair was dishevelled from my touch, and strands of it swirled about her face. I could see something of the fear I felt reflected in her eyes.

"It's all right," I said, my voice surprisingly calm. "It is my fault."

Eliza looked at me for a moment then said gently, "We ain't done nothing wrong."

I blinked at her. "We have, we…" I stopped and dropped my eyes. "I do not have the words for what we have done. But it is unnatural."

"No," Eliza said firmly. "Cos if God created everything, then He must have created this too."

"It is sin," I whispered. "He does not create sin. That comes from our weakness."

"All right. So ain't we allowed to be weak sometimes?"

I raised my eyes to hers. "I am engaged to be married," I said.

"Yes, and you'll spend your whole life married to him. What's a few moments set against that?"

I stood abruptly. "It is a sin," I said again. "We have sinned against God."

Eliza leaned back on the bench and regarded me calmly. "If God didn't want us to sin, then He shouldn't have made the world so fucking ugly."

She spoke quietly, but I flinched at the terrible bitterness that had come into her voice. "You must not say such things," I said.

"But it's true. This world is rotten and stinking. And I won't believe there's anything wrong in enjoying something good, just for a little while. You can spend your whole life atoning for it if it'll make you feel better." She leaned her arms on her knees and looked up at me, her eyes dark and shining. "Your whole life," she repeated, and I could bear it no longer. I turned and stumbled up the stairs leading from the kitchen, tears beginning to gather in my eyes.

I sequestered myself in the library where I dried my tears and renewed my attempts at sewing with a single-minded intensity. Whilst my finger fumbled and slipped over the thread, I forced my mind to recite the prayers and psalms that I knew by heart. *"Lamb of God, you take away the sin of the world. Have mercy on us."* The needle slipped and stabbed into my finger. I sucked at the globule of blood. *"If thine eye offend thee, pluck it out, cast it from thee."* I thought of Eliza's eyes, dark and watchful, and licked the metallic taste of blood from my lips.

I threw the sewing from me with an oath I had once heard our coal man use. What in God's name was I thinking? I was engaged to be married and I had allowed...this to happen. I thought of what my father would say. I imagined his face open with horror and dwelt on the image at length, to punish myself. But then a memory slipped unbidden into my mind: my father, sitting in our parlour and leaning forward in his chair to hold the hand of one of his parishioners. He was a burly docker who was sobbing into his handkerchief, for what reason I could not now recall.

"My son," I heard my father saying, "none but you and the Lord know the feelings of your heart. It is not for me to condemn you."

I smiled at the memory of my father's kindness. He was such a good man, a man with an endlessly open heart. I could have told him everything, and he would not have condemned me. He would have understood when I told him how lonely I was without him, how all the old certainties had passed away, and how Eliza had at least been kind to me, had been the only person I had been able to talk to in months and that was why this curious friendship—

I stopped. I saw my copy of St. Augustine lying on the table. In the previous few days, I had read again the early chapters describing his lust-filled youth. At that time, I had read about lust with no more feeling than if I had been reading about weaving looms. But now I felt my face grow hot as I remembered the feel of Eliza's wet mouth opening beneath mine. So this was what lust was. Even though my mind tried to erect a wall against what I had allowed to happen, the image and feel of Eliza pushed insistently to the front of my mind, and the curious ache again swept through my body.

I retired early to my room and rang the bell to request that my supper be sent up on a tray. I was both relieved and disappointed when Martha answered the bell and returned later with the tray. She set my bowl of stew down and enquired if I was ill.

"No," I said but felt I must give some explanation for why I had closeted myself in my room and added, "That is, I am not ill. I merely…feel a certain lowness in my spirit."

Martha nodded sympathetically. "Aye," she said, "tis this house. It can get you down."

"Was it ever a happy place?"

"Oh, it were, ma'am, once upon a time. And then it was as if one day, I woke up and realised that it had all leaked away somehow, like it had happened while I wasn't looking."

"Yes. I know what you mean."

"My dear mother used to pray every day for God to grant her a long life, and so He did. But sometimes, I think a long life must be more of a curse than a blessing. My poor old mum had plenty of time to feel her faculties slowly failing, to dwell long and hard on all the big and little regrets of her life, of all the years wasted." Her eyes travelled around the faded and shabby room before finally resting on me. She gave a little embarrassed smile. "Begging your pardon, ma'am. I don't mean to go on whilst your supper gets cold."

She left, and I picked miserably at the food before placing the tray outside my door. I got into bed and stared at the cracked ceiling. The wind rattled the window panes, and it took an age for sleep to finally come.

CHAPTER ELEVEN

The wood chopping woke me just after dawn. I lay in bed and listened to the regular rhythm of the axe rising and falling. I pictured Eliza chopping, her cheeks pink and breath white in the early morning air. I got up and splashed my face with cold water from the jug before wrapping my shawl around my shoulders and standing just behind the curtain at the window. I paused, having to steel myself before moving the curtain aside an inch and looking out.

Eliza had almost worked her way through the pile of logs on the ground. She placed one on the block and swung the axe through the air. It sliced through the log, and her arms shook with the impact. She was facing away from me, but she turned slightly as she bent to throw the chopped wood into the basket. Strands of hair were clinging to the base of her neck like dark veins against her pale skin. I stared, fascinated by the sight and imagining how soft her neck would be. An aching shiver passed through me, and I closed my eyes and drew back from the window.

I was like King David, I thought, spying on Bathsheba as she bathed. And look what happened to him, I told myself savagely as I splashed more water on my face.

After Martha had served my breakfast, I slipped out of the house before Beatrice could summon me and walked into the village. I had no aim other than to be away from Beulah Lodge and away from thoughts of Eliza. I succeeded in my first object at least. I toured the few shops listlessly before walking the long way back over the moors.

I took lunch in my room and then tried for the umpteenth time to settle with my needlework and again, I cast it aside after a few minutes. There was a reading lesson to prepare for Eliza, and I girded my loins to attend to this task. I could not neglect Eliza's education because of my own weakness.

I opened the big, heavy Bible and began to flick through for a suitable passage that I could use for our lesson. As the familiar words swam before my eyes, I felt a calmness descend. Scripture had always been my refuge in times of trouble.

I had often read the Bible with Daniel and my father in our small parlour in Poplar. One of us would read the daily passage, and then, after a moment's silence, one of the other two would comment on the meaning of the words, of how they might apply to our daily life in the East End. Yet somehow, the reading had changed once it was Daniel and I as a betrothed couple. Now, once I had read the passage, Daniel would expound upon its meaning. I had ventured on a few occasions to debate a few points of the interpretation with him, but his pained silence told me that my views were not welcome.

My thoughts were continuing down another unsettling path, and so I focused on the next passage:

"Behold, thou art fair, my love; thou hast doves' eyes within thy locks: thy hair is as a flock of goats that appear from mount Gilead. Thy teeth are like a flock of sheep that are even shorn, which came up from the washing; whereof every one bear twins, and none is barren among them. Thy lips are like a thread of scarlet…"

I slammed the Bible shut, causing a small puff of dust to erupt from the pages. Even scripture was of no help to me now. At that moment, there was a knock on the door, and Eliza poked her head around.

"Ma'am?" There was no mistaking the question in her voice, but I waved her in with as much aplomb as I could muster. She took her seat beside me, and try as I might, I could not prevent myself from staring at her lips and thinking of a thread of scarlet.

I took out my teaching materials and focused on them. I had not prepared for this lesson as meticulously as I would usually have done, and it felt unformed. After practising drawing a few letters, I flicked through the Bible and found a passage from Kings that we went through together. But it was too difficult. The sentences were long and complex, and Eliza struggled, and I felt her confidence waning. I closed the Bible and said that I would write out sentences for her.

I composed a simple passage about a man and a cow, but as I wrote, I could feel Eliza's eyes on me, and then I felt my face flush, and my hands became warm and clammy, and I felt her gaze as if it was a hot, heavy weight, and I could hardly concentrate on what I was doing.

The sentence was garbled and barely coherent, but Eliza read it well enough, and I felt I had regained some of the momentum of the lesson.

We finished up with more writing practice. Eliza wrote out some three letter words carefully, and I turned my gaze deliberately out the window because I knew she would be poking the tip of her tongue out of the corner of her mouth as she concentrated, and I would not be able to keep my composure.

The lesson came to an end, and Eliza thanked me, as she always did, but there was a marked formality in her tone. I stared at a point over her shoulder and wished her the best for the remainder of the day. Eliza then curtsied to me, which she had not done for weeks, and withdrew.

I collapsed into the armchair, feeling as drained as if I had just scaled a mountain. I closed my eyes, but that proved to be a mistake as Eliza's face and lips swam before me, and I felt something else within me respond to this, a tingling that seemed to begin somewhere deep in my belly.

In desperation, the only thing I could think of was to go outside again, to be out of the house. I fetched my hat and cloak from my room and slipped out through the kitchen, not lifting my head long enough to see if anyone was there.

I tramped over the moors with a single-minded intensity, but I could find no relief from the thoughts and images of Eliza that crowded my mind. My legs had begun to ache by the time I turned my footsteps back to Beulah Lodge.

I halted in the yard, staring up at the large, looming bulk of the house. A plover called from somewhere behind me, its plaintive cry rising and falling on the wind.

My gaze fell upon the chopping block with the axe resting in it and the remainder of the logs from the morning. I looked at it for a moment, and then, before I could change my mind, I placed a log on the block and pulled the axe free. It was heavier than I had expected, and as I swung it up, as I had seen Eliza do, I felt muscles pulling in my shoulders. I landed the axe awkwardly against the log, causing it to skid off the block as the impact travelled up my arms. I took a deep breath, reset the log, and swung again.

I got better as I went along, splitting the logs more evenly and with less blows. My shoulders burned, and my hands smarted, but the physical discomfort was curiously satisfying. I was mortifying my flesh, punishing my body for its sensations that threatened to overtake my reason.

Finally, I could chop no more. My shoulders screamed their protest, and my hands were so raw and tender that I could not tolerate another juddering blow. I rested the axe against the block and leaned forward with my hands on my knees, breathing hard. Sweat was pooling under my arms, but I finally felt some measure of relief. I became aware of the throbbing in my hands, and I looked down. There were two raw blisters on each palm, red and angry looking. I drew my breath in with a hiss as I moved my fingers, but the pain came with a kind of grim satisfaction.

I re-entered the house, went straight to the library, and wrote a letter to Daniel. The words poured out from my pen, flowing across the paper in an increasingly frantic scrawl. I wrote from the very beginning, from the very first moment when Daniel had arrived in Poplar as my father's curate, a blond-haired, earnest young man whose enthusiasm for God's work shone forth from his face. We had all liked him, even though my father and I had gently teased him sometimes for his overzealous ways, such as how he would frown at those parishioners taking communion whom he suspected were not baptised into the Church.

I had found Daniel's earnestness endearing, and he in turn seemed to be taken with my fondness for debate, declaring often that he had never known any young lady to be so forthright. And we had all rubbed along happily until Papa became ill. Then Daniel took on all of Papa's duties in the parish whilst I nursed him over long months.

My father died very slowly. And Daniel was always there, providing kind words at the end of a gruelling day, praying with me, and taking as much of the burden as he could from me.

I was so grateful to him, and in those dreadful few weeks after my father's death, Daniel was with me constantly. It was a comfort to be able to talk about Papa with someone who had known him. We worked together to arrange a suitable funeral, and Daniel's eulogy had been a touching tribute to my father. Somehow, grief and gratitude had become entwined so that when Daniel had asked me to marry him a few months later, saying yes had seemed to be both a way to repay him for his kindness and a way to honour my father, as I knew it was what he would have wanted.

And now here I was, writing desperately to Daniel that I feared I had made a mistake in accepting him, that we had been thrown together by circumstance but that there existed no real kindred feeling between us. I could not be the wife that he needed. I could not be a mother to his children, especially not now, not since everything that had happened at Beulah Lodge, not since I had been so thoroughly thrown into confusion that I barely knew who I was anymore. I felt as if I had aged ten years since being here, yet at the same time, I had felt moments of lightness and joy that I hadn't felt since before Papa died. I pleaded with him to see sense, to release me from an engagement that would doom us both to unhappiness.

My pen finally came to a halt, and I read back through my scrawl. I sounded like a histrionic heroine in a gothic novel. I screwed the letter up and threw it onto the dying embers of the fire. This was madness. I had accepted Daniel willingly, and my future path was clear. There could be no turning aside from it; one day soon, there would be a letter from Daniel summoning me to his side, and I would go.

When supper time came, I was in my room, and Martha came to enquire if I wanted a tray sent up. I thanked her but said that I was not hungry.

"You ought to eat something, ma'am," said Martha. "You look awful pale."

"I am fine," I said, waving my hand.

Martha caught sight of the blisters and exclaimed, "Mercy! Whatever happened to your hands?"

"Oh, it's nothing. I was chopping wood."

Martha looked at me as if I had just told her that I had been to the moon. "Chopping wood? Whatever for?"

"I wanted to *do* something," I said.

Martha's face cleared. "Ah, because you're going for the missionary life." She nodded as if to herself. "Yes, I hear that many ladies out on the mission have to do the rough work cos they han't got no servants out there. I suppose you're getting your hand in."

"Yes, I suppose so."

"Mr. Glossop is always asking us to remember the missionaries in our prayers. They have to endure such hardship to spread the gospel."

"Indeed, though there is hardship everywhere."

"True enough. It is a great thing that your fiancé does, but I can't help feeling sad 'bout it."

"Sad?"

"I mean that if you and he are in India being missionaries, you won't be settling in Beulah Lodge once you are married. I mean that as you are the mistress's only living relation." Martha must have misinterpreted my surprise, for she said hastily, "Not that I am thinking of Mrs. Groves departing from us anytime soon. She is as tough as old boots, she is."

"I had not ever thought of Daniel and I ever settling in this house."

"Oh, of course. Why would you? What would you want with a great, draughty place like this? I suppose you would sell it or at least let it. Yes, if it were let, then perhaps Tripp and Eliza could be found a place."

"You are anxious for the future," I said, voicing what should have been obvious to me.

"Not so much for me, ma'am, as my son has his position with Mr. Holt, but poor Tripp han't got anyone, and he is so attached to this house that parting him from it would be like parting a child from its mother. And then, Eliza doesn't have a soul in the world, far as I know."

"Yes, I see."

"I thought perhaps now that you've been with us a little while, ma'am, that you might have developed a fondness for the place and might one day call Beulah Lodge your home?"

Martha's voice was pleading. I knew with certainty that Daniel would never consider living in Beulah Lodge. He would see no possibility of his mission being furthered in the tiny villages of the moorlands, and his mission was the most important thing to him. But Martha's face was so full of hope that I could not bear to crush it.

"I have certainly grown fond of the beauty of the moors and of how kind everyone has been," I said. "And who knows where God's calling may take us next?"

"Thank you, ma'am," said Martha. "Now I'll fetch you some supper, as you ought to try to eat something."

Supper was a bowl of leek soup and a hunk of bread. I managed a few spoons before pushing the bowl aside.

I stared disconsolately out the window, watching the light slowly fading and lengthening the shadows across the low hills. I thought of Beatrice, who had watched evening fall over the moors every day for the last forty years and seen God's cold, unforgiving face staring back at her. Perhaps she was right. And perhaps she was right about the Indian mission too.

The black, undulating hills of the moors seemed to echo my thoughts; nothing but darkness and emptiness lay ahead of me.

I thought of my father's church in Poplar with its stained-glass window lit up by the sun, casting jewels of light upon the tiled floor. If I closed my eyes, I could almost hear the notes of my favourite hymn, sung so many times in that church: *"There is a green hill far away…"*

I could not stop the tears from coming. I wept as I thought of my father and how happy I had been at his side. I cried at the thought of my future life, as bleak and featureless as the moors and then sobbed at my own selfishness. I put my head on my arms and gave myself up entirely to my sorrow. I was still sobbing when I heard a knock at the door. My breath was coming so raggedly that I could not reply. The door opened, and Eliza entered.

"Oh," she cried as soon as she saw me, and she came at once and knelt by my side. "What is it?" she asked, her face creased with concern.

I could not look at her. That she should show me kindness was too much to bear. I laid my head back on my arms and cried again. I was aware of Eliza gently rubbing my back as the heaving sobs finally began to subside.

I lifted my head and scrubbed at the tears on my cheek. The blisters on my hand stung as I did so. "I am sorry," I gulped.

"What for?" asked Eliza gently.

"For making a fool of myself." I rose from the chair and went over to the washstand. I poured some water from the jug and splashed some onto my face. The shock of the cold made me feel more like myself, and I turned back to Eliza. "I am quite all right now," I said.

Eliza stood and looked at the tray. "I was come to fetch your supper tray, but I see you ain't had any."

"I am not hungry." I walked over and sat on the bed and began to unpin my hair so that I would have something to do. But my blistered hands were sore, and I fumbled awkwardly with the pins.

"What happened to your hands?" Eliza asked.

"I blistered them. As I was chopping wood."

Eliza came and sat beside me on the bed. "That is a crying shame," she said. "You have such beautiful hands."

I made no reply. I was still struggling to take my hair down.

"Here, let me."

I let her pull the pins from my hair, and the tresses fell gently down my back.

"Pass me your brush," Eliza said.

"There is no need—"

"You can't do it with your hands all torn up," Eliza pointed out. I handed her the brush from the bedside table, and she pulled it through my hair, gently working the knots out. "Were you about to retire to bed?"

"Yes, I think so."

"Do you need help undressing, ma'am? Cos of your hands, I mean?"

I reached up to the top button of my bodice and tried to undo it. The pulling of the skin on my palms made me grimace.

"Here, let me."

She began to undo the buttons, her head bent beneath my chin. Strands of her hair brushed against my neck, and I felt my face grow hot. She helped me pull my bodice off when it was undone. Her touch was cool and professional. In contrast, my skin felt as if it was on fire with the nearness of her. She unbuttoned my cuffs for me and then unlaced my corset, and I felt relief as the constriction on my torso eased.

I stood, and Eliza unfastened my skirt for me. I stepped out of it, and then she helped me to take off my petticoats. Finally, I was standing in just my chemise and drawers, feeling as exposed and vulnerable as if I was naked before her. Eliza saved me some embarrassment by turning away to fold my clothes neatly on the chest at the end of my bed as I managed to pull my nightgown over my head.

I sat back on the edge of the bed, crossing my arms protectively across my chest and shivering. Eliza fetched my shawl for me and then busied herself with setting the fire ready for the morning. I watched her go about her tasks, and then she finally stood before me and said, "Will there be anything else, ma'am?" She said it in her usual way, and that in itself made the tears start to my eyes. The thought of going back to the usual formal relations between mistress and servant seemed too heavy a blow to bear. I swallowed and tried to reply, but my throat was too constricted.

Eliza came and sat on the bed beside me. She laid her hand gently over my own. "Please don't cry," she said.

I turned to her, and the look of tender concern in her face, for *me* of all people, undid me completely. I put my hand to her cheek, my fingers gently stroking the soft skin. "You should not…care so much," I said, fighting back the tears.

Eliza didn't reply but simply looked at me, her eyes like the dark hollows of a tree.

I could not have said if I moved or if she did. But somehow, as I was looking into those dark hollows and stroking the softness of her cheek, our lips met. I closed my eyes as I felt Eliza's mouth on mine and her hands cupping my face.

I kissed her back, my mouth opening as I felt the tip of her tongue against my lips. Eliza's hands moved from my face to tangle in my hair. She pulled me closer against her, and our kiss deepened as something stirred within me. I knew the feeling now and knew what name to give it. It was desire, lust, concupiscence, and it came salted with a fear that I should fight it, should resist it somehow. But I could not. And as we lay back on the bed, I knew that deep down, I did not want to fight it.

The kiss broke for a moment as we lay down together. Eliza raised herself on her elbow and stroked my hair. Her face was serious and impossibly beautiful. "If you don't want—" she began.

"No. I do." I did not even know what I was agreeing to, exactly. I just knew that if I stopped too long to think about it, I would lose this moment.

She lowered her lips to mine again, and my mouth opened against hers, and I felt her tongue move questioningly, almost shyly against my own. The stirring feeling within me grew ever stronger, and I moved my tongue with hers, dancing and swaying. The kiss became harder, more insistent. I pulled her face toward me hungrily, as if I was trying to quench a raging thirst.

Her hands moved down my sides and across my stomach. They travelled up again, brushing over my breasts, and I jumped at the touch.

Eliza moved to lie on top of me. The feel of her weight on me intensified the yearning that was coursing through me. I wrapped my arms around her, wanting to pull her as tightly against me as I could.

I felt her hand move under my chemise and stroke across my stomach. The feel of her touch against my bare skin made me gasp.

"Is that—" Eliza began.

"Yes, yes," I said, wanting to feel her touch me everywhere. Eliza caressed my belly as we kissed ever more passionately. I became painfully aware of my breasts as her hand slowly travelled upward, and when her fingers grazed gently against them, I almost cried out. And then, as her fingertips trailed lightly around my nipples, a sound did escape my lips, a keening, moaning sound that I could not believe came from me.

A distant part of me was appalled that I could make such an indecent noise, but then Eliza's hands became firmer on my breasts, cupping them, her thumbs brushing across my nipples, and I writhed and gasped beneath her. It was like a kind of pain. I almost could not bear the touch, yet at the same time, I desperately wanted it.

The yearning feeling was centred between my legs, and I could feel a wetness, and one of Eliza's hands was tentatively moving in that direction. When her fingers brushed against the tight, curly hair of my sex, I stiffened.

Our kiss broke for a moment, and we looked at each other, both of us breathing heavily. As before, I had a sudden image of what this must look like to an outsider: me in my underclothes with a servant girl on top of me and her hand in my drawers. And touching me somewhere where no one had ever touched me before.

Eliza's hand had halted where it was. "Are you all right?" she asked.

The throbbing between my legs was almost painful, an insistent question to which I did not know the answer. "Yes, it's just..." I felt myself blush as I tried to find the words. "I have not...no one has really touched me there." I looked at Eliza's chin as I spoke, unable to meet her eyes.

"I don't have to," Eliza said. "Do you want me to stop?"

I raised my eyes to hers. I thought about stopping. I could do it. Stop this now, prevent it from going any further. Although I did not know what further meant. I was like a traveller hesitating at the gates of the city, consumed by curiosity for what lay beyond but afraid to enter.

The throbbing between my legs continued unabated, like an incessant chanting that could not be ignored. If I could just see into the city to know what it was like...and then I need never go there again. Then my curiosity would finally be sated, and I could assure myself that there was nothing worth seeing there after all. I slowly shook my head.

Eliza kissed me very softly as she gently explored my sex with her fingers, stroking and caressing. I had expected her touch to feel strange and new, but it felt as if I had been waiting for it, and my body seemed to sigh with relief. Then she found the core of wetness at the centre. I was embarrassed by its abundance and almost wanted to say something, but then Eliza shifted on to her side next to me. Our eyes met as I felt her slowly enter me. I gasped and held her tightly. Eliza's lips moved to form a question, but I cried out before she could speak.

"Yes."

Eliza lowered her head to trail kisses on my neck as her finger moved slowly inside me. I closed my eyes and gave myself up to the feeling. After a moment or two, I felt Eliza's hand shift against me, and I felt fuller as she added another finger. She moved them gently back and forth, and I felt the throbbing building, climbing ever higher toward some unknown summit. Her breath was hot on my throat, and I clutched at her head, coiling my fingers in her hair. I could not speak. I could barely breathe.

Eliza's thumb rested on the front of my sex, and she gently pressed down as her fingers moved inside me. The pressure was simultaneously delicious but almost too much to bear, and my legs began to shake.

My breath became shorter, coming in quick, stabbing gasps as the throbbing sensation seemed to narrow to a fine, white-hot pinpoint. I squeezed my eyes tightly shut, and it was then that I felt Eliza press hard against me, pushing herself in as far as she could. Her fingertips hit against the very deepest part of me, and I cried out as the hot pinpoint exploded, and white fire engulfed my sex and every part of me in a shaking, heaving convulsion. I clutched at Eliza, making incoherent noises as wave after wave passed over me.

I could not tell how much time passed before I came to myself again. Eliza had eased herself from me and was lying curled against my side, her hand on my stomach, and her face resting in the crook of my neck. The dying embers in the fireplace popped gently, and there was the sound of creaks and sighs as the house settled itself for the night. I listened to the sound of my breathing as it slowed to normal.

I traced the network of fine cracks in the plaster of the ceiling and felt a curious sense of surprise that everything was as it had been. Except that now I was surely different. I had entered the unknown city, and that could not be undone. I knew that there would be repercussions, things I would have to contend with, but I had not the strength to consider them now. For now, I wanted only this moment before the future, like a dark raging storm, would come crashing in around me.

"Eliza?" I said, softly.

She raised herself on her elbow. Her eyes looked sleepy, and her hair was tousled from my hands. "Yes?" There was a wariness in her look and voice, as if she tried to gauge how I was feeling.

I smiled reassuringly. Whatever the repercussions would be, they were mine to shoulder and mine alone. "What…what happened just then?" I asked, feeling a blush.

"I can't tell you a decent word for it, but it's what's meant to happen."

"I thought I was having some sort of a seizure."

"But it were nice, I hope?" Eliza asked, looking shy.

"Oh, yes," I said, but even as I said it, I could feel the dark press of the future, the questions and consequences threatening to burst upon me.

Eliza lay down beside me again and put her arm across my waist. "Don't think about it yet, ma'am," she whispered in my ear. "Not yet."

I pulled the bedcovers over the both of us against the deepening chill in the room. My eyelids began to droop, but before I could let sleep claim me, I muttered, "Eliza?"

"Mmm?"

"My Christian name is Ruth."

"Ruth," Eliza repeated sleepily, lingering on the final syllable like a kiss.

CHAPTER TWELVE

I awoke with a start, fancying myself back in my old room at the Poplar rectory and taking a few moments to remember that I was at Beulah Lodge. The events of the previous night came back to me in a rush, and I turned my head, but Eliza was not there.

Had I dreamed everything? Images and sensations came back to me in bursts, and my mind involuntarily recoiled from them, as if it had been someone else who had done and felt all those things and not the Ruth Mallowes that I had thought myself to be.

I sat up and threw off the bedcovers. There was a fire burning in the grate, which meant that Eliza or Martha must have already entered this morning. The curtains were drawn back, and I noticed that the room was flooded with daylight. My eyes darted to the clock, and I saw with horror that it was past nine.

I had never slept so long before, and I rushed through my toilet as fast as I could. As I buttoned up my cuffs, I looked at my Bible on the chest by the bed. My usual morning routine involved saying some prayers when I awoke, but I could not do so today. I was not yet ready to present myself before God.

The breakfast things were still laid in the dining room. I hastily ate some bread and butter and drank a cup of cold tea before walking through toward the library. I almost collided with Eliza, who was coming out of the door.

We both apologised and stood in the hallway, caught in an agony of looking and yet trying very hard not to look at each other. Eliza curtsied awkwardly. "Good morning, ma'am. The mistress has asked if you would attend on her."

"Yes. Of course."

Eliza led the way up the stairs and along the passage to Beatrice's chamber. She knocked at the door, and Beatrice's voice croaked from within.

I had not seen Beatrice since I had overheard her and Eliza in the middle of the night. I had been half expecting her to look different somehow, but there was no obvious change in her. She was hunched in her usual chair, huddled in a shawl, with her claw-like hands gripping the arms. I had to suppress a shudder as I remembered her soft, hate-filled words to Eliza.

"Miss Mallowes is here, ma'am," said Eliza softly.

"So I see," Beatrice croaked without turning her head to look at me. I took my usual low seat. I wanted to get through the interview as quickly as possible so that I would be free to go and be alone somewhere to think. I desperately needed to think.

Beatrice turned her milky eyes on mine. "What have you been doing?" she asked sharply.

I felt my face flame at once, and it took all my strength not to look in Eliza's direction. "I have been—"

"Sitting idle, I daresay. Whilst your valiant fiancé fights the good fight on behalf of our Lord?" Her tone was sneering, and I felt a great weariness settle on me. I had not the stomach to engage in a battle with her.

"No," I said simply. "I have been practising my needlework and reading."

Beatrice snorted and then dismissed Eliza with a wave of her hand. I was still watching Eliza's retreating form when Beatrice said, "You waste your time with books. They will not help you when you are sweating in the Indian jungle."

"Reading is never a waste of time."

"I can't imagine your fiancé would approve of you spending your time in such a way."

"No, he would not, not now. But before we were engaged to be married, we spent many happy hours discussing books."

"A man wants different things from a wife than from a sweetheart." Beatrice said it without malice, almost with sympathy. "My husband wanted me to always be the sweet, virgin girl that I was at sixteen. He was most put out when he realised I had grown into an adult woman."

"Was he unkind to you?"

Beatrice laughed with genuine amusement. "Unkind? He was not a nursemaid. A husband is neither kind nor unkind. He simply is, and a wife must adjust herself to him."

"But everyone has faults."

"Not to his wife. To his wife, a man must be perfect. That is the only way a marriage can succeed."

"You deemed Mr. Groves to be entirely without fault?" My scepticism was no doubt evident from my tone, but Beatrice merely smiled one of her peculiar, mirthless smiles.

"I deemed Mr. Groves to be my husband. The question of his faults I left to the Almighty."

"Perhaps that is wise."

"And perhaps Daniel made a mistake in engaging himself to you?" she said, looking at me shrewdly.

Perhaps he had, I thought. Perhaps our engagement had been the greatest mistake for both of us. That was what I had tried to tell him in the desperate letter I had scrawled, a letter I would never send.

"We are to be married. Nothing will change that." The words fell heavily from my lips, and there was a silence between us.

Beatrice seemed put out that I was not providing her with more sport. She tried another tack. "You have at least ceased your familiarity with my servants, I hope?" Again, my face flamed, and I cursed myself. Beatrice raised her eyebrows quizzically. "You are still chopping the wood for us?"

"That is better than sitting idle, surely?"

"I suppose it will prepare you for being the wife of a missionary. I hear it is a life of drudgery." Beatrice spoke with such malicious glee that I allowed myself to become riled and snapped back.

"And what do you consider your own life to have been? At least in India I may be of some use." I at once regretted my outburst, not because I had angered Beatrice but because I had pleased her.

She gave a slow, spreading smile of satisfaction. "I can assure you, I have made very good use of my time on this earth. I have seen things that your provincial little mind cannot even conceive of. You will go and waste your life tending to the damned, whilst I have spent mine enjoying the fruits that come with the membership of God's elect."

"And what fruits would they be?"

Beatrice merely leaned back in her chair and smiled. Then she nodded to the blisters on my hands. "Those pretty hands of yours will have to get used to hard work."

I touched my palms gingerly. The blisters were healing but still tender to the touch. "I have never shied from that."

"And what hard work was there to do in your little rectory?"

"My father worked tirelessly in the slums, and I assisted him in every way to provide what relief we could to the poor."

"Ah yes, I had forgotten you had wasted your time tending to the reprobates."

I ground my teeth together to prevent myself from giving her the satisfaction of another angry outburst. "It is never a waste of time to relieve suffering."

"Your idea of God is all very well for a charming little parlour in a sheltered vicarage, but it bears no relation to reality." She gazed out the window. "God is like these moors, unchanging, harsh, and unforgiving."

"That is not what my God is like."

Beatrice turned her eyes back to me, and they were as hard as flint. "You create a God in your own image, my dear. One who is pretty and kind and loving. Christ was not sent to love us but to take our punishment for us. A punishment that we justly deserve."

She turned back to look out at the moors, and I was glad that she did not look into my face at that moment, for I feared what she would see.

I left the house immediately after the interview with Beatrice and walked up onto the moors, following that path that Eliza had shown me. I traversed the ridge and descended into the village. The single main street was filled with men on horseback and a few carts rumbling along the rutted road. The sound of the blacksmith's hammer rising

and falling formed a steady rhythmic beat as farmers and villagers went in and out of the post office and store.

I continued up the main street until I reached St. Rumbold's. I entered the churchyard and spent a few moments wandering among the headstones. They were plain, simple affairs with none of the broken pillars and weeping angels that were fashionable in London. The same family names recurred on headstones: Smith, Greenwood, Simpson.

I walked all around the churchyard and came back to stand before the church porch. I felt a curious hesitation to enter. I had been here recently for the Sunday service, but since then, it seemed as if everything had changed, and I would be entering the church now as a new person, as someone quite remote from the Ruth Mallowes who had prayed and sung a few days ago.

I pushed open the heavy wooden door and went in. The church was empty and dim inside, with a faint smell of damp lingering in the air. I sat in one of the pews and looked down the aisle at the small stained-glass window over the altar. Coldkirk was not a wealthy village, and the window was the only finery St. Rumbold's possessed. It showed the child saint floating in mid-air above a landscape that looked very much like the moorland outside. At his feet were his mother and father, on their knees and looking up at Rumbold with pious expressions.

St. Rumbold was said to have lived for only three days, yet in that time had demanded his own baptism and preached a sermon on the Trinity. I gazed at the image of the chubby child. Was his saintliness supposed to shame the worshippers at the church? Because in three days of life, the child had shown more Christian faith and virtue than most of us would manage in a lifetime? But to live only three days meant there was no time for the grime of sin to build up, that fine dirt that accumulated on a daily basis as we continually fell short.

I moved my gaze to the simple wooden cross that stood on the altar, and for the first time since the previous night, I tried to pray. Prayer had been something that had always felt easy to me. I had prayed every night before bed since I was a small child. Yet since arriving at Beulah Lodge, my prayers had become desultory. I had been rushing through them because I had felt uncomfortable being before God for too long.

I sat in the cold dark church and finally laid everything before God. I did not love my fiancé, and I wished heartily that I had never accepted his proposal. I did not want to go to India, not because I did not wish to undertake missionary work, but because I would be doing so with him. I looked toward my future and felt a kind of sick misery. I knew that must be sinful when there were people starving on the streets in London. What reason had I to despair compared to them? And yet I could not help it, and I prayed fervently to God to relieve my feelings so that I could face the future with courage.

And then my thoughts turned to Eliza and all that had happened. My mind instinctively shied away from the thoughts and images that filled my head, but I forced myself to think through everything, to lay it all before God.

At first, I had simply welcomed someone congenial to converse with. The shock of Beatrice's maliciousness had made me cling to any sign of friendliness. And we had talked easily together, in a way which I had not been able to talk to anyone since Papa had died. When had this changed from a simple companionship into whatever it was? I could not pinpoint the moment, but I knew that in some way, her physical aspect had always been pleasing to me. I had liked her face from the moment I saw it and the dark sheen of her hair and eyes…

My thoughts began to wander, and I reined them back in sharply. I had enjoyed her physical presence from the start, although I had not acknowledged it at the time. When I had read of lust in books, I had never really understood, but now I knew. I lusted for Eliza, which was sinful enough, but then I had given in to it.

I had not the words for what we had done together, but I knew that it was wrong because I had not only betrayed my fiancé but betrayed him with an unnatural act. And yet…it had not felt unnatural. In fact, it had felt more natural than the brief kisses I had shared with Daniel. I laid this thought too before God and held it up before Him, turning it this way and that as I examined it critically. I knew that I should ask forgiveness for my unfaithfulness, but although the words formed in my head, my heart did not speak them.

A phrase of St. Augustine's suddenly entered my mind: "Lord, grant me chastity and continence, but not yet." Looking at the plain

wooden cross on the altar, I promised God that I would give myself in service to Daniel and the mission in India. As soon as Daniel summoned me, I would go and then do just as Eliza had said, spend the rest of my life atoning and serving Daniel and God faithfully. But until then, could I not be allowed to follow my heart? When Judgement Day came, would this one sin outweigh a lifetime of sacrifice and service?

The church was blanketed in a deep silence as I sat and waited. I did not expect God to answer me. I knew that one could not bargain with the Almighty. The silence seemed to deepen, and as it did so, I felt a kind of peace settle on me.

I got back to the house after lunch, and Martha scolded me for traipsing across the countryside as she set some cold mutton before me.

"I think I am growing to like the moors," I said to her.

"I'm glad to hear that, ma'am. They aren't as bleak as people think." Martha paused by the door and added, "Eliza asks to be excused from her lesson today. The mistress is having one of her bad days, and Eliza can't be spared. She said she was sorry that she couldn't come tell you herself."

I thanked Martha for passing the message on and hoped that I had managed to conceal the keen stab of disappointment I felt.

I sat in the library after lunch and prepared some reading materials for Eliza, comforting myself with the thought that at least I would be better prepared for our next lesson. When I had finished, I busied myself with my sewing. Now that I had made my bargain, I felt more content about spending time with my needle. I would need to be a good missionary wife, and so I would need to practise my needlework. I managed a good few hours before I laid it aside and went down into the kitchen.

Martha was preparing supper, peeling and chopping a pile of potatoes. I went out into the backyard, but there was no sign of Eliza. I returned to the kitchen and offered to help Martha. She looked very doubtful until I reminded her that it was very likely that I would need to cook in India. She grudgingly agreed, and we spent a contented hour peeling and chopping whilst Martha regaled me with stories of the village and its various scandals and happenings over the years.

"There were the time Parson Glossop got falling down drunk in the Red Lion, and John Baker and old Mr. Simpson had to help him back to the vicarage." She shook her head with barely concealed glee. "He ain't allowed to forget that. Bishop came to see him and have words with him."

"And his parishioners? Were they happy for him to continue?"

"Some were and some weren't. But you wouldn't get many clergymen volunteering for St. Rumbold's, so we can't afford to be choosy. And Mr. Glossop is a kind man. And I always say that kindness makes up for many other failings."

I smiled at her. "Yes," I said. "I quite agree."

"Your fiancé must be a kind man," she said.

I dropped my eyes. "He is devoted to saving the souls of his parishioners." There was a silence, and when I risked a glance at Martha again, she was looking at me with an unreadable expression, her hands still mechanically peeling potatoes.

"But he is a kind man?" she tried again.

I looked at her, unable to form an answer. I could not meet her open, honest gaze and lie. Her eyes remained fixed on me, waiting for a reply.

I finally cleared my throat and said quietly, "I am not sure."

Martha chopped up a potato and threw the pieces into the pan of water beside her. "Well," she said, "I am sure he must be. He wants to save souls. Now, if that isn't kindness, what is?"

I made no reply, and we finished the rest of the potatoes in silence.

I went up to my room to dress for dinner. It seemed increasingly absurd to do so when I always took dinner by myself in the dining room, but I knew that Martha liked at least some proprieties to be observed.

I sat in the dining room and waited. The door opened, and Eliza came in bearing a tureen of soup. My heart leapt at the sight of her. She laid the tureen on the table and gave me a shy smile.

"Good evening, ma'am," she said.

"Good evening. How is Mrs. Groves? Martha said she was having a bad day."

"Yes, she gets them now and again. She is settled now, but there was a lot of fetching and carrying needed." She blew out her cheeks as she ladled some soup into my bowl, and I saw how tired she looked. "And you, ma'am? Have you had a pleasant day?"

"Yes. I have been into the village. I went and sat in the church for a while. It gave me a chance to…think."

Eliza gave me another spoonful of soup and darted a quick, searching look at me. "Think 'bout what?"

"I think you were right. I will spend the rest of my life serving God…and serving my husband."

Eliza looked at me, her face still closed and guarded.

I took a deep breath, knowing that I was about to speak words that could not be taken back, that once I had said them there could be no further excuse. "Will you…come to me tonight?"

Eliza's face cleared, exactly as if a cloud had moved from the sun. "Yes," she said, simply.

My preparations for bed that evening seemed to take three times as long as usual. I studied my face critically in the looking glass as I sat before it and combed out my hair.

I threw some more wood on the fire, although it did little to warm the chilly air. I put on my nightgown and wrapped a shawl around my shoulders. I moved around the room restlessly, unable to settle. What would Eliza be doing now? She must have been seeing to Beatrice, helping her into bed. And then there must be countless other tasks which I could only guess at.

I lit a candle and went to the window. It was completely dark on the moors. There was a small circle of light from the house and beyond that, only blackness. It was as if Beulah Lodge existed in a separate, enchanted kingdom. Outside its boundaries, the world was turning, and lives were lived, but inside, we existed in a suspended state.

I turned from the window and sat on the bed. I took up my Bible and idly flicked through the pages. I landed on the Book of Job and read through the familiar lines by the flickering light of my candle. *"Where wast thou when I laid the foundations of the earth?"* Could God in all His majesty really be concerned with what took place in this obscure house on the lonely moors? Of all the sin that He saw, was what Eliza and I did together really so bad?

I was just finishing the final lines of Job when I heard a light knock upon the door. "Come in," I called softly.

Eliza entered, holding a candle and a basket of wood. "Just come to see that you had enough wood for the fire, ma'am," she said as she closed the door. She took the basket to the fireplace and then set her candle upon the mantelpiece. Then she looked at me, wiping her hands over her apron. She was nervous, I realised with surprise.

"Why don't you come and sit down?" I said.

Eliza came and sat on the bed beside me. She looked at her hands in her lap and then said, "How are your hands?"

I turned them over so the palms faced upward. The blisters were healing, although they still smarted if I wasn't careful.

Eliza took my hands in hers and stroked her thumbs gently over them. I shivered. "Sorry, do they still hurt?"

"No, they're fine." It seemed ridiculous after all that had happened that Eliza merely taking my hands could cause me to tremble.

"I'm glad they're healing. You have such pretty hands." She looked up at me through her lashes, her dark eyes glowing in the candlelight. I leaned forward and pressed my lips against hers. She kissed back gently, but I had a fire kindled within me.

I put my hand to the back of her head and pulled her mouth hard against mine. Our tongues entwined as I wrapped my arms around her. I fumbled at the bun of hair on the nape of her neck until I found the pins holding it in place and tugged them free. Eliza's hair tumbled down her back. I broke the kiss to tease it free, running it through my fingers.

"It's like a river," I murmured.

"You better not be saying it's like the Thames," Eliza said with mock severity.

I laughed. "No, more like a mountain stream that rushes and…" Eliza raised her eyebrows, and I blushed. "Never mind," I said. "Poetry was never my strong point."

We kissed again and fell back on to the bed, Eliza on top of me, and her hands moving under my nightdress, stroking up my thighs and across my stomach. I felt the intense yearning return, centred between my legs. Eliza's hands brushed over my breasts, sending a small jolt through me.

"Wait," I gasped.

Eliza withdrew her hands "What is it?" she asked.

I pushed myself up into a sitting position. "I want…to…to you. I mean, I don't know what to do, but I want to do for you what you did for me."

Eliza nodded and then slid off the bed and undid her apron. Then she began to unbutton her dress. Without thinking, I turned my head away to give her some privacy. Eliza laughed. "Bit late for that."

I turned back in time to see her step out of her dress. I watched with a kind of wonder as she dropped her petticoats and then her drawers until she was standing in just her chemise. She met my eyes boldly and then she pulled the chemise over her head and stood nude before me.

I had never seen anyone so completely naked before. The candlelight caressed Eliza's skin, and my eyes travelled from her shoulders to her breasts and down the flat expanse of her belly to the dark thatch of hair between her legs. Her thighs were thinner than my own, but I could see the muscles standing out beneath the skin. I even looked at her feet closely, noting that there was a sizeable gap between her big toe and the others.

My eyes went back to Eliza's face. I opened my mouth to try to say something, but Eliza tiptoed over to the bed and pulled back the covers.

"Budge up," she said. "It's bloody freezing."

I giggled like a nervous schoolgirl and moved over. Eliza climbed under the covers, shivering. I put my hand tentatively on her bare shoulder and stroked the soft skin. Eliza's hair was fanned out on the pillow like a dark halo. I stroked down the length of her arm and then ran my hand across her stomach. I lowered my mouth to hers, and we kissed gently as I marvelled at the softness of her skin. My fingertips brushed the underside of her breasts, and I felt her kiss me harder.

Very carefully, as if I was handling a precious vase, I allowed my fingers to trail over her breasts. They were soft and warm like fresh dough. I circled gently around them, and as my palm grazed over her nipple, she gasped.

"Is that—" I began.

"Yes," she breathed. And then after a moment, "You might try kissing there."

The idea would never have occurred to me, but I was eager to give some of the pleasure that Eliza had given to me. I kissed down her neck, inhaling her scent of fresh air and woodsmoke. I trailed kisses across her collarbone and then, very gingerly, I laid a kiss on her breast. Eliza's hands ran through my hair as I kissed more firmly, pressing my face into their softness. My lips grazed over her nipple, and I felt her body tense beneath me. Unsure as to whether this was a good sign, I kissed it more firmly, and a moan escaped Eliza's lips.

Pleased with my discovery, I placed my lips over her nipple and swirled my tongue around it. Then I ran my tongue vigorously back and forth, and Eliza cried out and writhed beneath me. She took my face in her hands and pulled my mouth back to hers. Her kiss this time was more imperious, and I responded in kind, thrusting my tongue into her mouth.

Eliza took my hand and placed it between her legs. I was amazed at the wetness, and I moved my fingers gently over her warm flesh. Eliza clutched at my shoulders, gasping into my mouth as I continued my exploration. I had no idea that a woman's private parts were so complex, and I felt as if I was discovering a new world as my hand moved over ridges and contours.

As I moved my fingers back and forth, I brushed against a hard nodule of flesh that made Eliza jump. I touched it again, and she yelped. I was intrigued and very gently began to explore, swirling my fingers around it and occasionally allowing my thumb to brush over it. Whenever I did so, Eliza's body would arch beneath me. I spent several more minutes experimenting with this new discovery until Eliza caught hold of my wrist.

"Are you trying to kill me?" she gasped.

"Does it hurt?" I asked, horrified to think that I might have been causing her pain.

"No, it's good. But there's only so much good I can take."

"Should I stop?" For answer, she moved my hand down to a spot where the heat and wetness seemed to centre. Remembering what she had done to me, I pushed with my fingers until I felt something that seemed to give way. I pushed harder, and my finger slid inside her like I was putting on a glove. Eliza gave a kind of sigh and kissed me again.

I moved my finger slowly back and forth, feeling the landscape that existed inside her. It was as if there were whole valleys and summits within her that were waiting to be discovered. My finger slid easily in and out, and I found a steady rhythm. Eliza's head fell back onto the pillows, her eyes closed. I kissed her stomach and stroked her thighs with my free hand. As the rhythm continued, Eliza's breathing rose with it. She gasped and cried in time with my finger moving in and out. Her cries spurred me on, and I found my hand moved faster as she sobbed. Her breath came in short gasps, and her hips moved up and down furiously to meet my strokes.

"Push," she cried, "Push."

I drove my hand hard against her, pushing my finger up to the very limits. Eliza gave a loud cry, her whole body arching off the bed as her insides throbbed and contracted around me. I held myself deep inside her until the crisis passed, and she came to rest on the bed again. I gently withdrew my finger and lay myself beside her. Eliza's eyes were closed, and she was panting as if she had just run a race. My own breath was coming hard, and we lay there, our breathing slowly returning to normal.

The candle had burnt so low that I could barely make out the features of her face. I reached out and touched her cheek. She placed her hand over mine and stroked it with her fingertips.

"Was that…all right?" I asked.

Eliza chuckled, a hearty, throaty sound. "Yes. Yes, it were more than all right." We lay there for a few moments more and then Eliza rolled up onto her elbow. She ran her hand up my leg and rested it on my stomach. "Would you like…" She tailed off, and I shook my head. A delicious, sleepy lassitude had crept over me. Eliza kissed me and then swung her legs over the side of the bed.

"You're not going?" I asked in dismay.

"I might be needed in the night. Wouldn't do for anyone to notice me being where I shouldn't."

"Stay a bit longer, please. If you leave right now it will feel… tawdry." Eliza hesitated and then got back under the covers. She put her arm about me and drew me to her. I rested my head on her shoulder. "If we are discovered, I will say that I seduced you."

Eliza laughed softly. "They'd never believe a lady like you would know of such things."

"I didn't, not really. I heard things, but I never would have imagined..." I could not complete the sentence and satisfied myself with nestling against her neck and feeling her pulse beating steadily.

"Do people speak of such things?" Eliza asked. "People like you, I mean."

"Not openly. But I heard whispers, snatches of conversation." I thought hard about how to phrase the question that I dearly wished to ask next. Eventually, I cleared my throat and said, "And you? How do you know of such things?"

There was a long silence and then Eliza said, "There was a girl I knew back in London. We both worked the same patch and used to watch out for each other."

"What was her name?"

"Alice."

"What was she like?"

"She were a good laugh. With the sharpest tongue you ever heard. Got her into trouble many a time. But she was kind and sweet when she liked someone."

"What happened to her?"

"She's dead. Cholera." Eliza said it shortly, but I could feel her jaw clenching.

"I'm sorry."

"Ain't your fault." There was a pause.

And then I said, "Were you...sweethearts?" This time, the pause lasted longer. I could feel Eliza's chest rising and falling beneath me.

"We were everything to each other."

I did not know what to say to this so I simply pulled my arms tighter around her. I felt her pull me closer in response, and we lay together like that for a long time.

CHAPTER THIRTEEN

When I awoke, the sunlight was streaming through the window, and Eliza had gone. I lay in bed listening to the birdsong outside and searched within myself for feelings of regret or shame. But there were none. When I thought of Daniel, I thought only of the years of service he would have from me as his wife. I thought of the years of duties faithfully performed that I had already given to him, to my father, to everyone who had asked it of me. And then I thought of Eliza and the feel of her body beneath my hands, and all other thoughts were burnt away.

After breakfast, I sat in the library as usual until Eliza came to tell me Beatrice was ready to receive me. This routine had been unchanged for weeks, yet now, as soon as Eliza entered the room, I jumped up and went straight to her. I put my arms about her and pulled her into a kiss, my lips moving urgently against hers. I could feel her surprise, but she kissed me back, and a white-hot heat flared in my core.

Eliza pushed gently against my shoulders, and the kiss broke. "The mistress," she said, smiling. It was all I could do not to hold her hand as she led me upstairs.

I fidgeted impatiently all through my interview with Beatrice, unable to concentrate on anything she said to me. She attempted to bait me in her usual way, but I gave distracted, incoherent answers. She became irritable that I was depriving her of her sport and dismissed me.

The day passed in a kind of delicious agony as I roamed restlessly from the library, my room, and the garden. I knew that Eliza would be about her work, and I could hardly go and seek her out for stolen kisses. But the only purpose of my day was to see her and touch her again.

Lunch, served by Martha, came and went, and I ate hardly anything because of the tight knot in my stomach. Then I sat outside in the sunshine underneath one of the apple trees that clung to the sloping grass above the back of the house. I settled with my needlework, darting glances up at the windows. I recalled the time that Beatrice had seen Eliza and I, although her window faced the front of the house. That must mean that she roamed the house occasionally, though I had never seen her outside the confines of her room. The thought was unsettling.

I saw Martha and Tripp emerge from the back door, both carrying wicker baskets. I raised my hand to them as they passed below me and headed off in the direction of the overgrown fruit cage that eked out survival at the base of the slope.

A few minutes later, I saw Eliza come into the yard and empty a bucket of dark, soapy water. She did not look up but hefted the bucket back through the door. I waited a few minutes, then rose, thrusting the handkerchief I was half-heartedly embroidering into my pocket.

I slipped through the back door and found her in the scullery, replacing the mop back in its place by the white enamel sink. She turned as she heard me enter and smiled, the corners of her eyes creasing. I kissed her at once, pushing her back against the high, smooth edge of the sink. I felt her mouth yield beneath mine, and her hands came up to my face, pulling me closer. My hips pressed against hers, and I felt the now familiar wetness building at my core.

As my tongue explored her mouth, I felt Eliza press the heel of her hand between my legs. Even through all the layers of my skirts, her touch electrified me, and it was all I could do not to cry out. I fanned my hands over Eliza's breasts, and I cupped them as she ground her hand against me. I wanted to tear her dress from her, to get at the soft flesh beneath, but just at that moment, we heard the faint voices of Martha and Tripp from somewhere outside.

We jumped apart and stood staring at one another. Eliza was leaning back against the sink, breathing heavily. "We must be careful," she whispered.

I panted. "Yes. Yes, we must."

"I will come to you tonight," she promised. I nodded and then turned and made my way back into the house.

I sat in the library until supper, reading St. Augustine. The passages where the saint struggled against his lusts were alive to me, and I read it with new eyes and a new sympathy for the man. If this was what concupiscence was, then I could understand why Augustine was powerless against it.

When supper time finally came, it was Eliza who served me. She entered with the soup dish, eyeing me cautiously. "Don't worry," I said, "I am not going to fling myself at you." Eliza set the soup on the table and took my plate. She ladled soup into it slowly, her eyes flicking to mine as she did so.

A smile tugged at the corners of her mouth. "Good things come to those who wait," she murmured.

I clenched my fists as she left the room.

When she returned with the main course of smoked fish, we said nothing. But our eyes each moved over the other, probing and pushing. Later, as she leaned across me to take my dessert plate, Eliza whispered in my ear, "I will see you later tonight." A shiver passed through me.

I waited for her, pacing my chamber in my nightdress with my shawl wrapped about me. Despite the heat of the day, my room was always cold at night. The candleflames flickered in the draught, making the shadows shift and heave in the corners. I sat at the window, looking out into the blackness of the night and then returned to pacing the room again. A horrible thought crossed my mind that perhaps she was not coming, perhaps she had thought better of it. And what could I do? I could hardly make my way up to the servants' quarters and demand an explanation. Eliza might even share a room with Martha.

It seemed ridiculous that I did not even know where Eliza slept at night, and I began to concoct wild excuses that I could use to go to the servants' quarters and find her.

Finally, I heard a gentle tapping at my door. I went to open it, and Eliza slipped in. She too was dressed in her nightgown with a shawl about her shoulders and a candle in her hand.

"I'm sorry," she said as she set her candle on my dressing table. "The mistress needed a lot of seeing to this evening."

"Is she ill?"

"Nah, she's just in one of her moods." Eliza looked at me, her eyes travelling up and down me in a way that sent a tingling down my spine. "And you? Are you quite well?"

Two short paces brought me to her, and I answered her question by pressing my lips hard against hers. Our arms tangled around each other, and I pressed her to me. I let my hands rove restlessly over her, trying to find a way in to touch her skin. We stumbled over to the bed, landing clumsily. Eliza lay herself on top of me, her hands lifting up the hem of my nightdress. I ran my own hands down her back until they came to rest on her hips. I pulled them tighter against my own as my tongue explored deeper into her mouth.

When I felt Eliza's hands move lower, I opened my legs wider for her. There was no hesitation this time, no uncertainty. I knew with crystal clarity what I wanted her to do, and when she entered me, my body gave a kind of sigh. I kissed her with even greater urgency, and she moved inside me, my hips rising against her. Eliza shifted her hand, and I felt her insert another finger, filling me up completely. I luxuriated in the feeling and wanted to savour the sensation, but it was as if we were in a race, and once the finish line had been sighted, there was no slowing down.

Our kiss broke, and Eliza moved down and layered kisses on my stomach as her hand moved rapidly inside me. Her rhythm seemed to go on and on, a constant refrain that was slowly building toward a crescendo. My breaths came in short, shallow gasps in time with her thrusts, urging her on. When the end finally came, I cried out and went rigid, squeezing my eyes shut as wave after searing wave passed through me.

Eliza laid her head on my stomach, and I idly stroked her hair as I slowly came back to myself. She withdrew slowly and then pulled herself back up the bed to lie on the pillow next to me. I could barely see her face in the dimming light of the candles. I reached to touch its now familiar contours, running my fingers along her jaw and down into the hollow at the base of her neck. I kissed her again, very gently this time, caressing her lips with my own. I stroked the softness of her cheek, and my other hand rested on the smooth expanse of her chest.

As the kisses went on, I felt my ardour rising again, a renewed need building between my legs. I pulled up the hem of Eliza's gown, my hand roving over her legs as our kisses became more urgent. I moved up until I was cupping her breasts and kneading the soft flesh gently. I carried on in this way for a few minutes until Eliza made an impatient sound and then stood, pulling her nightdress over her head and stepping out of her drawers. And then she was back at my side, kissing me hard, and my hands went straight to her breasts, kneading them and running my thumbs across her nipples. Then I lowered my head and kissed her breasts, tracing their outlines. My lips grazed across a nipple, and Eliza gasped. I took one of her nipples into my mouth, sucking it and running my tongue across it.

Eliza groaned, and her body twisted beneath me as if she wanted to get away but not really. I moved my lips from her breast and transferred to the other, sucking harder and harder. Eliza began to whimper. I continued in this way for several minutes, moving my mouth from one nipple to the other until finally, after Eliza had whispered, "Please," into my ear several times, I moved my hand between her legs.

It was like dipping my hand into warm honey, and my finger slid inside her easily. I moved in and out, keeping my mouth on her breast. As Eliza gasped and moaned, I felt a strange fierce longing overtake me. I pushed my hand into her hard, and her hips rose off the bed. I increased my pace, thrusting my fingers into her as hard as I could whilst my tongue flicked remorselessly against her nipple. I want you to, I want you to, I thought to myself, the words hammering around my head in time with my thrusting fingers.

Eliza covered her mouth to suppress her cries at the same time that a wave of moisture filled my hand. I felt her insides fluttering and contracting around my hand as her fingers dug into my shoulders. Her legs wrapped about my hips as she pulled me tight against her. I held on, my fingers still buried inside her as her climax peaked and then gradually pulsed away.

It seemed like hours later when I finally withdrew my hand and settled my head next to hers, both of us breathing heavily.

Eliza stroked my hair from my face. "Blimey," she murmured, "who would have thought it?"

I felt myself blush and was glad it was too dark for her to see. "Was it…I mean I hope I didn't hurt you."

"You didn't, not really. It ain't all tender kisses and caresses. Can be fierce sometimes." As if to prove her point, she kissed me hard, awakening a fresh passion in me.

The night passed as a series of storms, building slowly and then erupting in violent bursts before subsiding to build again.

The first streaks of dawn were seeping across the sky as I broke from kissing Eliza to say, "It's almost light. You should go."

"Not yet." She made to kiss me again, and I drew my head back, smiling.

"You must get some sleep."

"I can do without sleep," she insisted, pulling me close.

"Then think of Martha. Won't she be awake before too long?"

"Ah. You have seduced me, and now you cruelly cast me aside," she said, raising her hand to her forehead in mock distress.

I poked her arm. "Go now before I start screaming for help."

She planted one last kiss on my lips before getting up and wriggling back into her drawers and nightgown. She wrapped her shawl about her shoulders and took up her candle. She looked briefly at herself in the looking glass and ran her hand through her hair, combing it down with her fingers. She turned back to me and smiled.

"Good night, Ruth," she said.

❖

The next few weeks passed in a glorious, sun-filled haze. I still engaged in my usual activities. I read, walked, and fiddled with my needlework. I continued to teach Eliza to read and write, and I went to church on Sundays. And I still had my daily interview with Beatrice.

I struggled through these encounters as best I could, stifling my yawns and saying as little as possible in the hope that Beatrice would dismiss me sooner. She did not. She simply took the opportunity of my silence to rant on her favourite themes of predestination, the uselessness of all her servants, and occasional remembrances of her former life at Beulah Lodge. When she spoke of the past, Beatrice seemed to temporarily forget I was there. She did not speak of her husband with fondness exactly, but it seemed as if her hard edge was momentarily blunted. And then she would recall that I was present, and her malice would return.

The monotony of the days were punctuated by snatched moments with Eliza, a kiss stolen as she set my meals before me or a swift, passionate embrace in the hallway or scullery or library or wherever we happened to find ourselves alone together. Eliza came to me every night, and we spent the hours roaming over one another, as if we were each a newly discovered country to the other.

I hardly knew myself in those weeks. I would never have imagined that I could be so completely swept up and absorbed in another person. I thought of Eliza constantly, always anticipating where our next encounter would be. Even when we had made love repeatedly through the night, as soon as she left, I longed for her again.

I read the books of Kings and Chronicles, and the accounts burst into vivid life, the passionate loves and griefs of David mirrored my own feelings, and the intensity of the emotions echoed down the centuries in a way that I had never experienced before.

Somewhere, buried deep within me, was the knowledge that it could not last. It lurked there like a figure glimpsed just from the corner of my eye, and if I did not look directly at it, I could pretend that it did not exist.

One particularly glorious summer's day, after breakfast, I sat beneath the apple tree with my needlework until the time came for my daily appointment with Beatrice. I opened the back door and entered through the scullery into the kitchen, my eyes taking a moment to adjust from the bright sunshine outdoors.

Martha was heaving the copper kettle from the range, and as she set it on the table, Eliza came into the kitchen. "Don't bother with that, Martha. Mistress don't want nothing."

"She don't want any tea?" asked Martha in surprise.

"No. Nothing at all."

Martha wiped the sweat from her brow and frowned at the kettle. "I suppose I can use the water for that pan what needs scrubbing."

"Does Mrs. Groves still wish to see me?" I asked. They both jumped at the sound of my voice, and I could not suppress a smile.

Martha put a hand to her chest. "Lord bless you, ma'am. You're as quiet as a mouse. What did the mistress say, Eliza?"

"She said she ain't well and don't want to see anyone." She paused and then added with a wink, "Only she didn't put it quite as nice as that. I'm to go back at lunchtime and see if she wants for anything."

Martha nodded and then looked kindly at me. "It looks as though you are released, ma'am."

"I am sorry that Mrs. Groves isn't feeling good. But I shall be glad of the chance to be out of doors on such a beautiful day. Perhaps I shall go and pick some harebells for your mistress. You said there was a particular spot where they were in flower?" I turned to Eliza, who nodded.

"Yes, ma'am. On a bit of heathland down toward the river at Hawnby. I could show you the exact place." She looked at Martha and raised her eyebrows.

Martha shook her head, smiling. "I don't know why you want to be getting all hot and bothered traipsing over the countryside in this weather."

"I'll pick you some purple harebells," Eliza promised.

Martha waved her hand. "Oh, get away with you. I'm not some milkmaid who needs posies. Just mind you're back by lunch time for the mistress. You know how she gets."

Eliza whipped off her apron and cap with astonishing speed. "You're a diamond, Martha Greenwood. You know that? An even bigger diamond than that Indian one the Queen has."

"The Koh-i-Noor," I supplied.

"Exactly." Eliza pushed open the back door and shouted back into the kitchen, "Bigger than that."

I waved to the laughing Martha and followed Eliza out into the yard. We walked serenely beside each other until we reached the top of the ridge and dipped down out of sight of the house. And then we were like two schoolboys playing truant. We leapt and whooped our way down the track, taking hold of each other's hands and practically dancing with the joy of being free.

When we regained our composure, we walked hand in hand along the path, descending down toward the river, which I had only ever seen as a wisp of silver from the high points of the moors.

"It is good to be out of there, ain't it, Ruth?" said Eliza, swinging my arm along with hers. I always thrilled to hear her use my Christian name.

"Yes," I said. "There is something about Beulah Lodge that is oppressive."

"It's the mistress. She's in the entire house somehow, like she's seeped into the walls."

The thought made me shiver despite the heat of the day. "I keep thinking of that time she saw us in the yard. She must have been in a room on the other side of the house."

"She has been known to go for wanders sometimes."

"So she is not completely confined to her chamber?"

"Nah, she ain't such an invalid as she likes everyone to think. She's vigorous enough when she wants to be, like when she wants to chuck a paper knife!"

"Perhaps that is how she spends her time, practising like a knife thrower at the circus."

Eliza laughed. "You wouldn't catch me volunteering to be her assistant."

We walked for an hour or so until we came to a large expanse of heath. There were a few sheep grazing upon it who shuffled anxiously away from us as we approached. Eliza stopped and pointed.

"There you are!" she said triumphantly. I followed her gaze but could see nothing. Eliza pulled me toward a clump of trees nestled in a slight dip in the land. Interlaced amongst the long stalks of grass were the beautiful bell-shaped flowers, nodding slightly in the summer heat. We crouched amongst them, exclaiming at their vivid purple and white colour and tipping the flowers up to look more closely at their delicate petals.

"They look like fine ladies wearing bonnets," I said. I gently touched a snowy white flower. "This one looks like Mrs. Freebody."

"Freebody?"

"Mrs. Freebody and her daughters were very active in my father's church. The Miss Freebodys helped me run the Sunday School."

"I knew someone called Peabody once. He was one of them barrel organ players, and he had a little monkey called Smash. Don't think his name was actually Peabody, though, think he got called that cos he had a foreign name that no one could say." She settled amongst the grass with her back against the tree and took out her tobacco tin. I sat beside her, relieved to be in shade.

"We used to have organ players in Poplar too," I said. "There was an Italian chap for a while. But I don't know what happened to him. He was there one week and then gone the next."

"Prob'ly got coshed for his takings or something." Eliza struck a match and lit her cigarette.

"Did you ever get coshed?"

Eliza looked at me in surprise. "That's a funny question to ask."

"Not really. You mention every now and then what things were like for you, but I still don't really know."

"Why should you want to know?"

"Because I care about what happened to you."

Eliza blew out smoke and looked away toward the sheep ambling over the heath. After a while she said, "I got slapped about a bit, all the girls did. Alice got stabbed with a penknife once by some bloke who thought she'd given him the clap." Eliza grinned. "He soon regretted that, though. Alice headbutted him right between the eyes and then walked all the way to Saint Tommy's for help with the knife still sticking out her thigh."

"And the man who did that to her?"

"Never saw or heard from him again." Eliza laughed, causing several sheep to look up in alarm. "Alice never would stand for nonsense from anyone."

"What would Alice think of this?"

"Of you and me?" Eliza took another pull on her cigarette and smiled. "She wouldn't begrudge me a bit of happiness. And she'd be tickled, what with you being a lady and all. Would prob'ly tell me I was punching way above my weight." I blushed, and Eliza said hastily, "I don't mean...I mean I hope I ain't said something wrong."

"No, no. It's just I am not used to any of this."

"You ain't never had a love affair before?"

My blush deepened. I had certainly never considered the word *love* in relation to what Eliza and I were doing, and to hear it mentioned so casually completely unsettled me. "No. No I mean it's not the sort of thing young ladies in my position...from my family..." I trailed off.

"What would your family think of it?" Eliza asked, gently.

I plucked a stalk of grass and twirled it in my fingers, not looking at her. "I don't know what my father would have thought," I said. "Daniel would say it was a sin."

"And you?" She said it casually, but I could feel her eyes on my face.

"The Bible is clear about unnatural vices."

"But yet you still go to bed with me."

"I believe God is a loving God. He sees into my heart and knows what is there before I myself do. He knows I am prepared to give my life as a missionary. I hope, I pray, that that will be enough to atone for my sins."

We were both silent. The bleats of the sheep, like old men coughing, drifted across the heath. I wound the stalk of grass around my finger and pulled it tight, watching as the tip of my finger turned red with stopped blood. I felt the threat of the future, which I had so assiduously held at bay, begin to press around us, darkening the joy of the sunlit afternoon.

A high-pitched chirruping noise, like that of a grasshopper, sounded from somewhere behind us. Eliza stubbed out her cigarette on the sole of her boot and pocketed the end.

"It's a warbler," she said, cocking her head in the direction of the sound.

"You must draw one for me," I said.

Eliza smiled at me and then got to her feet carefully, taking care not to crush any of the harebells. She squinted at the sky. "I ought to be getting back to see if the mistress wants anything."

I stood and brushed down the front of my dress. My hand sought out hers, and we walked back in companionable silence, only dropping each other's hands when we came within sight of the house.

CHAPTER FOURTEEN

Beatrice recovered from her bad turn soon enough, and the following day I was summoned before her as usual. She wasted no time in getting straight to her point, "You waste ever more of my servants' time I see," she said as soon as I sat down.

I asked her patiently what she meant, knowing that Beatrice enjoyed drawing these things out.

"You are teaching Eliza her letters. Running your very own ragged school out of *my* house."

I wondered how she had come to know of this. Had Tripp told her? Or had she somehow seen something? The latter thought was so disconcerting that I quickly decided it must have been Tripp. "Do you object?" I asked with as much nonchalance as I could muster.

"It is a waste of time," Beatrice snapped.

"You know my thoughts on reading, Aunt. I can never regard it as a waste of time."

"It is the same as teaching a dog tricks, very amusing for a little while but of no real value."

"Again, I cannot agree. Reading can only improve the mind and character."

"And if I were to forbid these lessons?" She spoke softly, raising her eyebrows. I sensed I was on dangerous ground. I was, after all, completely dependent on Beatrice's goodwill as her guest, and I was already pushing my luck.

"If there is a concern about Eliza's work, I would be happy to conduct her lessons at a different time. Perhaps in the evening when her work is done," I said carefully.

"Or perhaps you could hold your lessons on the little walks you take with her." I was caught off guard by this, and Beatrice smiled triumphantly. "Oh yes, I see you go off gallivanting together. Where do you go?"

"Only to the village," I stammered.

"To do what?"

I felt the heat of a blush come over my face and cursed myself. "To post letters, run errands…" I met her eye and willed my face to return to its normal hue.

"And what do you talk about on these little excursions? What conversation can you and she possibly have?"

"Nothing much," I said as carelessly as I could. "We talk mainly of the places we knew in London."

Beatrice leaned forward and looked intently into my face, blinking slowly. "*My* servants are *my* concern," she said. "They belong to me. Do you understand?"

I felt my face grow hot again, and I nodded. Beatrice sat back in her chair, looking pleased with herself.

I felt somewhat shaken by the encounter with Beatrice but told myself again that she had not expressly forbidden me from continuing to teach Eliza. The lessons had come to be an integral part of my days at Beulah Lodge, and I was not prepared to give them up lightly.

Indeed, I was spending a considerable amount of time in the library. For not only were there Eliza's lessons to prepare and conduct, but I was increasingly coming across Mr. Tripp, studying his books intently. In fact, one afternoon, a few days after Beatrice's sharp reprimand, I came into the library to continue my sewing and was greeted by the sight of him examining his books and looking as if he might actually be smiling.

He looked up as I entered, and my original impression was confirmed. Tripp was smiling.

"Mr. Tripp," I greeted him. "Your account books bring you pleasure today?"

"It's the multiplying you showed me, ma'am. It has made things so much easier."

"Indeed? I am very pleased to hear it."

"And now the books ain't piled up in the corner no more, I was thinking I could look back over the last few years and see where things stand. Overall, like."

"A very worthwhile project." I approached the desk and cast my eye down the neat columns of figures. "How do things look?"

Tripp chewed the end of his pencil, the smile replaced by his more usual frown. "There ain't much coming in. And there always seems to be too much going out."

I saw that he had adopted a new way of recording his figures, with separate columns for income and expenditure across the whole of the previous year. I pointed to a large sum in the expenditure. "That will have made a dent." My eye ran up the column and saw similar large amounts occurring at least once, sometimes twice in the preceding years. "What are these payments for?" Tripp huffed slightly, and I realised that I had been too direct. "I beg your pardon, Mr. Tripp. I do not mean to pry into your handling of the estate. Doubtless these must have been for repairs to the house or other essentials."

Tripp sat there frowning to himself, and I let the silence stretch out. "There is no shortage of repairs that must be done," he said, finally. "The roof, the gutters, the chimneys. They all need attention."

"And such attention does not come cheap."

"No. That's why we have to take a care with our candles and suchlike."

"Just so," I said, thinking that it would take more than economising on a few candles to return Beulah Lodge to its past glories.

"But this money…" Tripp was clearly battling with himself over how much to tell me, and I bit down my impatience. "Well, this money was paid from the estate at the mistress's behest."

"To whom?"

"To a gentleman in London. Her solicitor, I assume."

I looked at the figures. They were substantial sums of money, and I could not imagine why her lawyers would require such payments. Tripp was looking at me rather anxiously, and I said, soothingly, "Ah, I see. Solicitors are never cheap."

Tripp looked relieved and turned back to his work. I took my usual seat in the armchair and picked up my sewing. If the estate was paying out such vast sums each year, it was no wonder the place was falling in around us.

I might have given the matter no more thought—it was, after all, none of my business how Beatrice managed her affairs—were it not for one morning when Mr. Tripp sought me out at the breakfast table.

This was highly unusual, and I sensed that something must be troubling him deeply, as he stood before me twisting his cap round and round in his gnarled hands. "I was wondering, ma'am," he began.

I knew that offering him tea or inviting him to sit down would only make him more flustered, so I simply said encouragingly, "Yes, Mr. Tripp?"

"You see, ma'am, it's Curran."

"Curran? Ah, the man who pays his rent in potatoes?"

"That's the one. Well, the final part of his rent is due this quarter, and I must go to his cottage and collect it from him."

"Quite so."

"Curran normally comes to the house last day of the quarter, as he lives close by, but he ain't come, so now I think I must go to him."

"That seems perfectly reasonable," I said, still baffled as to what it was Mr. Tripp required of me.

He twisted his cap some more and then burst out, "He's a clever one, is Curran. He always likes to make out as how I ain't done my sums properly, and I must have missed something, always trying to say that he don't owe what I say he does."

"But you have his mark against the last rent payment, do you not?"

"Yes, ma'am, but I know as how he'll say that I have entered the figures all wrong, and he'll try to give me more potatoes, I know it. And not as we can't use potatoes—Martha makes a wonderful cottage pie, you know—but I can't be letting more money slip through our fingers, not when the accounts is looking as bad as they are." He ran out of breath and came to a halt, staring miserably at the carpet.

"I do see how difficult it is for you, Mr. Tripp. Tell me, how can I be of assistance?"

Tripp's eyes roamed around the room before resting on the teapot in front of me. "I thought perhaps if you accompanied me, ma'am, that might make Curran think twice before attempting any of his usual tricks." I was surprised by the request, and it must have shown in my face, for Tripp at once said, "I understand if you think it would not be proper."

"Not at all," I said, anxious that this opportunity to be of use should not pass me by. "I would be very happy to accompany you. I used to visit parishioners with my father, so I think it very proper indeed."

Tripp looked mightily relieved and told me that we should set out directly, as it was a long walk to Curran's cottage. I made myself ready as quickly as I could and met him at the stable.

His first idea was that I should ride Prospero, and he would lead the horse, but this image seemed so ridiculous to me that I spent some time persuading him against it. We finally set off on foot, walking along the road away from the village and up across the moors. We followed the road for a good half an hour as it dipped down into a valley and then followed the river along a series of tracks.

Curran's cottage was one of half a dozen clustered on the hillside above a bend in the river. There was nothing else nearby, and I wondered aloud how these houses had ended up here.

"Used to be an ironstone mine hereabouts," Tripp explained. "They built houses for the miners. Most of 'em have fallen into ruin now."

We walked up the hill to a cottage in the middle of the group. The neighbouring houses were scattered far enough away for the house to seem fairly private. It was surrounded by a low drystone wall, with vegetable plots laid out and a chicken coop around the back. The house itself seemed in a reasonable state of repair, at least to my untrained eye.

Tripp knocked on the door, and it was opened by a woman of around forty wearing a patched dress and a haggard look.

"Good morning, Mrs. Curran," said Tripp.

"Good morning, Mr. Tripp. It'll be Curran you'll be wanting."

"Aye. Is he here?"

"No, he has gone down to weed the beets, but he will be back soon. Will you wait for him?"

"I think we better had," said Tripp gravely. Mrs. Curran noticed me for the first time and looked quizzically at Tripp. "This here is Miss Mallowes," Tripp explained. "She is the mistress's niece, and she is come to help me with collecting the rents."

Mrs. Curran nodded to me and then invited us both in to wait for her husband inside. We sat in the small dark kitchen, and Mrs. Curran served us weak tea from a chipped teapot. The poverty of the family was immediately obvious: their little furniture was rickety and cheap. There were some small children who clung to their mother's skirts and looked at us with large eyes but said not a word.

But more than any of this, it was Mrs. Curran's bowed shoulders and lined face that told me of the continual grind the family lived through, every day a trial of fortitude and endurance.

We made a little polite conversation, and presently, the back door opened, and Mr. Curran entered. He looked both surprised and displeased to see us. But he greeted Tripp cordially enough and then stood leaning against the mantelpiece whilst Mrs. Curran poured some tea out for him.

Curran's eyes flickered briefly over me, but he did not question my presence.

"I have come for the remainder of the rent," Tripp said sternly.

Curran took a cup of tea from his wife and sipped it slowly before saying, "I gave you all the rent last time Mr. Tripp. Remember? Them potatoes was the last of it."

Tripp took out his account book with a world-weary air and laid it on the table. He laboriously explained to Curran what he still owed and why. I watched Curran's face as he did so. The man's pale eyes flitted about the cottage, resting sometimes on his wife and children. He put me in mind of a hunted animal, and I saw the patches in his clothes and the same haggard look as his wife, and I was filled with sympathy for him.

"So you still owes a pound for this quarter's rent," Tripp finished.

Curran's jaw tightened as he placed his teacup on the mantelpiece and drew his pipe from his pocket. I glanced across the room and saw that Mrs. Curran was watching her husband closely, her face set in tense lines. I could see that Curran and Tripp were set on a collision course, and I feared that if I did not say something, there would be no way to divert them.

"But we do not necessarily need it all at once," I said. Everyone turned to look at me. I deliberately avoided Mr. Tripp's gaze for fear that I would lose my nerve. "It can be paid in instalments," I said confidently.

Curran frowned, his pipe held in mid-air. "That so, Mr. Tripp?" he asked.

I met Tripp's eye and after a moment, Tripp nodded slowly. "Aye, that's right."

"Instalments of how much?" asked Curran suspiciously.

"That is what we must discuss," I said carefully. "Aside from the cash, there could be payment made in goods—as you have already done with the potatoes—and perhaps payment made in labour as well." I could sense Tripp stiffening at this last, but I kept my gaze on Curran.

"In labour?" Curran tapped his pipe against the chimney breast and flicked his gaze back and forth between myself and Tripp.

"There is plenty of work that needs doing at the house, repair and maintenance, mostly. It could be that a day or two of your labour could count against your rent account." I risked a glance at Tripp.

His scowl had cleared, and he was nodding. "Aye, there's plenty to be done. And we ain't got no one to do it. I'm too broken down to be of much use."

"Oh, you ain't broken down, Mr. Tripp," exclaimed Mrs. Curran. "If you was only free of that place, why, you'd be springing like a newborn lamb."

The image was so comical that all of us, including Tripp, laughed out loud, and the tension in the room was broken. Mrs. Curran made another pot of weak tea, and Curran sat at the table with Tripp, and together, we worked out a plan for the next three months that would allow Curran to pay the pound he owed.

The discussion was amicable enough, yet it seemed painfully obvious to me that even if they cleared the debt they owed on this quarter's rent, the Currans were unlikely to be able to make the next rent payment. I said nothing, however, waiting until Tripp and Curran had shaken hands, and we had been seen out with many thanks and expressions of goodwill on either side.

It was only when we were out of earshot that I said, "I doubt they will be able to pay the next quarter rent."

"I agree, ma'am. I can't see as how they can do it. They make little enough from those crops just to feed themselves."

"What can be done?" I asked in consternation.

Tripp scratched one of his bushy eyebrows. "I don't rightly know. I can't drop the rent, not without the mistress's say-so, and she would never agree. And besides, it's not as if we can afford to be losing any rents."

"Perhaps you could relax it for a while, to give Curran a chance to increase his yields?"

"Mistress would never agree. And I don't see what else he could do with the land he's got. Mayhap he'd be better off moving to grazing sheep. There's a parcel of estate land higher up on the moors that'd be perfect for sheep, but there's no one to work it." I had barely opened my mouth before Tripp was shaking his head at me. "Mistress wouldn't agree to it," he said.

"But she cannot want the estate to go bankrupt," I exclaimed in frustration.

As ever, when any criticism of Beatrice was implied, Tripp retreated back into his shell. "Tain't my place to say, ma'am," he said stiffly.

We walked on for some way in silence before I said, "I understand the difficulties of your position, Mr. Tripp. It's just that the Currans' predicament seems so hopeless. I have seen families like that before, in my father's parish. Good people, honest people who do their best to make a living in whatever circumstances they find themselves. But they become worn down by the struggle and slip ever further into debt, as if they were stuck in quicksand. I just cannot accept that there is nothing that can be done."

"It is in the Lord's hands," Tripp said.

It is in our hands, I wanted to shout back, but I held my tongue. There was precious little I could do for the Currans and the other tenants of Beulah Lodge, but even that little would be endangered if I pushed Tripp too far.

And so, I held my peace as we continued the long walk back to Beulah Lodge.

I did not, however, forget the Currans, and they preyed on my mind constantly over the following days. I waited until the next Sunday, and then after church, when I knew that Tripp would be safely ensconced in the Red Lion, I sat down in the library with Tripp's summary book and applied myself to acquiring an understanding of the estate's financial position.

My father's churchwarden had been a Mr. Deakin, a vigorous middle-aged man with twinkly eyes, and one of his favourite maxims was that a well-kept account book could be as riveting a read as any novel. I had never quite believed him until I came to go through the Beulah Lodge account books. Several times, I checked back from Tripp's summary to the original dusty ledgers, unable to quite believe what I was seeing.

They told a story of an estate that had once been comfortably prosperous: rents paid in full on time, repairs and improvements routinely carried out, numerous servants paid regular wages with a bit extra given at Christmas. A sense of order and contentment radiated from the pages. Then, at about the time Mr. Groves had died, things seemed to change. All was quiet for a year or so, and then the first of the large payments I had noticed before began. The income columns began to shrink as the accounts became dominated by these huge withdrawals. Soon, it was clear that any savings had been run through, and then the lists of servants' wages diminished, and there was less and less of the repairs necessary to keep the estate in good order.

The last five years were the most eloquent. The outgoings of the estate dropped to bare essentials, and there was evidence of land being sold off and tenancies lapsing. The wages listed for the remaining staff were miserly at best, and there was no evidence that Eliza had ever been paid a wage at all. Yet still, the large sums being paid out continued, although the last of such sums had been made two years ago. It seemed clear to me that if another such sum was outlaid, the estate would surely go bankrupt.

I was chewing fretfully on the end of my pencil when the door opened and Eliza came in. "There you are," she exclaimed. "Martha was convinced you had fallen down a pothole on the moors."

"What?" And then I realised that the light was fading, and I had been poring over the books for the whole afternoon. "I did not realise it had got so late. Have I kept dinner waiting?"

"It were only some bread and cold meat left over from lunch."

"Is Mr. Tripp returned?" I asked, replacing the ledgers back on the shelf.

"No. He must be having a particularly good session at the pub tonight." She watched me return the account books with an amused smile. "You worried he'll catch you snooping?"

"Yes. Although I would not call it snooping. I am simply establishing the facts."

"That right, Inspector? So do you know who dun it yet?"

I was still too vexed by the estate's finances to return her banter. "You do realise that you have never been paid a wage the whole time you have been here?"

Eliza merely shrugged. "Never expected one. Mistress said she would give me my board and lodging, but she never promised a wage."

I replaced the last of the account books and stood chewing on my lip, the figures still swimming before my eyes.

"What's the matter?" Eliza asked gently. "Are the accounts truly that bad?"

"Yes, they are. If Beatrice continues to pay her solicitors the sums she has been, I fear the entire estate will become insolvent."

"Her solicitors?" Eliza repeated incredulously.

"That is Tripp's explanation. Though I cannot conceive why Beatrice would need to pay them such sums. It is not even the same amount each time. Sometimes it is five hundred pounds, other times almost seven hundred—"

I saw something shift in Eliza's face, and I stopped. My first thought was that I was being rather indiscreet in discussing Beatrice's finances so openly with her. But since we had spent so much of our time together over the past few weeks, I had ceased to think of her as a servant. I had also become more adept at reading her expressions, and I stared at her in amazement.

"You know all about it, don't you?" Eliza dropped her eyes and shifted her feet, which immediately confirmed my suspicions. "Well? What are the payments for?"

"Should you not ask the mistress that question?" I bit my lip again. She was right. Strictly speaking, it was none of my business. But the image of Curran's dark-eyed children and his own, haunted look rose before me.

"I would, if I thought for one minute she would tell me," I said. "Eliza, the estate is scraping by. It is in debt, its tenants are impoverished, and all it will take is one more unexpected outlay, and then it will be bankruptcy. All the land will have to be sold, which will mean the tenants being turned out of their homes. The house itself may have to be sold. You, Tripp, and Martha would all be homeless."

"All right, but none of that would be your fault," Eliza pointed out.

"No, but I cannot stand by and watch it happen. Not if there is something I can do to help."

"There ain't nothing you can do."

"How do you know?"

"Cos I know the mistress. Just as you do, and you know she won't listen to no one."

"She does not want to be destitute, of that I am sure."

"Look, you don't got to worry about it. She's an invalid now. She likely won't be going to London ever again."

"So these payments are connected with her trips to London?"

"Blimey, you are like a rozzer."

"Eliza, please. Just tell me."

I could see the conflict play out across her face. Finally, she sighed and said, "They are gambling debts."

I almost laughed. "Gambling? Beatrice?"

"Cards, mostly. Though she did once bet on a cockfight."

I stared at her. "But gambling is a sin. Beatrice would never—"

It was Eliza's turn to laugh now. "Oh, she would. She would lose hundreds of pounds in a single night. I guess you have to know a lot about sin to be able to preach against it," she added bitterly.

I put my hand on the desk to steady myself. Although I was shocked that Beatrice could run up such debts with gambling, there was another, creeping unease that was coming over me. "How do you know this?" I asked quietly.

Eliza looked momentarily stricken, as if she wished she could take back what she had said. But her customary bravado soon reasserted itself. "Cos she told me."

"When did she tell you?"

"I don't remember the exact date, Inspector."

"Why would she tell you that? Why would Beatrice confide in you that she was gambling huge sums of money away?" Eliza didn't reply, and another thought struck me. "And how on earth would she know where to find a cockfight?"

I already had an inkling of what was coming as Eliza took a deep breath and said, "Beatrice was in London a little while before she brought me back up here with her. And I showed her around some of the places she wanted to go. They used to have a cockfight at this pub out in Whitechapel."

"But it is illegal."

"That forms part of its appeal. Apparently." Eliza wrinkled her nose in disgust. "Mistress loved it. Loved the cruelty and viciousness of it."

"Why were you showing her round?"

"Cos she paid me," Eliza mumbled, looking down at her feet again.

My head began to swim. "You said you met her when you were having some argument with a man."

"Yes."

"And then she offered you a place here."

"That's right. There was just a bit in between where she wanted to see some sights of London and paid me to show them to her. So I took her to the cockfight, and she took me with her when she went to one of her clubs to play cards."

"You did not mention any of this before."

"That's cos it don't look good on me, does it?"

I was feeling increasingly queasy, and I sat back down in the desk chair. "She paid you to show her around?"

"Yes. She wanted to go slumming, to see all the seedier sights. So I showed her what I could. It weren't easy. After all, it's not like a lady like her can just wander into a pub on the Cally Road, is it? We only got into the cockfight cos she threatened to summon a copper if they didn't let her in."

"How long did this last?"

"About a week. And then at the end of the week, she says she's going back up north and offers me to go with her."

I closed my eyes, feeling my stomach churn. "You lied to me."

"I did not lie," Eliza said hotly. "I just left some bits out, that's all."

"Some quite important bits, wouldn't you agree?"

"No, I bloody wouldn't! You asked me how I came to meet Beatrice, and I told you. I didn't say one thing that was untrue. And why should I have told you the whole, wretched story anyway? You ain't told me why you agreed to marry your beloved fiancé."

Her mocking tone stung me, and I got to my feet again. "There is no point in us continuing this conversation," I said coldly.

Eliza was visibly biting back her words. "All right," she said with equal coldness. "I have my duties to attend to. I only came to tell you that your dinner was waiting." She curtsied formally and withdrew, leaving me with shaking hands and absolutely no appetite for cold mutton.

❖

Eliza did not come to me that night. I lay in bed, my feelings oscillating between wretchedness and indignation that Eliza could have left out all the important parts about how she had met Beatrice.

Eliza studiously avoided me all the next day. As the hours wore on, my indignation subsided and was replaced wholly by wretchedness. I sat in the library, my needlework lying discarded in my lap as I boiled with self-recrimination.

What right did I have to pry into Eliza's past? And she was perfectly correct. I had not told her about how Daniel and I came to be engaged. Did the fact that Eliza shared my bed entitle me to know everything about her past? But yet a more disturbing thought lurked under the surface.

I had been shocked by Beatrice's gambling debts and appalled by the hypocrisy of her condemning sin whilst indulging in it herself. But how different was that from what I was doing? Was I any better than Beatrice? Was I too taking advantage of a vulnerable girl?

I was mired deep in these dark thoughts when the library door opened. My heart soared and then fell again just as swiftly as Tripp's craggy face appeared around the door.

"Begging your pardon, ma'am. I didn't know you were in here."

"That is quite all right, Mr. Tripp. As you can see, I am not occupied with anything in particular." I stood up from the desk and gestured to it. "It is all yours if you wish."

"Thank you, ma'am. I have some entries to make for Prospero's feed this month. And if I do not do it straight away, I am liable to forget."

I watched him shuffle over to the desk and peer at the account books until he found the one he was looking for. He frowned over it as he painstakingly entered in the figures to the correct column. It was a heart-breaking sight.

"Mr. Tripp," I said. "You know that the estate is on the verge of bankruptcy." He raised his head slowly and looked at me. I had half expected him to bluster, to vigorously deny any such thing or, more likely, to say that it was all the mistress's concern.

But he did neither of those things. Instead, he simply regarded me seriously for a moment or two and then said, "Aye. I may not be a book-keeping clerk, but I can see when one number is less than another."

"Of course. Forgive me, I did not mean to imply otherwise. But is your mistress aware of the parlous state of things?"

Tripp dropped his gaze. "She is an invalid. I cannot bring this before her and risk her health. Besides, she has entrusted the running of the estate to me."

"But if she makes any more of those payments…to her solicitors, then it will be the end of the estate. People will lose their homes and their livelihoods."

Tripp's pained expression told me that he had considered all of this before.

I came and sat across the desk from him. "Mr. Tripp. You have stewarded this estate to the best of your ability. No one can fault you for that. But a good steward must inform the master if there are wolves at the door. I can perfectly understand that you find the idea of telling your mistress about all this difficult to contemplate. Which is why I will be the one to tell her." He looked up sharply and opened his mouth as if to protest. "It will be easier for her to hear it from an outsider," I said firmly. "I am not endangering my position here by speaking out. It may be that I can persuade her to take some action before it is too late."

"She won't thank you for it, ma'am."

"I do not need her thanks. And I know she will not like hearing it. But I cannot allow her tenants, her servants, everyone to be at risk of destitution if there is something I could do to prevent it."

He regarded me from under his heavy brows. "It may be that you're right, ma'am. Perhaps she will take it better coming from someone outside and with you also being a lady. But I beg you will not harangue her about it. Break it to her gently."

I suspected that he said the last to preserve the illusion that she was a fine lady of delicate sensibilities who would be deeply distressed by the discussion of anything as vulgar as money. "I understand. I will be very careful, I promise."

I spent the evening contemplating how I would approach Beatrice about the problems with the estate finances. I sat in my room after dinner, idly jotting thoughts and plans down as they came to me. I sensed that I would only have one chance at the conversation. If Beatrice did not like what I had to say, she would shut me down and refuse to let me address the topic again. I had to try to get it right the first time, to persuade her to at least take the threat seriously.

I fretted and worried over all the different ways I could approach this, feeling that if I failed, then the livelihoods of everyone connected with Beulah Lodge would be at risk.

I called distractedly in answer to the knock at the door. Eliza came in, looking slightly sheepish. "Came to ask if you needed anything else, ma'am, before you retire?"

I glanced at the clock over the mantelpiece. "I had not realised it had grown so late," I remarked. "But I need nothing further, thank you." I had been so absorbed in my thoughts that I had almost forgotten our earlier quarrel. It was only when Eliza coughed awkwardly that I remembered.

"I, er, might have spoke a bit hasty before," she said.

"Oh, that. Well, I did accuse you of lying. Which was somewhat hypocritical of me."

"I s'pose I should've told you the whole story."

"No, you were under no obligation to do so. What right have I to demand a full account of your history? As you correctly pointed out, I have not done the same." I stood from the desk and stretched my aching shoulders. I went and sat on the bed and began to take my hair down.

"You asked me why I accepted Daniel's proposal," I said. "The truth is that I don't really know. It seemed the right thing to do at the time. He was very kind to me when my father died, and that seemed sufficient. And I am getting old. There are not many women of my station who are unmarried past the age of twenty-five. Not without having independent means, anyway."

"What would you do if you had to do everything over?"

I closed my eyes. "I don't know. And there is no profit in thinking about something that can never be."

Eliza came and sat beside me. I could sense her shyness, so I put my hand on hers and stroked along the roughness of her palm.

"I am determined to speak to Beatrice tomorrow about the parlous state of her finances."

Eliza sucked her teeth. "You know she won't like it."

"Yes, I know. But I have to try. I have been thinking about what to say to her. I think I will only have one opportunity to present my case, so I must get it right." I frowned as my thoughts returned to worrying at the problem of what I should say.

"You don't have to say anything. This ain't your lookout."

"I told you, I cannot stand by and do nothing. I know that Beatrice will not listen to me. But I have to try."

Eliza squeezed my hand. "You got courage, I'll say that for you."

I rose from the bed and went to the dresser. I placed my hairpins methodically into their box. At that moment, I did not feel very courageous. Was I not, in fact, a coward for what I was doing with Eliza whilst outwardly appearing to be a good Christian, preparing for the missionary life?

Eliza came up behind me and slid her arms around my waist. I leaned back against her, enjoying the warm, solid mass of her. "Should I stay tonight?" she asked, her breath soft against my ear.

"Yes," I whispered as I turned in her arms to kiss her.

CHAPTER FIFTEEN

The night spent with Eliza helped to calm my nerves, and I awoke the next morning feeling distinctly more relaxed. As usual, Eliza had left before dawn, but I saw her briefly later that morning as she cleared my breakfast things away.

"Do you know what you will say to the mistress?" she asked me.

"Yes. I think I know how I shall approach it." I drained the last of the tea from my cup and rose to my feet. "Wish me luck."

Eliza clapped me playfully on the shoulder. "Break a leg, my lad."

She showed me into Beatrice's room and gave me a reassuring wink as she withdrew. I sat on my low chair in front of Beatrice and began, as I always did, by asking after her health that morning. Beatrice complained about aches and pains, and our conversation then proceeded along the usual lines. She asked me how I had spent my time the previous day. My normal reply involved mentioning any walks, sewing, or reading I had undertaken. I did not mention Eliza's lessons as I feared that reminding Beatrice about them might lead to her forbidding them from taking place at all.

On this occasion, she surprised me by bringing up the subject herself. "Do you continue to attempt to teach Eliza her letters?"

"We have had some lessons," I said cautiously.

"And how do they proceed?"

"Reasonably well. Teaching an adult to read is always a slower process than teaching a child."

"Especially if the pupil is lacking in intelligence."

"There is no lack of intelligence," I retorted before reminding myself that I needed to keep my cool if I was to present my argument well. I laid my hands slowly on my knees. "I believe we are progressing tolerably under the circumstances," I said.

"You may be able to get the girl to write a passable imitation of her name, but you will never make a reader of her."

"Perhaps not. All those that learn to swim may not end up swimming the Channel. But the skill may save their life one day."

Beatrice laughed mockingly. "You believe that reading will one day save the life of that wretched girl?"

"Who knows what the future may hold?"

"For her class, the future is written as clearly as if it were chiselled into stone. Depravity and damnation await them all."

"And probably destitution too," I said pointedly. As I had hoped, I caught Beatrice off guard, and she narrowed her eyes at me. "I mean, as the estate is heading for bankruptcy in the next few years."

"What do you mean?" she barked.

I took a deep breath. After all my deliberations of the night before, I had come to the conclusion that being straightforward and direct was my best course of action. "I have been assisting Mr. Tripp with the estate account books. It is clear that—"

"I *knew* that you would snoop into my affairs," Beatrice snapped.

I ignored her interruption and carried on. "It is clear that the estate's income has dwindled to practically nothing whilst significant sums of money continue to be outlaid. Such a situation cannot continue indefinitely." I held my tongue at that point and waited. Pleas and exhortations crowded my head, but I held them at bay, sticking to my policy to present the facts barely and without comment.

Beatrice's eyes glittered coldly at me. "Outlaid on what?" she asked.

"I do not know," I lied and sent a quick prayer heavenward, asking for forgiveness for the untruth along with all the other sins I was committing at Beulah Lodge.

"Tripp is responsible for managing the estate. It is his concern."

"Indeed, it is. But Mr. Tripp is somewhat in awe of you." I saw her ears prick up at this, and I pressed my advantage. "In fact, as you say, he has always been, um, sweet on you." Beatrice smiled smugly. "And therefore, he does not wish to speak to you of anything that might cause you distress. His only wish is to make you happy. But you will not be happy if you are forced to sell the house from over you and watch strangers treat Beulah Lodge as their own." I had calculated that an appeal on behalf of her servants and tenants would have no effect on Beatrice, and so I did not even try.

Beatrice looked at me for a long moment as I held my peace. There was no obvious sign of anger in her expression, only her usual cold distaste. "I have only a few years left to live. What happens to this cursed house after I am gone is of no concern to me."

"We none of us know the hour. It may be that God will bless you with many years yet."

Beatrice gave one of her shouts of bitter laughter. "I pray every day that He will soon release me from this present hell."

"The estate may be bankrupt this time next year."

"You need not concern yourself with that," Beatrice said. "You will be grubbing among the heathen by then, far away from all of us."

I bowed my head. At one time, being far away from Beulah Lodge was what I longed for, but now I could not bear to think of it. I refocused my mind on trying to deflect Beatrice's anger. "I am only concerned for your welfare, Aunt. I would not wish you to have to face financial ruin in what may be the final years of your life."

"Oh, it is *my* welfare that has inspired all this interference?"

"And the welfare of everyone who depends upon Beulah Lodge for their livings. Your tenants, your servants."

"Which servants in particular?"

"Why, all of them."

"I am not a fool," Beatrice spat furiously. She turned her face away from me and gripped the arms of her chair, clasping and unclasping convulsively. When she turned back to me, she had clearly mastered her rage somewhat. "You are no longer to interfere in my affairs. I forbid it. And I forbid you from wasting any more of Eliza's time. Your lessons with her are to cease."

Cold nausea welled up within me. "Aunt, please." I tried to keep the rising panic from my voice. "Eliza's lessons and my involvement with the estate's finances are entirely unconnected."

"I disagree. I regard them both as evidence of your unwarranted arrogance. You are here at my pleasure, as my guest. You will obey my wishes."

My heart had sunk so far that I could give no reply. I could not even bring myself to look at Beatrice because I knew how triumphant her expression would be.

❖

Eliza could tell that something was wrong as soon as she saw my face at lunchtime. She laid my plate before me and said, "I take it talking to the mistress didn't go well?"

"No, it did not. Not that I expected it to, but I did not imagine that she would—"

"What? What has she done?"

"She has forbidden our lessons from continuing," I said with a heavy sigh.

Eliza glanced over her shoulder quickly, as if checking that we should not be overheard. "Let's see about that," she said quietly. "I'll come to the library after lunch as usual, and we can talk about it then."

I nodded listlessly. I was already thinking of how I could perhaps prepare Eliza some materials, so she could continue the study in her own time, though it would be far from ideal.

I sat at the desk in the library after lunch and reviewed all my teaching aids thus far. When Eliza came in, I said at once, "I think you could continue to study by yourself and still progress tolerably well, provided that you applied yourself."

"I ain't doing it by myself," Eliza said shortly.

"I know it is disheartening, but you must not—"

"You can carry on teaching me," Eliza said, seating herself beside me.

"I cannot. Your mistress has forbidden it."

"She ain't the Queen of England."

"No, but she is mistress of this house. Within these walls, her word is law."

"Do you reckon she would've liked you riding out to see Curran with Tripp? Would she have approved of you looking at the account books?"

"No," I admitted, "But she did not expressly forbid those things."

"Only cos she didn't know about them."

I shook my head, feeling my lifelong certainty about respecting those in authority already being shaken. "It is of no consequence what she *would* have done. She has forbidden our lessons, and I cannot go against her wishes."

"Why not?"

"I am her guest, and I am only here because she allows it. She could ask me to leave at any time."

"You're in the same boat as the rest of us. We are all only here on her whim. She could dismiss all of us at a moment's notice. That is the only true power she has, and she knows it."

"There is nothing I can do." As soon as the words were spoken, I felt something within me condemn them for passive, mealy-mouthed acceptance. They were not words that my father would ever have uttered.

"You can disobey her."

"There would be consequences for you as well as for me—"

"I would rather get dismissed knowing how to read than not. You said reading was the most important thing in the world."

"I know, but-

"Is it as important as teaching Tripp long multiplication? As important as sorting out Curran's rent?"

I was silent. I could hear the appeal behind her words, despite her usual matter-of-fact tone. And I did truly believe that teaching Eliza to read would be the greatest gift that it was in my power to bestow on her. "Our lessons are very important to me," I assured her.

"So why stop them? Just cos *she* says so?" Every lesson and experience of my life thus far had taught me that I owed Beatrice respect and obedience both as my aunt and as the mistress of Beulah Lodge. But the cruelty and malice she had displayed to everyone around her had removed any possibility of my respecting her.

"There is a risk to your position—"

"Ain't it worth taking a risk for?" This time, there was no mistaking the appeal.

I looked at her face, and the risk seemed so small and inconsequential set against the worlds that would open for Eliza. The last vestiges of my hesitation crumbled away. "Very well," I said.

Eliza sat back in her chair, visibly relieved. "Thank you," she said. "Like I said, I'm better off knowing how to read so I got something going for me when she kicks me out."

"Why would she kick you out?" I asked distractedly, my head still spinning with the tension of the interview with Beatrice. "She has your labour for free."

"It ain't my labour she wanted."

Eliza said it in her usual offhand way, but it cut through the noise in my mind, and I looked at her sharply. "What do you mean? What else could she want from you?" I knew already. Beatrice's needling question from the overheard conversation in the middle of the night sounded in my head: *How much would you have charged me?*

Eliza looked at her hands. "She wanted what punters normally wanted from girls like me." The cold sickness passed over me again, and I closed my eyes. "I didn't know that, not at first," Eliza went on. "When she offered to take me back to Yorkshire with her as her maid, I thought she meant a housemaid. It was only later I realised that she was expecting something else."

"Did you—"

"No," Eliza shook her head vehemently. "She kissed me once. Just after I arrived here. And I suppose I let her cos I was grateful not to be sleeping in doss houses no more. She'd done me a favour, after all. But when I worked out that she wanted to go all the way"—Eliza shuddered—"I said no. And she was angry, really bloody angry. Said she wouldn't pay me for services that I wouldn't give. She called me a fool for thinking that I could possibly have anything worth paying for except for that what I'd been selling." Her cheeks were red.

"And that's why she treats you so abominably," I concluded.

Eliza nodded miserably. "I suppose I was foolish to think that she might actually want me for a housemaid."

"You jumped at a chance to escape your old life. How could you have known that Beatrice would want that from you?" I swallowed hard to keep down the bile that rose in my throat at the thought of Beatrice touching Eliza.

"That's all anyone has ever wanted from me," Eliza said quietly.

I placed my hand on hers. "Your worth extends far beyond what you had to do to get by. That is nothing, that *means* nothing. It is not the sum of what you are." I squeezed her hand, and she looked into my eyes. "Let's carry on with our lessons," I said. "And damn the consequences."

I stumbled over damn, as it was not a word I frequently employed, but it made Eliza laugh, which at that moment, was the happiest sound imaginable to my ears.

And so we continued with our lessons in defiance of Beatrice. If Tripp and Martha were aware that we were disobeying their mistress, they gave no sign of it. I was on edge at first, expecting that Beatrice might come bursting in at any moment and discover us, but after a few lessons, I began to feel more at ease.

I had always been taught to show proper obedience to those whom I owed it to—my father, my soon-to-be husband, God—and so rebellion was not something that came naturally to me. I did not dwell on it too much, however, as I saw how Eliza continued to blossom under my tutelage, and I felt a corresponding warmth and enthusiasm for teaching her.

The steady rhythm and progress of the lessons found its reflection in other areas of our life. Our nights together remained as ardent as ever, but a new softness came into our lovemaking, a kind of tender sadness that presaged what was to come.

Our lessons progressed until I was able to read through reasonably lengthy passages from the Bible with Eliza. We sat together one afternoon in the final days of summer, the light streaming through the library windows and lighting up the threads of gold in Eliza's hair. We had just finished going over a passage from Genesis together, and I was pleased by Eliza's progress and said so.

She sat back in her chair, smiling at me. "How long 'fore I can read the whole thing?"

"The whole Bible? Oh, you'll have read it cover to cover by Christmas," I teased.

"I like this bit we been doing. About the beginnings of the world. Beginnings are always better than endings, aren't they?"

"I suppose they are. I like the stories of King David best and the gospel parables."

"Ain't there a book named after you?"

"There is indeed a Book of Ruth," I said, smiling.

"And what's that about?"

"It's about a woman and her devotion to her mother-in-law," I said. I flipped the pages of the great Bible to the frontispiece of the Book of Ruth, which showed Ruth bending to retrieve fallen stalks of corn. "I'm rather fond of it, actually, and not just because I bear the same name." I ran my finger along the text until I found the passage. "And Ruth said, 'Entreat me not to leave thee or to return from following after thee. For whither thou goest, I will go. Where thou lodgest, I shall lodge. Thy people shall be my people and thy God my God. Where thou diest, I will die, and there will I be buried. The Lord do so to me and more also if ought but death part thee and me.'"

I stopped, and the silence in the room seemed to deepen. I looked into Eliza's eyes and she into mine. My heart felt so full that I struggled to speak. "It is beautiful, is it not?" I said finally.

"Yes," said Eliza hoarsely. "I ain't never heard it before. The church folk never read that bit to us."

"They should have done. It is about love, and that is the best, the noblest emotion that humanity is capable of. Jesus died for love of us." I felt my throat constrict as I looked at her and thought of love.

Eliza didn't reply but rested her head on my shoulder, her hair soft against my neck. She laced her fingers through mine, her thumb momentarily sliding against my engagement ring. "Read it again," she said.

I placed my arm around her shoulders and sounded the words out softly in the quiet, golden light.

Something had changed, had shifted somehow in that quiet moment. I knew it, and I felt that Eliza knew it also. I could not find the correct words to describe it, but it was a deepening, an enriching of what had already been there. I delighted in it, and yet I was also desperately afraid. Sometimes, when I looked at Eliza's sleeping face in the bed next to me, I was seized with a terror so overwhelming that I could hardly breathe.

It was a gloriously sunny day when the letter came. I was sitting at breakfast, drinking tea and stifling my yawns from the night before. Martha came in, bearing a letter on a tray. "This came for you, ma'am." I took it from her, recognising the handwriting. "Perhaps it's from your fiancé?"

"Yes. It is," I said, feeling a cold weight settle heavily in my breast.

I opened the letter slowly. The frequency of my correspondence to Daniel had diminished the longer I had been at Beulah Lodge, and it had been at least three weeks since I had last written. I braced myself:

My dearest Ruth,

I regret that I have not been able to write to you more often, but I have been ill with a fever these past weeks and am only now sufficiently recovered enough to pick up my pen.

The mission house here is a simple place, and even obtaining water and firewood is a laborious process. Reverend Joyce employs a native maid, but the girl is clumsy and stupid. Once you are here, I trust you will be able to manage these things more efficiently.

We have much work to do to spread the good news. Reverend Joyce has been at the mission for ten years, and I fear that in that time, complacency and indolence has set in. He spends more time trying to learn the native language and customs than preaching the gospel. Although we have a small and regular congregation in our chapel, they are the dregs of the town: drunkards, fornicators, and blasphemers. There is much work to be done to spread the news to those in the town with the power to make our little chapel respectable.

In view of the importance of maintaining this respectability, I think it necessary that we should be married in England and return to the mission as man and wife. In this way, we can present a picture of perfect Christian fidelity to the natives.

I will be returning to London and expect to be back in the city by the twenty-fourth of next month. Leave word for me with the Missionary Society when you have arrived in London, and we can be married at once. My recent illness has convinced me that time is of the essence. Our Lord tells us that we cannot know the hour when He will come again, and so we must toil ceaselessly to spread His word. You must set forth with all haste.

I trust that when you arrive here, you will show how well you have spent your time at your aunt's house. There will be numerous domestic tasks to occupy your time, and the native women are in sore need of an exemplar of Christian womanhood.

He went on to detail the arrangements he would make for our wedding, the church and the witnesses, and even gave me full instructions on what I should wear for the ceremony.

He signed off the letter by saying that he looked forward eagerly to returning to India with me, so that together, we could begin the solemn mission that God had entrusted to him.

I set the letter down on the table. So it had come. As I had always known it would. Beulah Lodge had only ever been a stopping point on my way to India, a temporary home until Daniel called me to his side. And now I would have to go.

I felt a sob rise within me, and I struggled to contain it. I should make arrangements, I thought. I would need to travel to London and find lodgings. The thoughts whirled in my head, but still I did not move. I merely sat and stared at the things on the table: the Delft teapot, the silver spoon sticking out from the marmalade pot, the edge of a tea stain on the white cloth that made Martha wince every time her glance fell on it.

I was still staring at the breakfast things when Martha returned to ask if I had finished. I looked listlessly at my untouched breakfast and cold tea and assured her that I was done. I rose and made my way upstairs before she could ask me anything about the letter.

When I reached my room, I lay upon the bed and stared up at the ceiling until the full force of events finally hit me, and I turned my face into the pillow and sobbed. I let the tears flow freely until I had cried myself almost insensible. After my sobbing had ceased, I splashed my face with water and gazed at my reflection in the looking glass. Although my eyes were red and puffy from weeping, my face was otherwise unchanged from the day before, which seemed extraordinary considering how far away that now seemed.

I should make arrangements, I thought again mechanically. But I would also need to tell Eliza. I should do that first, before anything else. Daniel's letter had been dated a month ago, a day or so delay would make no difference to him. Once I had told Eliza, it would become real, and then everything would be set in motion.

I decided I would wait until the evening. I could not tell her during one of our snatched moments during the day. I descended to the library and flicked idly through my Bible, only able to read a word or two before my mind wandered to thoughts of my life in India and everything that I would leave behind in England.

When the familiar knock came, I braced myself. I composed my face as well as I could and when Eliza appeared around the door, I even managed a smile.

"The mistress ain't feeling too good, ma'am. She's not up to seeing you this morning." I breathed a sigh of relief that I did not have to face Beatrice today. Eliza smiled at my reaction. "She'll save it all up for an extra strong dose next time," she said and winked. That made me smile, a genuine feeling of affection and warmth. She lingered by the door. "What will you do today?"

"I thought I might walk into the village. It has been a few days since I was last there."

"Good idea. It's washing day, so me and Martha will be in the tubs all day long. I wish I was walking on the moors with you," she added softly.

"Yes, so do I," I said, not quite able to meet her eyes.

I spent a miserable day traipsing across the moors, over to the village and back again. It was a beautiful day, and the landscape was a vivid patchwork of green and purple. I felt cheated that the moors looked so charming, as if they should have looked dark and brooding to match my mood. If the moors were the face of God, then they were rejoicing that I would soon be gone.

I walked idly around the village and lingered briefly in the church. I found the image of St. Rumbold's smug little face too much to bear and left again. I did not return to Beulah Lodge for lunch but simply wandered aimlessly on the moorland, pushing through thickets of heather and climbing on top of tors.

When I finally returned to the house, I was at least physically exhausted. After a desultory supper, I retired to my room and waited. I did not even attempt to read or in any other way distract myself. I simply lay on the bed, staring up at the ceiling.

I heard the clock in the hallway strike ten, and the familiar knock followed a few minutes later. I sat up on the edge of the bed as Eliza entered.

She set her candle on the chest and leaned down to kiss me. It was only a brief, touch of lips, and then she flopped on the bed next to me with a sigh, her legs dangling off the edge.

I lay back next to her, propping myself on my elbow. "You look tired," I said, brushing some strands of hair from her face.

"Mistress insisted that all the linens from all the beds should be washed."

"Are the beds in all the rooms kept made up?"

Eliza nodded. "God knows why. It's not like anyone ever comes to stay."

"Apart from me."

"Well, yes, apart from you. Some of the sheets get all mouldy cos the rooms is kept shut up all the time." She wrinkled her nose in disgust. "But I think Martha secretly loves doing it, 'specially on a sunny day. She was even singing as she pegged it all out. And it was a song about a sailor that gets a poor innocent country girl with child. I told her I never suspected her of knowing such filthy songs. Then she got all embarrassed, so we sang another song. Something about trees, I think." She frowned and then her brow cleared. "Oh yes. *'Singing home, dearest, home, and there let it be, Far, far away from me own country. The oak and the ash and the bonny elm tree, they're all growing green in the North Country.'*"

She sang it softly, and I could hardly tell what the tune was, but tears pricked my eyes.

Eliza stopped singing and sat up at once. "What is it? What's the matter?"

I dabbed my eyes with my sleeve. "I had a letter from Daniel today. He has instructed me to meet him in London. So that we may be married before we go to India together."

"When?"

"As soon as possible. I will have to make arrangements this week to travel back to London." I had not intended for it to emerge so suddenly. I had imagined gently building up to it, but now it had been said and could not be unsaid.

Eliza was silent for a long time, staring down at the bed covers. The candlelight flickered over the planes of her face, but her expression was unreadable, exactly as it had used to be when I first arrived at Beulah Lodge.

"Eliza?" I said softly.

She finally turned her eyes to mine. "What will you do?"

"I will go to him. I must."

"Must you?" she asked.

I stared at her. "Yes. I gave my promise to him."

Eliza picked at a loose thread on her dress. "But I won't never see you again."

I swallowed hard. "We don't know that. Daniel may decide to return to England one day."

"What, when he's converted every single soul in India?"

I looked at my hands. "I will write to you," I said.

Eliza flushed. "You'll have to use only easy words." she muttered.

"I'm sorry," I said helplessly.

Eliza stood and brushed down the front of her nightdress. "Well," she said, not looking at me. "I shall bid you good night." The sudden formality that had come into her voice pained me.

"You don't need to go." I slid off the bed and made to take her hand.

She turned away. "No. There ain't no point, is there? It'll just make it worse."

"We still have time."

"Time for what, exactly?" Her voice was so cutting that it made me wince.

"After all that has passed between us—"

"All that has passed between us clearly means sod all to you. You've had your dalliance, but now it's over, yes?"

"You were not a dalliance. But we always knew this day would come."

"And now it has. So what more is there to say?"

She picked up her candle and moved to the door. I followed her, wanting to kiss her or embrace her or do something to dispel this cold, yawning chasm that had opened up between us. But I could think of nothing to say, and Eliza did not turn to look at me again. The door closed behind her, and I was left staring at its solid, wooden indifference.

The creeping cold forced me back into bed, and I wept again, over and over as fresh waves of misery rose up within me.

At some point, I must have fallen asleep, and I awoke as the light drifted weakly in through the curtains. My head ached, and my eyes were sore from crying.

It was a familiar sound that had awoken me, the steady chopping coming from the yard. Since Eliza had been frequenting my room at night, I had been sleeping through her early morning wood chopping. But now I ran to the window and moved the curtain aside. I looked just long enough to confirm that it was Eliza before wrapping a shawl around my shoulders and hurrying downstairs.

Martha was leaning into the oven as I passed through the kitchen, and I did not stop to see if she had registered my presence. The early morning air was chilly, and my slippers did little to protect my feet against the cold flagstones of the yard.

Eliza stopped chopping as she saw me approach. She was pale, and her eyes were puffy from lack of sleep. We looked at each other for a moment or two in silence.

"You could come with me," I said finally. "To India. You could come with me."

"As your servant?"

"As my companion."

Eliza shook her head slowly. "So I can keep house for you and him? And watch you go to his bed every night?"

A sob rose within me at that brief glimpse of my future life. I spread my hands in a gesture of despair. "What would you have me do?"

"Break it off. Tell him you don't want to marry him."

"I cannot. I gave him my word."

Eliza's face darkened. "Right. You ignored your promise when you fancied a brush but remember it now that it gets inconvenient." Her lip curled contemptuously. "I've met lots of men like you."

I was stung to the quick. "I arrived here as a woman engaged to be married," I snapped, trying to keep my voice down. "You always knew that. And you always knew that one day I would leave for India. I never deceived you." Eliza turned her face away. "You want me to break my engagement? And then what? Stay here until Beatrice tires of me and throws me out? Or are we to run away together? And how should we live? I have no money of my own. I am staying here at your mistress's expense. And do you think Daniel will quietly accept my deserting him?" Eliza's gaze was still turned away from me. "We always knew it had to end."

The hens clucked contentedly nearby, and a breeze lifted some strands of hair from the back of Eliza's neck. "You are a coward," she said.

I closed my eyes. "You expect too much of me."

She finally looked at me then, her eyes burning. "So it would seem."

I could not bear it. "Eliza," I said, pleadingly and reached out to touch her arm.

She jerked it away. "No." She resumed chopping wood as if I wasn't there.

I stood for a moment, feeling a tear slide down my cheek. And then, as there was nothing more I could think of to say, I turned and went back into the house, feeling as if I was walking into my own tomb.

CHAPTER SIXTEEN

I had dressed and composed myself as well as I could when the time came to see Beatrice. Eliza came to fetch me. She did not speak to or look at me. I sat before Beatrice as Eliza was dismissed and enquired whether she was quite recovered from her illness.

"I shall never be fully recovered," Beatrice said. "I feel death stalking me like a cat stalking a mouse."

"I cannot picture you as a mouse, Aunt," I said.

That almost forced a smile from her. "Perhaps not. But there are times when I grow weary of this existence and would welcome death's embrace." She looked out at the moors, and I felt a moment of pity for her. Hers was a joyless life, leavened only by malice and bullying, and I could not imagine how she endured it.

"Daniel has written to me," I said. "He is to return to England for us to be married. And then I shall travel with him to the mission."

Beatrice turned her pale eyes on me. "When will you go?"

"As soon as possible. I must send some letters to London today, and then I expect to depart within a week or so."

She was silent for a moment, and I wondered if she would miss my presence in any way. I had at least been someone new to toy with. "And you will not return," she said.

"I do not know what will happen in the future."

"You will die of fever or be murdered in one of their uprisings."

"That is entirely possible."

"You do not fear death?"

"No. Why fear something that is inevitable?" And at that moment, I almost wished for it.

"And you are confident that your name is inscribed in the Book of Life?"

"No," I said, my voice trembling. "I hope. That is all."

Beatrice smiled a satisfied smile. "Accept that all has preordained, my dear, from before you were born. Then there is cause for neither hope nor despair, just a patient acceptance of what must be."

"Yes," I admitted, "there is wisdom in accepting that which one cannot change." I remembered Eliza's cold look at me and felt a lurch of despair at the thought of that never changing.

"And perhaps once you have gone, I may regain the full command of my servants without the various distractions that you devise for them."

"If you mean Eliza's reading—"

"And the little walks and the companionable wood chopping. To say nothing of your petting of Tripp."

"The servants here have all been extremely kind to me. Eliza has provided me with companionship."

Beatrice gave a shriek of laughter. "Companionship? You have found companionship with a harlot? It says much for your upbringing that you would allow yourself to be intimate with one of such low character and—"

For once, I interrupted her. I could not endure hearing her attack both Eliza and my dear papa at the same time. "My father taught me that we are all children of the same heavenly Father. And there is nothing low about Eliza's character. It is only due to an accident of birth that her life has been what it is. In fact, her circumstances make it even more remarkable that she has turned out so good and kind and courageous and..." I had become choked up with tears and pressed my handkerchief to my face.

When I looked up, Beatrice was looking at me with mingled surprise and suspicion. She narrowed her eyes as if trying to look into my heart to perceive what was there.

"Forgive me," I stammered. "I spoke hastily. I have not been sleeping well."

"I think the sooner you are gone from this house, the better." Her voice was quiet but dripping with fury.

I got to my feet. "I will make arrangements to leave as soon as possible. I am grateful Aunt, to the home that you have provided me."

Beatrice waved a hand to silence me. "Enough," she barked. "Be gone with you."

I left her room with all the speed I could muster.

I made straight for the library. I set my pen to the paper to write to my soon-to-be-husband. At first, I tried to adopt a joyful tone:

Dearest Daniel,
How pleased I was to receive your letter giving the longed-for news.

I screwed the letter up and threw it into the fireplace. Eliza had accused me of being a coward. Was I also now to show myself a hypocrite to boot?

I attempted a more sombre approach:

Dear Daniel,
I am ready to begin the work of Christ at your side and to labour with you for the salvation of souls.

That letter joined its companion in the fireplace.

After two more attempts, I finally wrote him a few brief lines:

Dear Daniel
I have received your last letter and will await your arrival in London. I will arrange lodgings via the Missionary Society, and you may write to me care of them. I hope you are fully recovered from your illness.
Ruth

I stared at it for a long time. I considered adding in the usual polite phrases such as, "I look forward to seeing you," but they simply sounded hollow. So in the end, I left it as it was.

I put on my shawl and hat and tucked the letters into my pocket. Martha greeted me as I passed through the kitchen on my way out, and so I stopped to tell her that I would be going to London to be married as soon as possible and thenceforth to India. She looked stricken and leaned her hands on the kitchen table.

"Oh, ma'am. I am sorry to hear that. I know that it was always intended, and that you and your fiancé will be doing the Lord's work." She stopped and bit her lip. "I suppose we have all become somewhat accustomed to you."

"And I you," I said, trying to smile.

"I know Eliza will miss you, ma'am."

"I will miss all of you. Very much." I hastened from the kitchen before the sight of Martha's kind, matronly face undid me completely.

I trudged to the village and back again over the moorland path. The weather was still fine, and the moorland sheep coughed and bleated as I passed. I had grown fond of this landscape, the heather, the tors, and the wildflowers. Never mind, I told myself briskly. India would be a new landscape to come to know and appreciate. There would be many new things to learn and much work to be done. If I applied myself diligently, I could forget Beulah Lodge.

I flung a quick prayer up to Heaven as I descended back down to the house. *Lord, let me atone through hard labour. Let me work my penance.*

Eliza did not appear for her lesson after lunch, and so I spent the afternoon with my much-neglected needlework. Martha served me a dinner of beef stew, which I had complimented her on many times.

"I shall definitely miss your cooking," I said to her as she cleared my plate.

"I will give you the recipe, ma'am. Then you can make it yourself."

"Alas, the cow is considered sacred in India."

Martha raised her eyebrows. "Well, I never." She lifted the pot of stew onto the tray. "I suppose you must commit my beef stew to memory then."

"I shall feast on it in my dreams," I promised.

I sat up later after dinner, reading my Bible and pretending to myself that I was not listening for Eliza's step outside my door. I finally gave up when I heard a clock striking midnight and retired.

CHAPTER SEVENTEEN

It seemed inconceivable that the next day had to go on churning out its minutes and hours.

I woke to the usual sound of wood chopping, but I did not so much as look out the window for fear of the pain that would stab me at the sight of her.

Martha served me breakfast, and I concluded that Eliza was deliberately avoiding me. I could hardly blame her. I ate very little and sat in the library as usual with a grey heavy misery resting on me. I worked on my embroidery whilst the same gloomy hopeless thoughts revolved round and round in my head. It was only when I heard the clock strike ten that I realised that Eliza had not come to take me to my usual morning interview with Beatrice. I did not know what that might mean.

I gave up on embroidery and tried to read my Bible, but my mind could not settle to it. I paced up and down the library shelves restlessly, taking down first one book and then another and flicking through the pages.

During my time at Beulah Lodge, I had succeeded in convincing Martha that not all meals needed to run on rigidly formal lines. For lunch, I had now established the protocol that it should be something small and cold. Martha or Eliza would lay it out in the dining room at one and then clear it away at two.

Martha was setting out dishes of cold meats and cheese as I entered the dining room. I mentioned that Beatrice had not sent for me and enquired as to whether she was in good health.

Martha fiddled with the butter dish for a moment before saying, "I don't believe the mistress is unwell but…there was a set-to this morning. From what Tripp said, anyway."

"A set-to? What do you mean?"

"Tripp says he was coming back downstairs from mending a latch on one of the upstairs windows, and he heard a dreadful row from the mistress's room."

"And?" I prompted impatiently.

"Well, ma'am, Mr. Tripp is not given to eavesdropping."

"Yes, yes, I am sure. But obviously he could not help but overhear and wanted to be sure that his mistress was not in any need."

Having received this assurance of the propriety of Tripp's conduct, Martha continued. "The mistress was having a terrible row with Eliza. I say a row…Tripp says he didn't hear Eliza say nothing. It was all Mrs. Groves shouting and screaming at the girl."

"What for? What about?"

"Tripp don't rightly know. A lot about how ungrateful Eliza is, how shameful her position is, and that kind of thing. He didn't want to linger too long."

"No, of course not. Is Eliza all right?"

"I ain't seen her. Could be as she's still with the mistress." Martha heaved a sigh. "It ain't unusual for her to get at the girl like that, but even Tripp was shocked by how the mistress sounded. Like she had quite taken leave of her senses, he said."

I could eat hardly any lunch. My stomach was a hard knot of nerves, concern for Eliza mixing with guilt that I had made her position at Beulah Lodge more difficult and would be leaving her to a bleak future with Beatrice. Far bleaker than my own, for I would have some status and position as the wife of a mission leader. And then I berated myself heartily for having dwelt on my own future without having once considered Eliza's. I resolved that I would speak to her again, assure her of my concern for her, even if she couldn't bring herself to look at me.

As it happened, I had no need to seek her out. I retired to the library after lunch, and there shortly came a knock upon the door. Eliza's head peered round. She looked pale and tired. She still did not look at me directly but spoke to the bookshelf above my head.

"It's time for our lesson," she stated.

I looked at the clock. "It is, but are you sure you wish to continue?"

"Seems to me I should have some good come out of this," she said coldly.

"All right." I moved over to the desk and took out our paper and pencils from the drawer. Eliza fetched the heavy Bible from the shelf, and we settled ourselves into our usual positions. Eliza's nearness was agonising. Our arms rested on the desk, almost touching but not quite. I could smell her now familiar scent and wondered if the smell of woodsmoke would forever remind me of her.

"Where did we get to?" I asked aloud, flipping through the sheaves of paper.

"You read that bit from the Book of Ruth," said Eliza.

"Oh, yes." I felt my face grow hot. "We can move on to something else." I turned the pages of the Bible over and back to the book of Genesis. "Let's continue with where we were." I ran my finger along the page until I found the passage. "There. See how you get on with this one."

Eliza began to read slowly but with a steady voice: "'And it came to pass when men began to…mul-ti-ply on the face of the earth and daughters were born unto them…'" And so she continued, hesitating when she didn't know the word. We sounded the letters out together and moved on. When we had completed a few passages, we went back to the beginning, and Eliza read it again, now confident on the words she had not previously known.

We lost ourselves for a while in the focus of the lesson. We moved on to practising writing out sections of the passage we had just read, and as I handed Eliza a pencil, my fingers brushed hers. I looked up and met her eyes. She did not look away.

My heart was full with feelings that I did not know how to express. Despite all the intimacy that I had shared with Eliza, I struggled to find the words. "Martha says that your mistress shouted at you this morning."

Eliza shifted slightly in her seat, putting a small but definite distance between us. "She shouts at me most mornings."

"Martha said that Tripp overheard. And that even he thought it was worse than usual."

Eliza looked at me coolly for a moment and then sighed. "It were sort of about you," she said.

"About me?"

"I think she suspects that there might be something between us."

I stared at her, aghast. "But how could she possibly…why would she even *think* of such a thing?"

"She knew about me and Alice." Eliza dropped her eyes and fiddled with her pencil.

"Did you tell her?"

"I dunno exactly. That first time when she called me over to her, it wasn't long after Alice died. Once I'd got into the carriage with her, I started to cry. She asked me why I was crying, and I told her that my friend had died. Stupid, really, but it was so long since anyone had even pretended to be kind to me." Her voice caught, and she swallowed. I placed my hand on her arm and felt an absurd joy when she did not shake it off.

"I didn't say exactly about me and Alice," she continued, "but she guessed somehow. She was always good at that," she added bitterly. I was about to reply, but something in Eliza's face made me wait. "I think that's partly why she tried to…to kiss me that time. I suppose she thought that I would be more receptive."

There was another silence as Eliza doodled flower shapes on the paper in front of her.

"I told her that if that was what she was expecting, then I would leave Beulah Lodge and take my chances on the moors. She just laughed and said I would freeze to death within a week. She never tried it on again, but she'd get at me all the time, finding fault with everything I did. I started to withdraw from her, to say as little as possible, and that just seemed to make her even angrier. She started to pinch and slap me sometimes to get a reaction. But I don't react, and that makes her hate me even more."

Eliza scored through the flowers she had drawn.

"I suppose I should be grateful that she didn't throw me out. I dunno what I should have done if she had. I used to think that she had some regard for me. She must have done, to have brought me here away from that life in London." She shook her head. "But I don't believe she ever had any affection for me. I might have briefly been of interest, but she soon tired of me."

"I get the impression that is how she views people in general. As mere things for her amusement that she may drop at will."

"I feel sorry for her sometimes," Eliza said. "She must be awful unhappy."

"Unhappiness is no excuse for cruelty." We were silent for a moment, and I felt an enormous sense of relief that the cold awkwardness that had existed between us seemed to have dissipated, even if only temporarily. "I worry about you. With her. When I am gone, I mean."

"You don't need to," she said curtly. "I'm used to it."

I reached out and took her hand, feeling as if I was taking a great risk. "I will worry about you. And I will think about you every day. And I will pray for you every day."

She looked at me, and I could see the conflict within her, the angry reply that almost burst forth until she blew out her cheeks and placed her hand over mine. "I know you will," she said. "I've been thinking on it. I know that there's people out there that need you. Need your kindness and your goodness and…" Tears gathered at the corner of her eyes, and she turned her head away.

I pressed her hand. "Eliza. Please don't cry," I begged, my own voice catching.

"I can't help it," Eliza said, her face still turned away from me, and her words coming in short gasps. "I love you, and you are going to leave me."

She said it so simply, as if it was the most obvious thing in the world, and yet it struck me like a blow. No one had ever said those words to me. My father had shown his love in a myriad of ways, yet it was not in his nature to speak of his feelings openly. And Daniel had spoken of his regard and affection for me but always in formal, distant language.

I reached for Eliza and pulled her close against me. She buried her face against my neck and sobbed. My own throat began to choke with tears, and I swallowed hard to suppress them, for I knew that if I gave into my sorrow, I would be lost.

After a while, Eliza's sobs slowed, and her breathing became regular again. I stroked her hair and murmured, "It will be all right. Everything will be all right."

Eliza raised her tear-stained face to mine.

"I wish I could—"

"Shh." Eliza kissed me, her lips salty with her tears.

This was unwise, I thought. But I could not stop the wave of longing and sadness that came over me. I cupped her face and kissed her back. It felt as if we were fighting to erase all the misery and despair of the last few days, and I gripped her as if I was drowning.

We were so absorbed in our passion, that we did not hear the library door open. We heard nothing until a piercing shriek made us jump apart and turn to the door. Beatrice was standing in the doorway, her expression wild. She clutched her black shawl around her thin shoulders, and with her free hand, she pointed at Eliza.

"You, you filthy whore!" Her scream echoed around the walls of the library.

I was so shocked that I was rooted to the spot.

Eliza recovered faster than I did, rising quickly to her feet. "It's my fault," she said. "I took advantage—"

But Beatrice had already turned her attention to me. "And you," she said, her voice spitting with rage. "You come into my house like a viper. So pious, so upright, but here you are committing foul deeds with this strumpet."

A wave of hot sickness passed through me. I got to my feet slowly and came around the front of the desk to face Beatrice.

"You will leave my house," she continued. "At once. And I will write to your fiancé and let him know just what a hypocrite he has promised himself to."

"It weren't her fault. It were all me," cried Eliza desperately.

"It's all right, Eliza" I said quietly. "Mrs. Groves is perfectly within her rights." I turned to Beatrice. "I will pack my things and leave at once," I said. "But I would ask that you do not punish Eliza for my sins. I, and I alone, am responsible."

"Ruth, you know that ain't true." Eliza's face was pale and creased with worry.

Without thinking, I reached out and took her hand. "It will be all right," I said. "It will." Her eyes looked into mine, and for a moment, I forgot where we were.

But a sudden scream from Beatrice made us both whip our heads round. With a speed I would not have thought possible, she flew at Eliza with clenched fists and struck her hard across the face. Eliza stumbled back from the blow and lost her footing, falling to the floor. Beatrice, still screaming like a banshee, stood over her and began to rain blows down on her, her eyes wild.

I shoved Beatrice hard, pushing her away from Eliza, who had curled into a defensive ball on the floor. Beatrice stumbled back toward the fireplace but regained her balance swiftly.

I crouched by Eliza, putting my arms protectively around her. Beatrice had a poker clasped in her right hand. At first, I could not comprehend what I was seeing. And then horror coursed through me as Beatrice raised the poker above her head. At the same moment, the door opened, and I heard questioning voices.

Beatrice charged me like a bull. I began to rise, to try to defend myself and Eliza, but Tripp came between us and caught Beatrice's arm just as it was swinging down. Beatrice flailed against him, clawing at his face while she screamed curses and insults such as I had never heard before. He struggled with her before finally wrenching the poker from her grasp and pushing her back.

Beatrice stumbled a few paces and lost her balance. She spent a moment suspended, her arms whirling before she keeled over onto the edge of the fireplace. Her head struck the tiled hearth with an almighty crack, and she lay still.

We were all frozen for a moment. And then Martha rushed from the doorway and knelt beside Beatrice, saying desperately, "Mrs. Groves. Mrs. Groves, ma'am, are you all right?"

Eliza sat up and said groggily, "What's happened?" Her face was red and swollen, with scratch marks down her cheeks.

"I have killed her," said Tripp heavily.

Martha looked up from Beatrice's side. "No, no Tripp," she said desperately. "Mistress is just stunned is all. Eliza, you must go for the doctor at once." Eliza stood unsteadily and made for the door.

I went over and looked down at Beatrice. Her face had lost its snarling fury of a few moments ago and was now calmer. Her eyes were closed, but she was still breathing. I shook her shoulder gently. "Beatrice?" She made no response. "Perhaps we should move her onto the sofa."

Tripp picked her up as if she were a baby and carried her over to the sofa. He lay her down gently, and Martha retrieved Beatrice's shawl from where it had fallen and draped it over her. Then we all three stood looking at each other, not sure what to do.

Martha made Tripp sit down and went to fetch him some brandy. Tripp clasped his hands together and looked at Beatrice's still form. "What have I done?" he asked softly.

"It was not your fault. You were protecting us."

"I shouldn't have pushed her so hard. I should've—"

"It all happened in an instant. And you could not have known that she would fall."

Martha returned with the brandy and made Tripp swallow it. He coughed slightly and wiped his mouth with the back of his hand. "They'll hang me for it," he said.

"Nonsense, Tripp," said Martha, trying desperately to sound cheerful. "She'll regain her senses, and all will be well." She threw a pleading glance at me. I could offer no reassurance as the sound of Beatrice's head hitting the fireplace reverberated sickeningly in my mind.

"She would have struck me with the poker if you had not intervened," I said quietly. "And she had already beaten Eliza. It is my belief that you saved my life. And for that, I can only thank you."

Tripp's dark eyes met mine. "What happened?" he asked gruffly.

"She was angry that I was teaching Eliza to read. She did not approve. And she resented how friendly I was with Eliza."

I watched their faces carefully. Tripp's face was unreadable, but Martha puffed out her cheeks distractedly. "Aye. She was always jealous like that, especially with Eliza. And it wouldn't be the first time she's struck one of the servants." She looked at Tripp, who closed his eyes. "She'll come to, though," she said confidently. "She's as tough as old boots, she is. She'll be back to herself in no time."

And then there was nothing else to do except sit by Beatrice and wait. We watched her chest rise and fall in silence. Every now and then, Martha would try to rouse her but to no avail.

After an hour or so, Martha went to Beatrice's bedside and listened closely to her breathing. "She's getting worse," she said in alarm. I came over to Beatrice's side and placed my ear by her mouth.

Her breathing was shallow and hoarse, a sound that I recognised from my dear father's deathbed.

I placed my hand on Martha's arm. "She is leaving us," I said. Martha stared at me uncomprehendingly. "No. She can't be." She looked at Tripp, whose head was bowed and then back at me. "She can't be."

I took hold of Beatrice's hand, which was cold and dry to the touch and began to recite the Lord's Prayer with Tripp joining in. The familiar words seemed to have a calming effect on Martha. She knelt by Beatrice's head and tenderly stroked her hair, murmuring to her as if she was a child.

"There, mistress," she whispered. "Don't you worry about nothing. Everything is just fine."

I clasped Beatrice's hand harder as I prayed for God to "forgive us our trespasses." I recited the prayer twice more and then stopped.

Martha looked up at me, tears gathering in the corners of her eyes and said, "She's gone."

Tripp collapsed back onto his chair and buried his face in his hands. Martha gently raised the shawl over Beatrice's face. Then she went to Tripp's side and laid a hand on his shoulder. "There's nothing more we can do for her, Mr. Tripp," she said through stifled sobs. "When the doctor has been, then we can tend to her properly. Make sure she's taken care of."

And so we carried on sitting, keeping watch. Once Martha had dried her tears, she went to make tea. She could not persuade Tripp to drink any, but I sipped mine listlessly, gazing out the window at the moors. They remained as they always did, harsh and unchanging, and I drew some comfort from that, thinking that they would remain as they were for all the ages. They would still be here once Beulah Lodge and all of us had long since crumbled into dust.

I shivered and looked back into the room, noticing for the first time how dark it was getting. Tripp had not moved from his chair. He stared blankly at the shrouded figure on the sofa. Martha was sitting nearby, her head nodding on her chest.

I too must have fallen asleep, for I was startled awake by the sound of heavy footsteps along the hallway outside. The room was almost completely dark, and for a moment, I could not discern where

I was. Then the remembrance of all that had happened struck me afresh.

A male voice from the doorway said, "Can we have some light in here?"

I heard Martha mutter something, and then some candles were lit that threw a feeble light on the room.

The doctor was a short, rotund man with a reddish face. He took in the situation quickly and crossed to the sofa. "What happened?" he asked as he lifted the shawl from Beatrice's face.

"The mistress fell and hit her head on the fireplace, sir," Martha said.

"How did she fall?"

"I pushed her," said Tripp. It was the first time I had heard him speak in hours, and his voice sounded unnaturally loud in the stillness of the room. The doctor turned sharply and looked at him.

"He was protecting me," I explained. "Beatrice...Mrs. Groves was about to strike me with a poker. She had already hit Eliza."

"Is that the girl with bruises who fetched me?" the doctor asked.

"Yes," I said. "Where is she?"

"She is in the kitchen. I told her to make some tea."

I left the doctor opening his bag with Martha and Tripp looking on and made my way down to the kitchen. Eliza was standing by the range, gazing at the copper kettle that was set on it. She turned as she heard me come in. Two large bruises bloomed across her face, and even in the poor light of the kitchen I could see she was exhausted. I went and put my arms around her and felt her shivering against me. We remained like that for a while until I finally released her and bade her sit.

She sank into Martha's rocking chair whilst I poured some water into the teapot. "Is she dead?" she asked in a low voice.

"Yes."

Eliza took a deep, trembling breath. "I knew she was. I mean, I kept hoping that maybe she wasn't, that she'd be all right but that noise of her head..." She shuddered.

"She did not regain consciousness," I said. "She just slipped away very quietly."

"There weren't nothing quiet about it."

"No. I know. But I suppose it was swift, at least." I spooned tea leaves into the pot, glad to have something to do.

Eliza watched me. "How can she be dead? How can this house still be here without her?"

"I don't know." We said nothing more as I finished the tea and laid it on a tray, ready to take upstairs. But we were forestalled by the doctor appearing in the kitchen doorway with his bag.

"There is nothing more I can do here," he said, pouring himself a cup of tea. "I have noted the cause of death, and I shall have to inform the coroner. There is likely to be an inquest." He saw our faces and added, "The circumstances are somewhat unusual." After a pause, he said, "Who is the next of kin?"

"I am," I said. "I am her niece. As far as I know, she had no other family living."

"I see. I will note that for my report." The doctor drained his cup. "I must be on my way." He gestured to Eliza. "Keep applying a cold compress to your face, and the swelling will go down." Eliza rose but the doctor waved a hand. "Do not trouble yourself. I can see myself out."

He made for the door and then turned as if a thought had struck him. "My condolences on your loss," he said.

His boots creaked on the stairs as he made his way up to the hallway. Eliza and I looked at each other in silence.

CHAPTER EIGHTEEN

The next week passed in a haze. Beatrice's absence seemed to echo around the house even more forcefully than her presence had. Martha, Eliza, and I took care of the arrangements between us. I wrote letters to the undertakers, to Beatrice's solicitors, and to the district registrar, just as I had done when my father had died. I spent a whole morning agonising over a letter to Daniel, unsure of exactly what to say of how Beatrice had died. In the end, I settled for writing "accident" and simply resolved to explain it more fully when I was reunited with him. I wrote that I would be delayed from travelling to London until Beatrice's affairs were settled.

I took to eating my meals in the kitchen with Martha, Eliza, and Tripp. These were generally quiet affairs, with myself and Martha trying to keep up some semblance of normal conversation. Eliza picked at her food, and Tripp was barely speaking at all. He seemed to be literally sagging under the weight of his grief.

The inquest was held within the week. It took place in the Red Lion, which was full to bursting, as the sudden death of the mistress of Beulah Lodge was quite the most exciting thing that had occurred in years. The coroner was a wiry man of about fifty, with piercing grey eyes who sat behind a table by the bar.

The doctor was called first, and he gave a brief account of what he had seen when he had arrived and confirmed the cause of death was the injury to the back of Beatrice's head, received when she had fallen.

I was called next, and I could not control my trembling as I took hold of the Bible to swear my oath. I described as best I could what had taken place. The coroner asked the question that I knew was inevitable.

"What prompted Mrs. Groves' violent attack on you?"

"She perceived me as being overfamiliar with her servant."

"What caused that perception?"

"I was teaching Eliza to read. And I had challenged Mrs. Groves previously over her treatment of Eliza."

"What was it about Mrs. Groves's treatment of her servant that caused you to confront her?"

"In that particular instance, she threw a paper knife that struck Eliza in the face." There was a murmur and a few tuts around the crowded room.

"When Mrs. Groves came into the library, what were you doing?"

"I was teaching Eliza to read." My face grew hot, and I felt sure that everyone in the room would be able to see through me, would be able to see that I was not telling the whole truth.

"And did this anger Mrs. Groves?"

"Yes. She…she did not want me to give Eliza lessons."

The coroner looked at me over the rim of his glasses. "What did Mrs. Groves say and do in the next few minutes?"

"She…became very angry and screamed first at Eliza and then at me."

"Screamed what, exactly?" His eyes were flinty and hard upon me.

"She called me a hypocrite and told me to leave her house."

"And what did you say?"

"I said that I would leave at once, if that was what she wished. But I asked her not to mistreat Eliza on my account. I took Eliza's hand, to reassure her, and that was when Mrs. Groves struck her."

"And then what happened?"

"Eliza fell, and Mrs. Groves continued to beat her. I pushed Mrs. Groves away from Eliza, and when I looked up, she had a poker in her hand and was raising it to strike me." There was a deathly silence in the room. "I…I thought she was going to kill me. And then Mr. Tripp appeared and grabbed her arm. There was a struggle, and then Mrs. Groves fell back and hit her head on the fireplace. She was unconscious. Eliza went for the doctor and myself, Mr. Tripp, and Mrs. Greenwood waited with Mrs. Groves until he arrived."

"Did Mrs. Groves regain consciousness at any point?"

"No, sir."

After a few more questions, I was released. I felt all eyes on me as I returned to my seat. I kept my gaze downcast and prayed that God would forgive me.

Eliza gave testimony next, explaining briefly how long she had been in service at Beulah Lodge.

"Did your mistress ill-treat you?" the coroner asked.

Eliza shifted and looked uncomfortable. The bruises on her face were fading but were still unmistakable. "She weren't an easy mistress. She could get very angry."

"Did she strike you prior to the altercation that led to her death?"

"Yes, sir."

"Did you give her cause to strike you?"

"I don't believe so, sir. I always carried out my duties as best I could."

He did not spend much longer on questioning her, and Eliza's relief was evident when she was dismissed. I saw some of the spectators smirking and whispering to each other as she regained her seat, and I pressed my lips angrily together.

Martha came next. She firstly confirmed that she had been in service at Beulah Lodge for many years.

"How would you describe your mistress?"

"She was a bonny lass once. But in recent years she had become...different. Morose."

"Did she ever strike you?"

"No, sir."

"Did she ill-treat you in any way?"

"She could say unkind things when the mood took her."

"And how often did the mood take her?"

Martha looked uncomfortable again, glancing around at her neighbours who were listening, agog.

The coroner repeated the question with a touch of impatience. "How often did the mood take her?"

"Most days, I would say, sir," said Martha quietly.

"Did you see her mistreat the girl, Eliza?"

"I heard the mistress screaming at her sometimes. And on a few occasions, Eliza would come back from the mistress's room with bruises on her face."

"Did the girl complain of mistreatment to you?"

"No, sir. She never said nothing about it."

The coroner proceeded to ask Martha in detail about the day of Beatrice's death and then dismissed her.

Finally, Tripp was called, and there was a stir in the room as he approached the coroner's table. He looked tense and haggard and spoke in a low monotone. Like Martha, he gave a brief account of how long he had been in service. The coroner asked him the same questions about Beatrice's ill treatment of Eliza, and Tripp replied that he had heard his mistress berate the girl and had seen her face with bruises.

The coroner then moved on to the day of Beatrice's death. As Tripp described what happened in the library, his voice began to shake. "I had just come into the kitchen from hoeing the veg, and I heard the mistress screaming from somewhere overhead. She sounded... demented. I hadn't ever heard anything like it. I raced up the stairs, and I could tell it were coming from the library. The door was open, and I could see the mistress running at Miss Mallowes with a poker raised. Miss Mallowes was kneeling on the floor by Eliza and had her arm raised, like, to protect herself." He swallowed hard. "I...I didn't barely have time to think. I ran in and grabbed the mistress's arm. She screamed and swore something terrible at me. She scratched and clawed at my face like, like she had taken leave of her senses. I pushed her back, and...and she fell. I heard her head strike the side of the fireplace-" He closed his eyes and shuddered. "I never meant any harm to come to her," he whispered. "I just meant to stop her. To stop her striking Miss Mallowes. That was all."

The silence was so deep, I could have heard a pin drop. The faces turned toward Tripp were full of sympathy. His devotion to Beatrice was widely known, and there was something touching about seeing this great hulk of a man on the verge of tears.

There was a brief adjournment, and then the coroner returned and summed up his findings. "It is clear from the evidence of Dr. Holt that Mrs. Beatrice Groves died as a result of injuries she sustained when she fell and struck her head on the fireplace. It is also clear from the evidence of multiple witnesses that this fall was the result of a brief struggle between herself and her manservant, Tripp. Mr. Tripp, Mrs. Greenwood, and Miss Mallowes have all testified that the struggle arose due to Mrs. Groves threatening Miss Mallowes with a poker. The household servants and Miss Mallowes all testify to the fact that Mrs. Groves had been known to strike and beat her servants in the past. There is further evidence from Dr. Holt that Mrs. Groves had been an invalid for many years prior to her death.

"Having heard the testimony of all the witnesses, I am satisfied that their accounts are consistent with each other. It is clear that an altercation took place between Mrs. Groves and her maidservant, Eliza Chambers, leading to Mrs. Groves striking Miss Chambers. Miss Mallowes intervened to protect the girl and was herself threatened by Mrs. Groves. Mr. Tripp attempted to prevent Mrs. Groves from striking Miss Mallowes, and in the process, Mrs. Groves fell and struck her head on the fireplace, resulting in her death. I am confident that there was no intent to harm Mrs. Groves on the part of Mr. Tripp. I therefore record a verdict of accidental death."

There was a collective exhalation of breath that echoed around the room. Tripp dropped his head into his hands whilst Martha patted his shoulder. I too let out a breath that it seemed I had been holding for an age.

We all four of us returned to Beulah Lodge in silence, and our strange, half-life there continued. Now that an official verdict had been reached in the inquest, the funeral could be held. I made all the arrangements, and the funeral took place a week later.

The service was well attended by the villagers of Coldkirk. Although few of them had even seen Beatrice in recent years, they could not remember a time when she had not been mistress of Beulah Lodge.

Mr. Glossop's eulogy was sketchy. Beatrice had never attended St. Rumbold's, and he had only met her a handful of times. The manner of her death gave him some difficulties too, but he nevertheless commended her for her long life and said that it was an acknowledged fact that she feared the Lord.

We gathered in the churchyard and watched Beatrice's coffin being lowered into the ground. Tripp's shoulders heaved with dry silent sobs, and Martha cried softly. Eliza stood perfectly still, her eyes glistening like dark pools in her pale face.

I threw a handful of earth onto the coffin and prayed that Beatrice was now at peace as she had never appeared to be in life.

As Mr. Glossop prayed for the Lord "shortly to accomplish the number of thine elect," I wondered if Beatrice was now among them, waiting for the Day of Judgement. I looked at the ring of low hills surrounding the churchyard and fancied that Beatrice was somehow joined with them now and that I could see her face staring back at me from the desolate sweep of rock.

There was a wake of sorts back at the house. A few former servants came and sat closeted in the kitchen with Martha and Tripp. I stood in the dining room where the table had been set with sherry and cold luncheon meat.

I made desultory conversation with Mr. Glossop and worked my way around the few mourners, thanking them for coming. I sat in the library once it was all over, feeling exhausted.

Martha came in with a letter for me, and I read it in the fading afternoon light. It was from Beatrice's solicitor, a Mr. Elias Chalcraft. The letter was densely worded and full of superfluous legal phrases, but on a second reading, I was able to grasp the contents. I folded it into my pocket.

As had become usual, I took my supper in the kitchen with the others. Once we had finished our helpings of bread-and-butter pudding and Mr. Tripp had lit his pipe, I told them about the letter from Mr. Chalcraft.

"He wants me to visit his firm in Chancery Lane so that he may read Beatrice's will to me as her next of kin. He also wishes to have an inventory of the contents of the house and the financial records of the estate. I thought perhaps I could take those with me."

Tripp nodded and removed his pipe from his mouth. "I was working on preparing a summary of the estate finances anyway. Mr. Chalcraft may have that."

I thanked him and turned to Martha. "And perhaps you and I may work on the inventory?"

Martha nodded. "If we work hard at it, we may have it done within a week or so." She paused and then said shyly, "And then what, ma'am? What will become of the house?"

She didn't add, "and us," but it hung heavily in the air. I swallowed hard. "I don't know. As I understand it, the estate is in debt, so there will doubtless be creditors who need to be paid." I stared unhappily at my plate.

"Perhaps your fiancé may decide to return to England?"

Eliza looked at me sharply, and I shook my head gently. "I don't believe so. He is devoted to the mission in India. That is where our lives will be." There was silence.

Tripp shifted in his chair and said gruffly, "Our days are as grass. Been in this house man and boy, but in the eyes of the Lord, it's no longer than the beating of a fly's wing."

"That's as may be, Tripp," said Martha, "but this house means a lot to me. To all of us. This place has been my livelihood for so long. I am not sure that I would find another position."

"I know," I said quietly. "I am sorry that I cannot give you the answer you want."

I felt miserable as they all looked away from me.

I sat up late in my room, reading my Bible by the light of a flickering candle. Scripture had always been a comfort to me, no matter the circumstances, and that night, I was reading of Jonah and his reluctance to travel to Nineveh. The account of the insistent compulsion of God's will did provide me with some small comfort. We were all of us subject to His will, though we might chafe and rage against it.

I closed the book and got into bed. I blew out my candle and lay in the darkness, imagining, as I did every night, the moment that I would leave Beulah Lodge. I fell asleep but was awoken by a dim light coming into the room. I opened my eyes and saw Eliza standing before the bed with a candle in her hand. She was dressed in her nightgown with a shawl wrapped around her shoulders.

"Eliza?" I mumbled, still half-asleep.

She sat on the edge of the bed beside me, placing her candle on my bedside table. "I'm sorry to wake you."

"No, it's fine." I sat up and rubbed my eyes. "Is anything the matter?"

"No. No, not really." She was looking at her hands in her lap. The weak light of the candle meant I could not read her expression.

"Is there something troubling you?" I asked.

"Just the night time, really."

"What about the night time?"

"It seems to be the worst time."

"The worst time for what?"

"For thinking about it. About what happened." She took a deep, shuddering breath. "I think about it all the time, Ruth. All the bastard, bleeding time. Every time I close my eyes and try to sleep." She shuddered again. "I see her face. The way she looked when she was going for you, her face all twisted like, like something from hell."

I placed my hand on her shoulder and felt her trembling. "You must try not to dwell on it so."

"I know. And in the day, it's all right cos I can work and not think about it. But in the night, there ain't nothing else to do 'cept brood on it. And I keep thinking that I should've done things differently, that I shouldn't have argued with her, that I shouldn't have used your Christian name in front of her. And maybe I should have just let her have what she wanted of me in the first place and that I shouldn't have refused her."

"No," I said firmly. "It was not your fault, Eliza. Nor was it Tripp's fault. There is no one to blame here."

There was a silence, and then Eliza asked, in a barely audible whisper, "But will God see it that way?"

"God knows the secrets of our hearts. He knows that we did not wish to harm Beatrice. And He will know what was in her heart."

"I think she must have been kind once. Martha and Tripp swear that it was so."

"People can change. What was once good can turn like soured milk."

Eliza was silent for a while. "I wish she hadn't died like that," she said finally. "I wish she had been in her bed, cursing us all till the end."

"So do I. But none of us has the luxury of choosing the hour or manner of our death."

Eliza was silent. My hand was still on her shoulder, and I could feel the warmth of her skin through her nightdress. She stood up abruptly. "Thank you," she said awkwardly. "And I'm sorry for disturbing you." She made as if to go, and I gripped her hand.

"Must you?" I whispered.

She looked at me for a long moment and then climbed into bed beside me. She laid her head on the pillow, only inches from mine. I almost cried at the sweetly familiar scent of her hair and skin. I stroked her head, bushing the strands of hair away from her face.

We lay there contentedly for a while, Eliza's hand resting on my waist. "You're still going to India, aren't you?" she said.

I didn't answer, and there was a long silence where there was nothing to hear but the gentle rise and fall of Eliza's breath and the creaking of the house as it settled. I was thinking about what I had said to Eliza, that none of us knew when the hour of our death would come. I might never make it to India. The boat might sink, or I might die of some tropical disease the minute I set foot there. Or perhaps, I would live to a ripe old age with plenty of time to reflect on the past and regret.

"I will think of you always," I said finally. "And I shall love you always. Until the end of my days."

There was a long silence, and then Eliza raised her head and kissed me softly on the cheek. She kissed her way along until she found my mouth. Our lips met tenderly, almost shyly, as Eliza's hands moved through my hair.

We kissed for long minutes, our tongues gently dancing together. When we lifted our nightgowns from each other and lay naked together, it was with sadness as much as with passion. Eliza trailed tender kisses over my breasts, bringing me ever so slowly to a fever pitch. When she finally entered me, it felt like both a greeting and a farewell. I shuddered against her as I reached my climax, clasping her tightly.

And then I took my time roaming over her body in the darkness. I caressed and kissed her breasts before moving lower and tasting the wetness between her legs. I drank in as much of her as I could, pressing my face against her and moving my tongue inside her. I held myself against her as she reached her climax, her thighs pressing against my cheeks.

And then we began again, a sad, bittersweet dance that felt as if it could be endless, but everything in this world had an end.

We finally collapsed into an exhausted sleep, our limbs tangled together as the first light of dawn tinged the sky.

CHAPTER NINETEEN

W e awoke late and dozed together before Eliza gently disengaged herself from my embrace. She kissed my cheek as she slid from the bed. I wanted to say something reassuring, but the sadness of the night was still there, running like a current between us.

There was nothing for it but to press on with another day. After Eliza left, I rose and took my breakfast in the kitchen. I then went upstairs with Martha to begin our inventory of the contents of the house, as Mr. Chalcraft had instructed.

It was a depressing job, going through dusty cupboards filled with motheaten dresses and mouldy linen. But we made good progress and swiftly worked our way through all of the unused guest bedrooms. The next stage was to move up to the top floor where the servants' quarters were. I had never been up there before, and Martha became shy when showing me the way.

"You must forgive how things are up here, ma'am," she said as I ascended the narrow stairs behind her.

The quarters consisted of a long, low corridor running along the spine of the roof, with rooms branching off under the eaves. Martha gestured at the first door, which was slightly ajar.

"Eliza's room is in there. She don't keep it as tidy as she should."

I glanced through the crack in the door and had a brief glimpse of a cast-iron bedframe and dresser but nothing more. I would have dearly liked to have gone into the room just to see where Eliza spent the nights when she was not with me.

We passed Tripp's and Martha's chambers, and then there were three further rooms beyond this. Martha took out a large bunch of keys. "These rooms have always been kept locked," she explained, stopping before one of the doors.

"Always?"

"Tripp says they were used as bedrooms for the servants when there was more staff here. But ever since old Mr. Groves died, they have been locked."

Martha tried several of the keys in the lock until she found the right one. The door creaked open on a dark, cluttered room that smelt strongly of damp. There was one small window that was so covered with grime that it admitted hardly any light.

The room seemed to be full of an odd assortment of furniture. Old chests, dressers, and tables with spindly legs were pushed back against the eaves, leaving a narrow passage between them.

Martha walked to the window and with some difficulty, forced it open. Fresh air and the chatter of birds at once entered the room like sunlight entering a tomb.

Martha placed her hands on her hips, looked around the room and sighed. "Where shall we begin, ma'am?"

I took out the notebook and pencil that I had been using to record the inventory. "Let's start near the window and work our way to the door."

We set about our task and quickly established a routine. Martha heaved the furniture out and described it to me as I noted it down. "Occasional table. Wood all rotted. Pair of upholstered dining room chairs. Dreadful pattern on 'em. One washstand with cracked jug. One iron fire guard. Still covered in soot. One chest." Martha paused whilst she lifted the lid. "Heavens above," she exclaimed softly.

"What is it?"

"It's full of papers, ma'am." I came over and looked into the chest. Bundles of yellowing letters were tied together with frayed ribbon. I picked up one of the bundles and glanced at the faded writing.

"My darling Beatrice," I read out loud, "it seems as if the days conspire against me, as if extra hours are surreptitiously added in order to increase the time that I must wait until I see you again." I put the letters back into the chest. "We should not read any more."

"No," said Martha, with a touch of regret in her voice. "I suppose Mr. Chalcraft won't be interested in these, will he?"

"I will note them down, and he can advise on what we should do with them." I added them to the list whilst Martha rummaged through the remainder of the papers. I heard her exclaim again and looked up to see her pulling out a framed painting that was leaning behind the chest. It was a wedding portrait. The groom was seated with the bride standing behind him, her hand resting on the back of his chair. I peered at the picture closely.

"Is that Mrs. Groves?" I asked in amazement.

"Yes, ma'am. Didn't I say she was bonny once?"

The girl in the portrait was as far removed from the Beatrice I had known as an elephant was from a sparrow. Beatrice looked directly at the viewer with an intense, focused gaze. Her cheeks were smooth and plump, and her pale hair was piled high on top of her head. Her slim waist was highlighted by the elegant wedding gown. I stared at the picture for a long time, hardly able to comprehend that it could be the same woman, even with all the intervening years.

"I cannot believe it," I said.

Martha nodded sadly. "Aye. You can see why Tripp might have lost his foolish boy's heart to her."

"Do you remember her when she was like this?"

"A little. Mr. Groves died not long after I entered service here. But I'm sure I remember her laughing in those early days."

My eyes rested on Mr. Groves' face. It was a stern face, and the age difference between him and his bride was such that Beatrice could have been taken for his daughter. "What happened?" I wondered aloud.

"I don't think Mr. and Mrs. Groves was ever what you called sweet on each other. Old Mr. Groves had been a bachelor for most of his life, and then he married Mrs. Groves when she was ever so young. And brought her here to this place. Tripp says Mr. Groves weren't ever the sociable sort, just spent most of his time in the library and tramping over the moors. There weren't much to keep a young girl occupied. And they never had any children."

"But that letter I read, was that not from Mr. Groves?"

Martha coloured. "Oh, no, I don't think so, ma'am. But there was talk."

"Yes?"

"It was probably only gossip, but there was a story that Mrs. Groves had had a prior understanding with a young man before she married Mr. Groves." I raised my eyebrows. "It was said that the young man was deemed unsuitable, and her father was keen to see her married to someone swiftly."

I looked at Beatrice's youthful face. "I wonder what her young man was like. Would he have made her happy?"

"Who can say, ma'am? What a great sorrow it is that we can't revisit the past and know these things."

I gazed at Beatrice's pained eyes and felt a heavy weight of sadness settle on me.

"But when Mr. Groves died," I began tentatively, uncertain of how to word my thoughts.

Martha finished it for me. "You would've thought she might have had a new lease of life. After all, she was still under forty when he died. But she seemed to follow the example of Mr. Groves. She never had any visitors and rarely went beyond the gardens, when there were still gardens. She would go down to London once a year to see her solicitors and the rest of the time, she seemed to brood and grow more and more melancholy."

"Like being in prison," I said with a shiver.

"Aye. And one she had made for herself." Martha shook her head. "I've always said a long life is only a blessing when it is a life that is lived. And life is a gift from God, ain't it? Surely, it's a sin to squander it."

I was unable to reply. Beatrice's eyes seemed to stare miserably at me from the portrait, as if she was looking ahead to her own desolate future. Martha leaned the picture back against the chest with the faded, dusty letters and closed the lid.

"Let us continue," I croaked, impatient to be done with the task.

We worked steadily and by dinnertime, we had completed the inventory of the servants' quarters.

"D'you find anything interesting?" Eliza asked. She was holding the bowls as Martha ladled spoonfuls of soup into them.

"We found a wedding portrait of Mr. and Mrs. Groves," I said.

"Really? How did she look?"

Tripp shot an irritated glance at her and harrumphed loudly as he sliced some bread to go with his soup. "That ain't a decent question to ask. Those things is private."

"Can't be that private if she stuck them in the servants' attic," Eliza retorted.

"She looked very pretty," I said swiftly.

There was a silence as Martha finished serving the soup. "Will you say grace, ma'am?" she asked. We bowed our heads.

"For what we are about to receive, may the Lord make us truly thankful. Amen." We tucked into our soup in silence.

Eliza was the first to break it. "How long will it take you to finish the inventory?"

"I think if Martha can be spared from her work, then we should be able to complete it in another few days," I said.

"And then you will be leaving us?" Eliza said. She said it blandly, but the question struck me like a blow.

"Yes, I suppose so," I began and then made a conscious effort to pull myself together. "I had a letter from the Secretary of the Mission Society saying that they had secured lodgings on my behalf." I met Eliza's eyes briefly and then looked away.

"And you will be married in London?" asked Martha, smiling at me. I nodded, not trusting my voice. "And then India," Martha continued. "Why, it shall be so different, I can hardly imagine it. You will see so many new sights and meet so many new people. And doing God's work, too, you must be so excited."

"Indeed." I looked intently at my soup.

"And we'll be without a mistress whilst you're gone," said Eliza with a cheerfulness that sounded forced to my ears. "I'm looking forward to being a lady of leisure."

"You'll be no such thing," muttered Tripp.

"You and me is going to learn to dance, Mr. Tripp. We'll be waltzing round the stable yard before the week is out. We'll give Prospero a proper good show."

"Get away with you," said Tripp good-humouredly.

I said nothing else as the talk continued and excused myself as quickly as I could.

I had not intended to return to the servants' attic but my feet seemed to lead me there of their own accord. I pulled out the wedding portrait of Beatrice and her husband and stared at it for a long time. The light from the window faded as the dusk settled, and it had the effect of accentuating the sadness in the young Beatrice's painted features. What would she have done if she had been given the chance to go back? Could she have done anything differently? Could she have defied her father? I was lucky that my father had been such a good man who would never have forced me into a marriage I did not want.

If he was here now, and I told him I did not want to marry Daniel, what would he say? I knew the answer as surely as I knew my own name. He would tell me to think and pray and then to do as my conscience dictated.

I went over to the small window and looked out at the sweep of the moors still visible in the failing light. I prayed for a long time, until all I could see was darkness beyond the glass.

I didn't knock on Eliza's door but walked straight in. She was sitting on her bed, her hair unpinned and swirling about her shoulders. She was in her chemise with her shawl wrapped around her. She jumped as I entered and looked at me in horror.

"You can't be here," she whispered frantically. "What if Martha should see?"

"I don't care," I replied, coming to sit beside her on the bed.

"It's all right for you to not care," Eliza complained. "But I still have to live here. You may be off in India—"

"I'm not going to do it," I said.

Eliza frowned at me. "Not going to do what?"

I held her hands. "I'm not going to India. I can't." Eliza looked at me in silence, her eyes watchful and wary. I took a deep breath. "And I'm not going to marry Daniel." Eliza still said nothing, and I could see the conflict play out across her face. She was guarding herself against hope, against disappointment. I squeezed her hands. "I am in earnest, Eliza. I cannot marry a man I do not love. I never loved him. And now…now I love you."

Eliza said nothing for a long moment, her face entirely still. "Do you mean it?" she asked finally, "Do you really, *really* mean it?"

"As God is my witness. I will not marry him because I love you and only you."

Eliza's eyes widened, but that was the only outward sign she gave. "But I ain't got nothing to give you, Ruth. I got nothing. I *am* nothing. What kind of life could we have—"

"I don't care," I said. I held her face and rested my forehead against hers. "I don't care about any of that. I will be with you, and that's all that matters." I saw tears gathering at the corner of her eyes, and finally, her face creased into a joyful smile. I kissed her then and spent several long moments caressing her face and stroking her hair.

I could not contain myself and moved my hands under Eliza's chemise. Eliza gently caught hold of my wrist. "We can't, not here. This bed creaks something awful. You've got to go back to your own room."

"Will you come to me there?"

"Yes, I'll come in a little while."

"Do you promise?" I was anxious that what I had grasped might slip out of reach already.

Eliza put her arms around me. "I promise," she whispered against my ear.

I slipped out of Eliza's room and tiptoed along the corridor to the stairs back down to the main house. I entered my own chamber and made myself ready for bed. And then, as I had done so often, I lay in bed and stared up at the ceiling. But for the first time since arriving at Beulah Lodge, my heart was light. Eliza kept her promise.

CHAPTER TWENTY

M y heart was singing with happiness the next morning as I exchanged smiles with Eliza over breakfast. But Martha and I still had to plough on with the inventory, a task that grew ever more monotonous and depressing. We folded and catalogued every piece of motheaten clothing that we found in wardrobes and chests of drawers. I made a list of all the books in the library whilst Martha took out all the silver that was stored in the locked kitchen cupboard.

By an unspoken agreement, we left Beatrice's room until last. When we finally opened the door, it looked much as it had the last time I had seen it. It was only her empty chair that seemed to scream silently of her absence.

Martha began to take out her clothes from the wardrobe whilst I looked through the papers in her bureau. Most of them were old letters of business, to and from her solicitors or notes to tradesmen in the village. The majority were dated several years ago, proof of her declining interest in the estate. And stuffed at the back of one of the drawers was a pile of promissory notes made out to various establishments in London. I looked at the sums involved and knew that these were the gambling debts.

I bundled the official papers together and then leafed quickly through what remained. The knowledge that Beatrice would have hated me looking through her private papers spurred me on to complete the task as quickly as I could.

There was surprisingly little personal correspondence, and I read none of it closely. I simply placed it into a separate pile from the business letters. Beatrice's small copy of the New Testament and Psalms was in the final bureau drawer I looked in. I flicked through the pages and saw Beatrice's own notes and glosses crammed into the margins. As the pages fell open on Revelation, I saw one passage heavily underlined with countless notes added around it:

"They shall hunger no more, neither thirst anymore; neither shall the sun light on them, nor any heat. For the Lamb which is in the midst of the throne shall feed them, and shall lead them unto living fountains of waters: and God shall wipe away all tears from their eyes."

I closed the small book and placed it on the pile of personal letters. Despite all our endless theological discussions, both Beatrice and I wished ultimately for the same thing: to be with our Lord and Saviour.

I tied the two piles together with string and helped Martha sort the rest of the room.

We were finished a few days later, and I packaged up the inventory and the business papers into an envelope addressed to Mr. Chalcraft. I packed it into the corner of my trunk along with the few possessions that I had brought with me to Beulah Lodge.

I closed the lid and thought that it seemed a lifetime ago that I had come bumping across the moors from Thirsk with such high hopes for my stay. Beatrice had turned out to be the exact opposite of what I had hoped for. But then there was Eliza, whom I could never have hoped for because what had occurred between us would never have entered the mind of the woman who had stepped down from that coach all those months ago. I was a different person now.

Eliza came into my chamber as I was packing the last of my things, ready for departure the following day.

"Do you need any help?" she asked, sliding her arms around my waist.

"No, I don't have much to pack."

"How long will you be in London?"

"I'm not sure. Daniel may already be there, or perhaps I may need to wait for his arrival."

"It will be hard to be here without you," Eliza said, nuzzling my neck.

As I turned to face her, a sudden thought struck me. "Why don't you come with me?" I said.

Eliza blinked. "Come with you?" she repeated.

"Yes, why not?"

"But you will have to meet with Daniel—"

"You need not accompany me for that," I said hastily. "But I should like to have you with me the rest of the time. It would be hard to leave so soon now that we have..." I didn't yet have the words for what we had become, but Eliza nodded.

"I would like that," she said, smiling. "And I should like to see London again."

"That's settled then," I declared.

Martha looked relieved when I told her later that afternoon. "Oh yes, ma'am. I would feel so much better if you had someone to accompany you. Don't seem right for you to be in London alone, though I suppose once you are married, you will have your husband with you."

"Yes," I said, feeling my face redden. I felt unable to explain to Martha that I was not intending to marry after all. I reasoned that explanations on that subject could be left until later; "later" being a hazy point in the future that I could not yet envisage.

And so, the next morning, Eliza stood beside me as the coach that was to take us to the station drew up on the driveway.

Mr. Tripp bumped my trunk awkwardly down the stairs.

"Hope you ain't got any precious china in that trunk, Miss Mallowes," Eliza called as a puffing Tripp pulled it across the hall floor.

Martha elbowed her in the ribs. "Oh, let him alone Eliza. You must part on good terms."

"Yes, we must all part on good terms," I said, pulling on my gloves and looking sternly at Eliza. Tripp pulled the trunk out onto the front steps, and I was relieved to see the coachman hurry over and help him. I turned to Martha. "I will write to you once we are safely in London."

"Thank you. And..." Martha shuffled her feet awkwardly. "And if you did ever have the time, ma'am, to write us a brief note from

India and let us know how you and your husband fare, I'm sure we would all be glad to hear of it."

I held out my hand. "Good-bye, Martha. Thank you for all your kindness."

"And thank you for yours, ma'am. God bless you."

I pressed her hand quickly, feeling awkward that I could not reassure her that I had every intention of returning. I stepped toward the coach as Martha and Eliza said their farewells. My trunk had been loaded onto the luggage rack, and Mr. Tripp stood waiting by the open door. He met my eye as I approached. Was it my imagination, or had his face softened somewhat over the last few months?

I held out my hand to him. "Good-bye, Mr. Tripp," I said.

"Good-bye, ma'am," he said gruffly. "And thank you for all you have done." He held my hand in a strong grip.

"And thank you," I replied.

Mr. Tripp nodded gravely and helped me up into the carriage.

Eliza followed shortly behind me. "Ta-ra, Tripp," she called. "Hope you won't miss me too much."

Tripp muttered something into his whiskers about how he would enjoy the peace and quiet once she was gone but did lift his hand in farewell.

Eliza settled herself beside me, and we both turned to look through the carriage window as the squat block of Beulah Lodge receded into the distance.

I sat back against the seat and watched Eliza's face in profile as she gazed out at the house retreating from view. There was a suppressed excitement in her expression, and her eyes shone as she turned to me.

"We're going to London." she exclaimed.

It was late morning by the time the carriage pulled into Thirsk station. Porters came and took our luggage and showed us into our train compartment. It was pleasant to be able to stretch our legs after the cramped coach.

Our second-class carriage was full. Eliza and I settled in opposite each other in the middle of the compartment. At York, the rest of our travelling companions disembarked, and I settled back into my seat, removing my hat and unpinning my shawl.

"Are you excited at the prospect of being in London again?" I asked.

Eliza nodded vigorously. "It's been nigh on six years since I were last there. I s'pose lots must have changed. They was forever pulling buildings down and putting new ones up. But all the usual places will still be there, of course. St. Paul's, Tower Bridge, the Monument."

"Ah, yes, the Monument. I always meant to climb it but never got round to it."

"Oh, you should. You get amazing views of the city when it's a clear day." Her face creased into a sudden smile. "Me and Alice used to spit our cherry stones from off the top, see if we could land 'em on the gentlemen's hats below."

I laughed and noticed the other people in the carriage looking curiously at me. I settled down to read my Bible, and Eliza dozed off in the corner.

The afternoon shadows were lengthening over the pages of Revelation as we reached the outskirts of London. I had glanced up every now and then to note the landscape changing from the hills and dales of Yorkshire to the factory chimneys of the Black Country, the flat farmland of Buckinghamshire, and now to the suburbs of London itself.

I closed my Bible and looked out the window, watching the gardens that backed onto the railway line flow past. Eliza leaned forward too, her face lit up with anticipation.

"Almost there," she exclaimed. She kept up a running commentary as we drew closer to Euston. "I knew a Harry from Harrow once. Right bastard he was. Used to keep a flick knife in his boot. And I been to Bushey Park once. A young man called Charlie once bought me an ice cream there."

"Charlie?" I asked, smiling.

"Charlie," she said with a sigh. "He was the potboy from the Coach and Horses, and he was a bit sweet on me."

"Was he handsome?"

"Oh, he were beautiful. He had this fair, curling hair and a face as smooth as a girl's. Big blue eyes 'an all." She looked over at me and blushed.

"And did you let him kiss you?" I asked, teasing.

"We never got that far. I let him hold me hand, and he went so red in the face, I thought he would burst." She shook her head sadly. "He was a nice lad but far too kind."

"Can one be too kind?"

"Kindness ain't a virtue in London. It's a weakness. People will take you for a mug if you let them. And Charlie was the type to let them."

"What happened to him?"

"He got the sack from the Coach and Horses for some reason, dunno why. He was from the country originally, Norfolk, I think. I hope he found his way back there and ain't at the bottom of the Thames."

The buildings grew squatter and blacker as we came into Euston. We disembarked to the dense smoke and bustling crowds of the station. After the loneliness of the moors, the sheer volume of people around me took me aback. I could not understand where they had all come from.

A porter took our bags, and we made our way out to the taxi rank. We climbed into a Hansom, and I gave the address of our lodging house in Islington. The driver whipped up the horses, and we trotted though the traffic and crowds of Euston Road.

Eliza stuck her head out the window and drank in the scene, exclaiming at the familiar sights. She shouted questions up at the driver. "What happened to that chophouse that used to be round the back of King's Cross? And weren't there a church with a white tower used to be on this corner?"

The driver jovially shouted down answers, and we slowly left the throng of trams and carriages at the junction of Caledonian Road and made our way into the quieter streets of Barnsbury. Quieter by London standards, for to my eyes, the pavements still seemed unaccountably crowded.

Our lodging house was a genteel property on Thornhill Square. Its proximity to the tile kilns and factories on the Caledonian Road meant that its prices remained reasonable. I paid the driver as Eliza and a manservant took the luggage indoors.

The landlady, a Mrs. Dawson, greeted me and showed me to my rooms. There was a bedroom and small living room with a folding camp bed for Eliza. It was plain but comfortable. I paid Mrs. Dawson twenty shillings for a week's lodgings in advance.

Mrs. Dawson asked if I would be requiring supper that evening. Eliza, who was standing behind our landlady, shook her head vigorously and made a retching motion. I thanked Mrs. Dawson for her kindness but said that I would not require anything as I was exhausted by the journey and had little appetite. Mrs. Dawson looked relieved but said if there was anything I wanted, I should let her know.

"I'll nip out and get us some pies if you like," Eliza said, dragging the trunk into the bedroom and opening the lid.

"You do not trust Mrs. Dawson's cooking?"

"That and the expense. She'll charge you at least two shillings for some supper. I can get us a couple of pies for twopence, and I bet you anything they'll be tastier than whatever stringy chop she'll serve up." Eliza began lifting my clothes from the trunk and folding them carefully into the small chest of drawers at the end of the bed.

"It has been a long time since I bought something from a pie man," I said, recalling with a sudden, vivid nostalgia a winter's morning many years ago when I had held a steaming hot pie under my nose and inhaled its pastry scent. I was so transported by the memory that I didn't hear Eliza's question and had to ask her to repeat it.

"I was saying that I'll go out now and get them. There'll be loads going up and down the Cally Road at this time. Do you want to come with me?"

"No, thank you. I feel too weary and travel-stained. I will stay here and finish my unpacking."

After Eliza left, I lay down on the bed and closed my eyes. After the quiet that had always seemed to permeate Beulah Lodge, it felt as if a veritable cacophony of noise surrounded me. There was the creak of floorboards overhead as someone moved about above me and the slamming of doors from somewhere else within the house. From outside came the distant toots from the train line, dogs barking, and voices raised on the street below.

After resting for a while, I rose and unpacked the rest of my trunk, fretting about what I would say to Daniel when we finally met again. How on earth could I find the words to explain? I could hardly tell him that I had fallen in love with a servant girl. Would he be angry and refuse to accept whatever explanation I gave him? What if he somehow found out about Eliza and I? Would he make a scandal and ruin any chance I might have of living some kind of life together with Eliza?

My thoughts ran around in unending circles, and I became aware that it had grown dark and that Eliza had been gone for almost two hours.

And now fresh worry overtook me, and I paced the sitting room, formulating plans for what I should do if she didn't return. Should I go out and look for her on the Caledonian Road? Summon a policeman and report her missing? But then a terrible thought struck me. What if she had deserted me? Perhaps she had come to her senses and realised that we were doomed, that we could never live together openly. Perhaps being back in London had somehow broken the spell of Beulah Lodge, and she had simply decided that she was better off on her own.

My nerves were so worn that I jumped almost a foot in the air when the door opened, and Eliza appeared clutching two pies in a page of newspaper.

"Sorry about the wait," she began.

"Where have you been?" I snapped.

She looked at me in surprise. "I got talking to a bloke on the way, and it turned out he knew Lil."

"Who on earth is Lil?"

"She were the barmaid at the King's Head. Anyway, we got talking, and then we nipped into the pub for a jar."

"Oh, so you have been drinking?"

"Only a small one."

"And you did not spare a thought for me all this time?"

She frowned and looked genuinely perplexed. "What do you mean? You said you weren't that hungry."

"I have been here worrying about you and what might have happened to you. I only expected you to be gone for half an hour or so."

"But London is my patch, Ruth. You know I wouldn't have come to any harm."

The tension and the nerves of the last few hours got the better of me and I burst out, "I don't know that at all. I was worried sick. You could have spared a thought for me whilst you were gadding about in the pub like a…" I stopped myself, but it was too late. Eliza's face darkened.

"Like a what?" she demanded furiously.

I bit my lip and said nothing. Eliza adopted a mincing parody of my voice and said, "You seem to have acquired a most unfortunate habit of not finishing your sentences. Madam." The sarcasm that she poured into that final word made me wince, but I was still too angry to make amends.

I held out my hand. "Just give me the pie, would you?"

Eliza thrust it into my hand and then turned and left without another word, slamming the door so hard that the frame shook.

The pie tasted of nothing in particular, but I could not tell if that was due to the quality of the baking or because of the argument with Eliza. After I had eaten, I undressed and got into bed and allowed myself to weep unrestrainedly for a while.

A few days ago, I had declared that I would abandon my engagement for Eliza's sake, and now I had allowed a stupid quarrel to drive her away. When my tears had finally ceased, I sat up in bed and read my Bible for a while, listening out all the while for the door to open and Eliza to return. As the evening wore on, I heard the sounds of the other residents returning, some of them clearly the worse for wear for drink. One of them even attempted the chorus of "Champagne Charlie" before being shushed by a giggling companion.

Their sounds of merriment only deepened my gloom. I heard the clock in the hall strike midnight and resigned myself to having to sleep and see if Eliza returned in the morning. I prayed fervently that she would, that I had not ruined our future before it had even begun. I turned out the lamp and settled myself on my pillow.

I must have fallen asleep almost instantly. The next thing I was aware of was of a coldness on my back, followed by a warm presence sidling up to me.

"Ruth?" Eliza's voice whispered in my ear. "Are you awake?"

"Yes," I mumbled, turning over onto my back. There was enough light from the street lamps coming through the curtains for me to see the outline of Eliza's face in the darkness. I could smell a lingering scent of alcohol on her breath, but I had learnt my lesson from earlier and said nothing.

"I'm sorry," Eliza whispered. "I shouldn't have left you for so long."

"I'm sorry, too," I said. "I had no right to be angry with you. And thank you for the pie." There was a pause, and then I said, "Where did you go?"

"I had an idea that I would walk down to the river."

"To the river?"

"Yes, though I didn't make it that far. I only got as far as Clerkenwell."

"And then?"

"Then I had a few in the Butcher's Arms. And then sat on the steps of St. James's for a while, watching the tramps settling themselves for the night." I felt a cold fear seize me at the thought of her alone at night in such a place, but I held my tongue. "That could've so easily been me," Eliza continued. "I've spent enough nights under the arches to know what that kind of life is like. No one lasts long." She was silent, and I listened to her breathing beside me. "I thought I would feel like I was home coming back to London."

"Does it not feel like home?"

"In some ways it does, with all the familiar sights and sounds. But I reckon I've been gone too long. Now it just feels a bit overcrowded and smelly."

"I know what you mean. I have lived my whole life in London, and yet after only a few months away from it, I find myself yearning for the moors."

"Yes," Eliza cried, raising herself on her elbow to look down on me. "I keep thinking about how you could take a lungful of air up there without taking in half a pound of coal dust at the same time."

"And how you can hear the birds."

"I know. I ain't seen no birds since we arrived 'cept a couple of dirty looking crows picking over a dead cat."

"Perhaps you have become a Yorkshire lass?" I teased.

Eliza sighed heavily and lay back down beside me. "Nah, I ain't one of them. Never will be. But now, I don't feel like I'm a Londoner neither. I dunno what I am."

Her words echoed within me. I too had felt cut adrift, as I cast aside the future that had for so long seemed set in stone.

"You are yourself," I said, wanting to anchor us both.

Eliza was silent for a long time. So long that I felt my eyes begin to grow heavy again.

"I don't know myself anymore," she said quietly. "So much has happened since I left London. I ain't the same person now."

I reached out and took her hand. She squeezed it, and after a moment she turned toward me in the bed and planted a hesitant kiss on my cheek.

I understood what the hesitancy meant, and I reached up and kissed her on the lips to show that all was forgiven. And then I kept kissing her, and then I rolled my body over on top of hers and allowed my hands to make amends.

CHAPTER TWENTY-ONE

The next morning, I had the novelty of waking up to find Eliza still slumbering beside me. I revelled in the newness of this and spent some time watching her sleeping face, smooth and beautiful on the pillow. After a while, I rose, threw on my dressing gown and slippers, and slipped quietly from our rooms to the lavatory.

When I returned, Eliza was stirring. She smiled sleepily at me from the pillow and looked about her as if she had forgotten where she was.

"Good morning," I said.

Eliza sat bolt upright and began to hastily throw the covers off. "You should've woken me. I'll get the fire going and the tea."

I sat on the bed beside her and placed a restraining hand on her leg. "Do not trouble yourself," I murmured, leaning in to kiss her warm, sleepy lips. I fell back onto the bed beside her, unable to tear my mouth from hers. Eliza raised her hips to push against my own, and we found ourselves repeating our lovemaking from the night before.

Later, as we lay entangled in the sheets, I said, "I don't want you to call me ma'am anymore. In public, if you must, but not when we are alone. And you are not to wait on me anymore, either. We are to be as equals."

Eliza mumbled her agreement as she trailed kisses along my neck.

I knew that our blissful cocoon could not last all morning, and by nine o'clock, we were both dressed and breakfasted. It was lucky that we were, for shortly after, there was a knock at the door, and

Mrs. Dawson's adolescent son handed me a telegram. It was a brief message from Daniel saying he had heard of my arrival and would call for me at my lodgings that afternoon.

I gave the boy a penny and sat in the armchair as he left.

"What is it?" Eliza asked, her face creased with concern.

"Daniel is coming here. This afternoon."

"Oh. That's very quick."

"Yes." I bit my lip. I had not expected that the encounter with Daniel would occur so soon.

"Do you know what you will say to him?" Eliza asked gently.

"No. I mean, yes, I know what I must say. But how I shall say it, I do not know." I stared at the faded whirl of flowers on the carpet, my mind whirring uselessly.

"Come on," Eliza said briskly. "Let's go for a walk. You was always going for walks at Beulah Lodge when you needed to think, so let's do the same here. Course, it won't be quite the same."

"I think we are unlikely to see a plover."

"True. But we may see a pigeon that still has all its toes. Imagine that."

I smiled and allowed her to bustle me into my hat and coat and out of the house.

Eliza insisted that it was necessary to look at the river in order to think, and so we walked down Gray's Inn Road and Chancery Lane, crossed over the choking bustle of Fleet Street, and thence through the quiet courtyards of the Middle Temple until we were on the Embankment. We strolled along in the morning sunshine, and I could almost have forgotten that in a few hours, I would need to break my engagement.

Once we passed under Waterloo Bridge, we paused for a rest, taking a seat on one of the benches facing the river. We watched the multitude of small steam tugs, barges, and rowboats hurrying across the dark water.

"All right," said Eliza, withdrawing her tobacco pouch. "You have a ponder about what you're going to say to him. You want a smoke to help you think?" I had not attempted to smoke again since that one occasion in the kitchen and declined her offer. Eliza rolled a cigarette and struck a match.

We sat in silence for a few minutes, watching the endless stream of boats passing back and forth before us.

"So many journeys beginning and ending," I murmured, half to myself.

"I'd go to Norway," Eliza said.

"What?"

"Thinking about journeys and that. If I could go anywhere in the world, I'd go to Norway."

"Why?"

"I met a Norwegian called Jack once. Least, that's what he said his name was. And he said they got snow there so deep and so white that it was like God covered the world in fresh white bedsheets every morning."

"'Though your sins be as scarlet they shall be as white as snow,'" I said.

"Exactly. All that snow, like a fresh start every day." She dragged on her cigarette and asked, "Where would you go? If you could go anywhere?"

"The Holy Land," I said after some thought. "I would dearly love to walk in the same places where our Saviour walked, to see some of the same sights that He would have seen."

"P'raps we can go there together someday," Eliza said.

I did not reply. I had spent so long imagining myself travelling to India, picturing what life would be like there that I now struggled to think of a different path, a different future. I was not a person who thrived on uncertainty. The plan of my life and future had been upended, and I was struggling to adapt to the ambiguity of my situation.

I allowed my hand to rest next to Eliza's on the bench and brushed my fingers against her. I took a deep breath and focused my mind on the task before me, how I would explain all this to Daniel.

When Eliza and I finally left the Embankment sometime later, I felt that I had an idea of what I would say to Daniel. All of this was forgotten as soon as we returned to our lodgings, and Mrs. Dawson's boy informed us that a gentleman was waiting for us in our sitting room.

I froze, completely incapable of speaking. Eliza thanked the boy, who shuffled off, darting a curious glance at me. We stood in the dingy hallway, and Eliza looked earnestly into my face.

"All right?" she asked.

"No. But I will have to be." I threw a glance up at the stairs, steeling myself.

"I'd best make myself scarce. I'll come back in an hour or so."

I squeezed her hand. "Do you promise?"

Eliza glanced quickly around the hallway to confirm we were alone and then cupped my face in her hands. "Of course," she said. "I promise."

I nodded and began slowly to make my way up the stairs. I heard the front door click as Eliza let herself out.

I opened the door to our rooms, and Daniel rose from the armchair where he was seated. I felt the shock of seeing him again as if I had been struck. I noted at once the change in his appearance. He was thinner, and his skin was tanned. He stood with his hands clasped behind his back and inclined his head to me gravely as I entered.

"Ruth. I am very glad to see you." Nothing in his tone or manner gave any indication of gladness, but I knew that Daniel was a man who weighed his words carefully. If he said he was glad, then he was.

"And I am pleased to see you safely returned." I held out my hand to him, and he took it, grasping it firmly. I asked him to be seated and took the other chair before him. I enquired if he desired any refreshment, and he declined.

"We have much to discuss," he began.

"Yes, indeed," I said and took a deep breath, preparing myself to say the words that I knew would cause him pain.

"The first thing to arrange is our marriage ceremony. I have spoken to Mr. Westcott. You may recall he was a friend of mine from theological college."

"Yes, I remember. But—"

"He has agreed to perform the ceremony, and his parish church is in Holborn, which would suit our needs perfectly. We will need witnesses, of course. I trust you did not travel to London alone?"

"No, I was accompanied by Eliza. From Beulah Lodge. But Daniel—"

"Excellent. She may act as witness tomorrow, and perhaps Mr. Griffin from the Missionary Society may act as the other."

"Tomorrow?" I exclaimed with an irrational flash of irritation. I had no intention of marrying him tomorrow but still felt annoyed that he had arranged it all so hastily.

Daniel looked at me in mild surprise. "Yes. I see no point in delaying the ceremony."

"Daniel, I—"

"For once we are married, we may start back to India immediately. There is a steamer that leaves in a week's time. That may give us time to dispose of any business relating to your late aunt." He paused. "My condolences." It was so obviously an afterthought that I grimaced.

"Thank you," I said, distractedly. "But I must tell—"

"If there should be further matters to arrange, I think there is no reason why these could not be managed by correspondence from India. It is vital that we return there with all speed. There is much work to be done, so many souls to be brought to Christ. With a wife at my side, I shall have greater respect amongst the natives. The accommodation is somewhat basic, but you will no doubt—"

"Daniel!" He stopped and raised his eyebrows at me. "I cannot marry you," I said. It was louder and brusquer than I had intended because I did not want him to interrupt me again.

He looked at me for a moment in silence, his pale grey eyes resting thoughtfully on my face. I returned his gaze steadily, determined that he should not doubt my sincerity.

"It does not have to be tomorrow," he said finally, bowing his head to emphasise his concession. "There would be no harm done if the ceremony were to take place later this week. I'm sure Westcott could—"

"No," I said, taking my turn to interrupt him. "I mean, I cannot marry you at all."

He sat back in his chair. "We cannot complete our missionary work unless we are married," he said with the air of one explaining to a child why they had to put their shoes on.

"I will not be undertaking missionary work." In all my imaginings of this conversation, I had been gentle and kind, but now I wished to be as blunt as possible so that he would understand.

"But it is God's will."

"For you perhaps, but not for me."

Daniel stood abruptly and walked to the window, his hands held behind his back. I waited, giving some time for my words to sink in. Daniel turned back to face me. "I understand that the death of your aunt must have come as a grave shock, especially considering the circumstances of her death. If you require more time in England to settle things, then by all means, you may have it."

"You have always been kind to me, Daniel. Especially after my father died and I will always be grateful to you for that. But I do not love you in the way a wife should love a husband. It would be wrong of me to marry you, and I cannot do it."

Daniel turned back to the window and said, without looking round, "Marriage is a union of souls, Ruth. It is not reliant on mere earthly passions." There was nothing "mere" about them, I thought to myself.

"I cannot speak any plainer, Daniel. I cannot and will not marry you."

He turned around then and looked at me. "You gave your promise not only to me but to your late father."

"And I never intended to break that promise. But things have changed since then. I have changed."

Daniel's eyes narrowed almost imperceptibly. "Have you formed an attachment that has prompted this change of mind?"

My heart thumped almost painfully within my chest. "Yes," I said. "And I would not have wished to cause you pain. But I am also glad, for if it had not happened, I might have married you, and we would both have been desperately unhappy."

Daniel said nothing for a long while. I gazed at the stiff set of his back and waited. He was not a man governed by his passions, so I had not expected a violent scene. But this silent waiting was almost worse. Eventually, he turned to face me again.

"When was this attachment formed?" he asked, his voice as hard as granite.

I knew at once what he was getting at. "After I had accepted your proposal. When I did so, I fully intended to keep my promise, but I cannot do so now. I am sorry."

"Who is this man who would pursue a woman already promised to another?" Daniel asked with the first hint of anger he had shown.

"There was no pursuit on either side. It happened naturally."

"Naturally? How can it be natural to cause a woman to break her promise? I ask again, who is this man?"

"I am not obliged to tell you anything more," I retorted, feeling my own temper beginning to rise. I had not wanted to hurt Daniel, but I had been rankled by his manner ever since he had started speaking. And I was convinced that his anger arose not because he was losing me but because he perceived that I had been stolen from him.

I took the engagement ring off my finger and placed it on the small table by the fireplace. Daniel followed the gesture with his eyes.

"I disagree," he said coldly. "I think you are very much obliged to tell me who this man is." When I said nothing, he asked, "Will you marry him?"

"I don't know."

"Ah. Because he is married already?" Daniel said it with such a sneer in his voice that it was all I could do to keep my composure.

"I have nothing further to say on the matter," I said, my voice shaking. I stood, hoping that this might hasten his departure. He looked at me with such disdain that I felt a chill pass through me.

"God commands us to keep our promises," said Daniel, in the manner he adopted for his sermons. "Your father would be ashamed of you." I felt at that moment like St. Paul must have felt as the scales fell from his eyes. I saw, as if for the first time, the vast gulf between the man my father had been and the man Daniel was.

"No," I said, calmly. "He would be ashamed of me if I entered into a marriage whilst being in love with someone else. Such a thing would be self-evidently wrong to him. As it is to me." I picked up the ring from the table and held it out. "Please take this. It is yours."

We looked at each other in silence for a long moment. Finally, Daniel took the ring and placed it in his pocket. I breathed a sigh of relief.

"Very well," he said curtly. "I see you are determined to cause a scandal."

I almost laughed. "I fear we are not grand enough to cause a scandal."

"The mission in India will be greatly disrupted," he said reproachfully. "I had counted on having a helpmeet."

"I am sure you will find a worthier companion for your work," I said blandly.

Daniel harrumphed and smoothed down his waistcoat. "I have many matters to see to. I suppose I should thank you for your candour..." He trailed off.

I made a conscious effort to recall how I had leaned on him in the days after Papa's death and said, "There is no need. It was the very least I owed you. I shall never forget your support after my father died. And I will pray for you and the success of your mission."

Daniel picked up his hat from the table, no hint of emotion visible on his face. "I will take my leave. I intend to return to India at once and have much to attend to." He paused and then held out his hand to me. "It is possible that we will not see each other again."

I took his hand and pressed it. "It is in God's hands." Daniel nodded and went to the door. He paused a moment and looked back at me. And then he shook his head as if trying to clear an unwelcome thought, and then he was gone.

I listened to his steps down the stairs and heard the front door close after him.

I sat in the armchair for a long time, my mind wandering back over the memories of the time when Daniel had first come into my life, and he, I, and my father had all lived together. Although I had no regrets at breaking my engagement, I was sad that a link to my father had been severed. A great weariness came over me, and I rose from the chair and went to lie upon the bed.

I had no recollection of falling asleep, but I must have done, for when I awoke, it was getting dark outside. I felt headachy and disorientated. I rose groggily from the bed and went into the sitting room. Eliza was standing by the window, gazing out at the street.

"What time is it?" I asked.

"About six o'clock, I think."

I poured myself a glass of water from the washstand and walked over to the window to stand beside Eliza. She jerked her chin at the street outside. "Look at that," she said.

I looked but could see nothing. There were a few pedestrians walking up and down and a young woman standing under a lamppost opposite. "At what?"

"Her. Under the lamppost."

I looked again but could see nothing remarkable about her. Her clothes proclaimed that she was not a lady, but aside from that, I could deduce nothing further. "What about her?"

Eliza looked at me hard. I looked again at the girl, and it finally dawned on me. I had taken her for a street seller but could now see that she had nothing with her that she was obviously selling. As a gentleman walked past, the girl spoke to him, but he ignored her.

"Oh," I said, quietly. "I see."

"She's picked a poor spot. This neighbourhood ain't the place for that."

"Then why is she here?"

"Maybe something happened in her usual patch. She's got some bruising on her neck."

I looked again and saw that she was right. And I noticed other things. "She is very thin."

Eliza nodded, grimly. "She is. And pale. I'd bet you a guinea that she won't be seeing Christmas this year."

I gaped at her, appalled. "You can't possibly know that."

"She looks like she's dead on her feet already. And it'll be winter soon."

I looked at the girl, my own problems at once forgotten. "How old is she?"

"About fifteen, I reckon. Maybe younger."

I turned aside from the window and rummaged in my purse. I gave the small change left in it to Eliza. "Go and give that to her," I said. Eliza looked at the coins in her hand. "I know it's not much, but it's something."

Eliza went out, and in a few minutes, I saw her approach the girl and hand the coins to her. The girl nodded her thanks briefly. Eliza paused and spoke to her for a few moments, but the girl made it clear that she did not wish to talk and moved off.

As Eliza came back into the room I said, "How long will that last her?"

"Not long."

I sank into the armchair and rubbed my eyes.

"How did it go?" Eliza asked, coming to kneel beside me.

"As well as could be hoped, I think. There were no ugly scenes. Daniel accepted it all with remarkably good grace."

"And you? How do you feel 'bout it?"

"I am relieved that it is done. And also, a bit sad," I confessed. "Daniel was someone I could share memories of my father with. But it seems of little consequence compared to what that poor girl faces."

Eliza squeezed my hand and sighed. "I s'pose I'd better go and see Mrs. Dawson about some supper," she said.

CHAPTER TWENTY-TWO

I awoke the following morning and remembered at once that I was no longer an engaged woman. I lay still and listened to Eliza's steady breathing beside me. What did the future now hold for me? I had spent so long with the course clearly mapped, and now I felt directionless. Almost without thinking, I reached out and laid a hand on Eliza's hip.

After breakfast, we set off for the offices of Beatrice's solicitors. I had made an appointment for ten o'clock and had been all for hailing a cab, but Eliza had scoffed and said it would take us a mere half hour to walk to Chancery Lane. So we picked our way slowly down Caledonian Road and through some of the quieter streets that ran parallel to Gray's Inn Road.

We talked as we went. Eliza had a seemingly endless series of stories involving people she had known, all with monikers that described either their profession or their appearance. Thus, there were tales of Mick the Milk and Baldy Susan.

A few times, I ventured to ask where they were now, but Eliza would only shrug and say, "God knows. And maybe even He don't."

It was a quarter to ten when we arrived outside a door on Chancery Lane where a brass plaque informed us that Chalcraft and Sons were located on the third floor. I rang the bell, and we were admitted by a boy who looked to be no older than sixteen, with a morning coat that was shiny at the elbows.

He showed us to Mr. Chalcraft's door. As he was about to knock, he glanced suspiciously at Eliza, who winked at him. Mr. Chalcraft bade him enter, and he showed us in, saying "Miss Mallowes to see you, sir."

Mr. Chalcraft rose from behind his immense mahogany desk and came to shake my hand. He was a tall, thin man with a keen pair of grey eyes that looked out from under beetling grey brows.

"A pleasure to see you, dear Miss Mallowes," he said warmly. "That will be all," he said to the lad, who withdrew, closing the door behind him.

Mr. Chalcraft waved us to two padded chairs seated in front of his desk. He showed no surprise at Eliza's presence and merely glanced at her occasionally with a vaguely puzzled expression.

"My condolences on your loss," he said, folding his long fingers together.

"Thank you, Mr. Chalcraft."

"I have Mrs. Groves's will here, which she lodged with us some years ago. You have no objection to my reading it to you?"

"None at all."

"It will not take long." Mr. Chalcraft withdrew a document from a thick envelope on his desk. There was a lot of legal preamble, and I did my best to concentrate, but I found my mind wandering back to my conversations with Beatrice and if she had ever imagined this moment. I was brought back to myself by Mr. Chalcraft saying, "And so it really is quite simple. The estate and all the vessels, et cetera, were left to your mother, and in the event of her pre-deceasing Mrs. Groves, they were to pass to her issue. As you have no siblings, you are the sole heir to Mrs. Groves's estate." I blinked at him. "Does this come as a surprise?"

It had never occurred to me that Beatrice would have remembered my mother in her will. But even if she had no regard for my mother or for me, who else did she have?

"Is there any mention of the servants in the will?" I asked to cover my confusion.

"No. There are no bequests or anything of that nature." How like Beatrice, I thought grimly.

I withdrew the papers from my pocket and handed them to Mr. Chalcraft. "Here is the inventory of all the contents of the house and the summary of the finances prepared by the estate steward."

Mr. Chalcraft ran a practiced eye down the inventory. "Nothing particularly out of the ordinary, it seems. Though rather a lot of theological tomes," he observed, turning over the leaf of paper that covered the library. He took up the summary of the finances that Mr. Tripp had prepared and studied this in silence for some minutes, his brows drawn tightly together.

"The finances are not in a healthy state," he remarked disapprovingly.

"That is unfortunately the case."

"There seem to have been considerable outlays made in the last few years." Mr. Chalcraft looked questioningly at me.

"Yes. They were payments for…that is, Mrs. Groves incurred—"

"Gambling debts," said Eliza bluntly. Mr. Chalcraft raised his eyebrows.

"I'm afraid so," I said.

Mr. Chalcraft sighed with the air of someone who had seen too much to be surprised at the depths of human foolishness. "Most unfortunate."

"What will happen next, Mr. Chalcraft?"

He placed the papers on his desk. "The inventory, plus the valuation of the house and the estate will be put before the court of probate. And then probate should be granted in due course. As executor, I can then settle any outstanding debts and then distribute the assets to the beneficiaries. Meaning that the house, its contents, and the estate shall belong to you."

"And I may then do with it as I wish?"

"Of course. Though I would advise you that the estate is not, in its present condition, a profitable venture."

"But it could be made so, with sufficient investment of time and effort?"

A ghost of a smile seemed to play about Mr. Chalcraft's lips before it was swiftly vanquished. "It has always been my belief, dear lady, that there is nothing that cannot be achieved if only the necessary amount of time and effort is expended," he replied gravely.

I stood and shook his hand. "Thank you for all your help."

He inclined his head graciously. "I would say that I look forward to our next meeting, but as my profession is not one which features in the joyous moments of life, I will simply wish you all the best for your endeavours, whatever they may be."

Indeed, I thought as we took our leave of him. Whatever they might be.

We stood on the pavement outside Chalcraft & Sons, and Eliza replaced her battered straw hat on her head. "Well, then," she said. "That's that."

"Yes." I watched the bustling street with a feeling of disconnection, as if I wasn't quite anchored to the world anymore.

"Back to Mrs. Dawson's, is it?" Eliza asked.

"No," I said. "I need to think. Somewhere quiet." I looked around the bustle of Chancery Lane.

"What 'bout the abbey? That ain't far from here."

"Yes. That will do." I set off at once in the direction of the Strand, feeling an urgent need to escape the pressing crowds and traffic and noise.

I set a brisk pace, and in half an hour, we were standing before the gothic splendour of Westminster Abbey. I paid our sixpences to the robed official on the door, and I walked slowly down the nave, gazing up at the great vaulting arches and ceiling. I stopped in front of the great stained-glass window of the nave, with its depictions of the twelve tribes of Israel. I gradually became aware of Eliza fidgeting beside me. I turned my head to look at her.

"I might take a turn round by myself," she said. "Leave you to have a think." I smiled gratefully at her, and she moved off down the nave.

The vastness of the abbey made me feel very small indeed. Of what significance was I in God's eyes? I would very soon be the owner of Beulah Lodge, a place I had hated for some of the time I was there. What on earth was I to do with it? I did not know the first thing about managing an estate and grand house. My attempts to help Mr. Tripp seemed small and vaguely pathetic set against the enormity of the estate's financial problems.

What if I sold the estate? I winced, imagining the looks on all their faces if I were to tell them that. And even so, what then? What was I to do with myself now? How would Eliza and I be able to have a life together?

I worried at these thoughts over and over until I exhausted myself. The stained-glass window was not going to give me any answers. I turned from the window and wandered the length of the nave. I passed through the quire and past the high altar, looking about me to try to find Eliza. I passed the tombs of all the medieval kings and queens and climbed the small flight of steps into the Lady Chapel.

I finally spotted Eliza standing before the tomb of Elizabeth I. I stopped for a moment and observed her profile. She was frowning intently at the inscription written in gold on the black plaque above the tomb. I felt my heart lighten at the mere sight of her.

As I stood there, a man approached Eliza from the other side and stood beside her for a moment. Eliza turned, and he inclined his head toward her, speaking to her so softly that I could not hear. I saw Eliza tense and shake her head. The man continued to speak and placed a hand on her elbow.

It was not a particularly violent gesture, but it was proprietary, as if he had every right to touch her. And it filled me with a swift, sudden rage. I walked quickly over to them and said loudly, "Ah, there you are."

They both turned to look at me, Eliza with relief and the man with an irritated look. He was around fifty, with light hair that was turning grey at the temples. He looked supremely calm and unruffled, which annoyed me even more.

"A friend of yours?" he asked Eliza.

"Who are you, sir?" I snapped coldly.

He tried a charming smile on me, but seeing my face, he abandoned the attempt. "I was merely engaging the young lady in conversation."

"Your conversation is at an end. Please leave us."

"Certainly," he murmured and raised his hat to us. "Ladies." He looked significantly at Eliza as he said the last word, and she flushed.

I clenched my fists as he walked away. "Of all the sly, deceitful—"

Eliza laid a calming hand on my arm. "It's only a gentleman trying his luck. It's common enough."

"In Westminster Abbey?" I asked incredulously.

"Men like him don't get put off by the thought of God watching." Eliza turned back to Queen Elizabeth's tomb. "I was trying to read the inscription but couldn't make head nor tail of it."

I glanced up at the plaque. "It's in Latin," I said.

Eliza's face cleared. "Oh. That makes me feel better. I was thinking that I was so dense that I had already forgotten everything you taught me."

I smiled and linked my arm with hers. The hushed sounds of footsteps and voices echoed around us, but we were alone in the chapel.

"You done your thinking?" Eliza asked.

"Yes. But I don't know that it did me much good." I felt weary, and as ever, Eliza seemed to know exactly what I was feeling.

"Look, let's get you home, eh?"

"Home," I repeated quietly, painfully aware that I did not know where my home was anymore.

"Back to our lodgings, I mean." Without another word, Eliza took my arm and steered me out of the abbey. Once outside, she flagged down a Hansom, and we were soon back in Islington. I paid the driver and went upstairs to our rooms whilst Eliza sought out Mrs. Dawson.

After an indifferent luncheon, we sat in the armchairs by the fireplace. Eliza was frowning over a newspaper, and I tried to read my Bible. But I could not concentrate. I got up and stood by the window. The girl from the previous evening was no longer standing in the street. I watched the pedestrians and the odd hawker ambling back and forth.

"What's this word?" Eliza asked.

I looked over her shoulder. "Specious."

"And what's that mean?"

"Misleading. Something that sounds good but actually isn't."

"Hmm." Eliza frowned for some moments and then read slowly, "'Mr. Gladstone accused Mr. Disraeli of presenting specious arguments to the house.'"

"Someone is always accusing someone else of something," I said wearily.

"Are you all right, Ruth?"

I turned and looked out the window again. "I don't know what I'm doing," I said.

"About what?"

"About everything. What am I to do with Beulah Lodge?"

"Live in it, I s'pose."

"Oh, Eliza, it's not as simple as that."

"Ain't it?"

"The estate is on the verge of bankruptcy. And I know nothing of estate management."

"I didn't know nothing about birds till I came to Beulah Lodge. And I didn't know how to read. But I do now. Cos I learnt."

"There is so much to running the estate that I have not the least idea about."

"That's what Tripp's for, ain't it? And he'll have to let you know what's going on now you're the mistress." She looked at me with complete assurance.

I twisted my fingers together. "But what if I fail? If the estate goes bankrupt, then you will all be without a position or a place to live."

"You ain't gonna gamble the money away like Beatrice did. You'll try your best, I know you will. And if you do that, and it still goes pear-shaped? Then you ain't got nothing to reproach yourself with."

"I wish I had your faith."

"What's the worst that could happen? Even if the estate goes under, we still ain't likely to end up like that poor girl on the street last night."

I looked at my clasped hands. "You must think me very silly."

Eliza rose and came to stand by me. She took my hands in hers and bent her head to look up into my face. "I think you very lovely," she said. She took my face and raised my eyes to hers. "You don't got to have all the answers. We'll figure it out as we go along." She put her arms around me and hugged me tightly. I relaxed against her, enjoying the feeling of safety and reassurance provided by her embrace.

CHAPTER TWENTY-THREE

I awoke early the next day. I lay in bed and stared at the ceiling. I remembered the ceiling of my room at Beulah Lodge. I had spent so long gazing at it that I could recall it in almost perfect detail. Did my future now lie in that house? I tried to picture what daily life there would be like, but I could not. Beatrice's presence would surely haunt the place. How was it possible I could be happy there?

Eliza stirred and rolled over toward me, snaking her arm about my waist. "Are you still worrying?" she mumbled.

"Yes. Sorry."

"You don't have to be sorry." She nuzzled my neck. "We don't have to go back up north straight away. So let's go out and see the sights today. Take your mind off things."

"Yes," I said thoughtfully, "that's a good idea. I would like to go and visit my father's old church in Poplar."

"Course," Eliza murmured contentedly. "Whatever you want." She kissed my neck, sending delicious tremors down through my body. I turned toward her and kissed her warm, sleepy lips.

It was some time later when our cab pulled up on Poplar High Street. The crowds and smells were oppressive, and I found myself longing for the tors and fresh air of the moors around Beulah Lodge.

I knew, of course, that there would be a new incumbent and a new family in the rectory. But as I took Eliza's hand and stepped down from the cab, the sight of the old familiar church rendered me momentarily speechless.

I stood on the pavement and gazed up at the tall, elegant spire that reached into the blue sky. It had been less than a year since I had last stood here, but it felt as if a lifetime had passed. I walked up to the heavy wooden door and lifted the latch.

The interior was dim and cool, with the smell of incense lingering on the air. I walked down the aisle, past the rows of pews, until I stood before the plain wooden pulpit where my father had preached every Sunday. I could almost see him there, in his characteristic preaching pose, clutching both sides of the pulpit.

I heard Eliza's step and she came to stand beside me. "This where your father preached his sermons?"

"Yes. He was usually the most mild-mannered of men, but when he was preaching, he was passionate and fiery."

"Fiery?"

"Yes, but not in a hell and damnation kind of way."

"I didn't think he could have been a fire and brimstone preacher. Cos you ain't like that."

"I never thought that fear of Hell was the message Jesus sought to bring us."

I looked at the light from the stained-glass window bleeding its colours across the tiled floor. My gaze travelled up to the plaque beside the pulpit where the names of past rectors and their dates of service were inscribed. I read my father's name with a shock: *Henry George Mallowes 1848–1871*. It seemed impossible that the years of memories had been reduced to mere words and dates on a plaque.

I sat down heavily on the nearest pew. Eliza looked at my face and said, quietly, "I can wait for you outside."

"You are constantly loitering elsewhere on my behalf," I said.

"Don't you worry about me. Loitering is my speciality. You take your time." She squeezed my hand, and her footsteps echoed back up the aisle, and then, with a creak of the door, she was gone.

I sat and listened to the silence thickening inside the church. I felt the presence of my father in this building so forcefully that he could have been sitting beside me. I gazed at the crucifix on the high altar and thought of all the years of devoted service that my father had given to his parishioners and to the destitute and desperate of London. As the jewelled light on the floor shifted with the passing clouds, I prayed that God would grant me just a small part of the strength and determination of my father.

I looked up into the pulpit where Papa had preached and promised him that I would continue with everything he had believed in: to relieving the suffering of the poor and making the love of God manifest. Although I might no longer be a missionary in India, I would further the mission of God wherever I was. *"Not my will but thine be done."*

I waited in the silence. The song of a blackbird came to me from outside the window, sudden and sweet. I stood and took one last, lingering look at that dear, familiar church. And then I walked back outside and joined Eliza.

We took a cab from Poplar to the Monument. Eliza was insistent that we could not leave London without climbing to the very top.

"Only three hundred and eleven steps," she said cheerfully as I paid the entrance fee at the base. She began ascending, and I followed her up the narrow spiral staircase.

Talk was impossible, and so I focused instead on the steady placing of my feet on each step. I held my skirts up to avoid tripping and kept my eyes on the stairs in front of me. I developed a rhythm as we climbed steadily higher and higher, my breathing and my steps aligned together. I became unaware of everything around me as my world narrowed to the placing of my feet and the intake of my breath. All the thoughts and feelings of the past few hours and days receded into the far distance.

It felt as if the climb lasted for hours, but in reality, it could not have been more than ten minutes, and then I was in the open air, the wind lifting the strands of hair from beneath my hat. Eliza was already ahead of me, her cheeks pink from the exertion of the climb.

"Not a bad view, eh?"

I nodded, too out of breath to reply. The river lay close by like a streak of silver running through the city. It was crowded with boats of every description, mimicking the traffic crowding the streets far below us. The people swarmed along like tiny black insects whilst the sky above them was a brilliant blue.

I took a deep breath. The air was clearer up here, and my heartbeat began to return to normal.

"Nothing seems so bad when you're up here, does it?" Eliza was leaning against the stonework, the wind blowing her dark hair back from her face.

"No," I agreed. "Everything down there seems insignificant."

There were two young men finishing their sightseeing. They tipped their hats to us as they went back through the narrow doorway and began their descent. And then Eliza and I were alone, high above the city.

I leant back against the wall alongside her, and we both looked out over the river at the city sprawling eastward alongside it toward the docks.

"So much has happened in the last few months. I can scarcely take it in," I said.

"I know. You think things is set, that the path is clear, and then something happens, and everything goes topsy-turvy." Eliza paused and then added, "And sometimes you can't tell if it's for the best or not."

"I always believed that God had a plan for me. That He had a path laid out for me and that I could discern it if only I prayed and listened hard enough for His voice. I thought His plan for me lay in India. That it was my destiny to support Daniel in his mission."

"You get to decide your own destiny now. You could do whatever you want."

"But I need to know what God wants me to do."

Eliza made an impatient noise. "Can't what you and He want be the same thing? Or does serving God always mean having to do something that makes you miserable?" Her voice had an edge to it.

I didn't answer immediately but turned to look back out at the seemingly limitless spread of London. "Things have changed so fast," I said, quietly, "that I am lagging behind."

Eliza bit her lip in a way that I knew would presage her hunting for her tobacco pouch. "I'm just...scared." She said the last word so quietly that it was almost swept away on the wind.

I looked at her in surprise. "You? Scared?"

"Yes! Of you deciding that you gotta go and do something else and—" She waved a hand toward the sky. "And leaving me."

I could see the fear, then, written clear across her face, and I took her hands and brought my face close to hers. "I will not leave you," I said. "I promise." I kissed her then, the wind blowing her hair across my face. A sudden noise made us leap apart, but it was only a pigeon landing on the ledge above us. We both laughed with relief, and some of the fear left Eliza's face.

Though she was not fully reassured because she said, "So what will you do? Will you make your home at Beulah Lodge?"

"Yes, I suppose so."

Eliza rolled out a cigarette on the balustrade and drew her matches out. "You don't sound very excited by the prospect. But then it is the arse end of nowhere, I s'pose." She struck a match and cupped her hands carefully around the flame to light her cigarette. "But maybe God's calling you up there for a reason. To help what's-his-face who can't pay his rent."

"Curran."

"That's the one. He ain't got it as bad as the poor sods in the slums here, but then you can't take all the urchins of London back with you, can you?"

"No," I said.

Eliza smoked her cigarette, and I stood beside her, looking out toward the slums of the East End and imagining all the human misery that was contained within them.

We made our way back to our lodgings later than afternoon. Our route took us past St. Paul's cathedral, and we stopped for a moment in the square. Pigeons gathered hopefully around our feet, but Eliza shook her head at them.

"Sorry, ladies and gents. Ain't got nothing for you." I stood beside her and gazed up at the great dome of the cathedral. Eliza nodded at it. "You been inside?"

"Yes, a few times. Have you?"

She shook her head. "Nah. Too grand for me."

"That is how I felt." Eliza raised her eyebrows at me. "It is full of marble statues and tombs to the great and the good. It is very much their cathedral. I think the presence of God can be felt much more strongly in a humble parish church." A smile tugged at the corners of Eliza's mouth. "Oh, I know you think I am only one down from a duchess. But if not for an accident of birth, our positions could have been reversed, you know."

Eliza laughed. "Good thing they weren't. I can't see me being any good as a vicar's daughter." She became more serious for a moment. "And I wouldn't wish my lousy beginning on anyone. Especially not you."

I allowed my fingers to brush against hers for a moment. "I would give anything to have been able to spare you that…somehow."

"We got Beatrice to thank for everything, you know. We would never have met if it weren't for her. We could have spent our whole lives in London, and our paths might never have crossed."

I looked up again at the dome and sent a vote of thanks upward to Beatrice.

We continued onward. Eliza assured me that she knew a shortcut, and her route took us through the Clerkenwell slums.

I had been to the slums many times before. The narrow, crowded streets of Whitechapel and Bethnal Green were familiar to me. But there was still a sense of shock at seeing the rows of dilapidated housing, their bricks blackened with coal smoke, looking as if they were leaning against each other for precarious support. There were numerous dark alleyways and doorways, all of which contained people who moved around like shadows, even in the late afternoon sun. It was the women who caught my eye in particular. Their dark rimmed eyes and pallid faces stared at us as we passed.

I looked at Eliza and could see from her face that she was struck by the sight too.

"Blimey," she muttered. "You forget what it's like, don'tcha?" I nodded in silent agreement. There was a stench of decay everywhere, and the thin cries of children added to the general atmosphere of misery. No wonder that preaching hellfire had so little impact here. The people were already living in a kind of hell.

As we turned onto the main road leading up to Angel, I was surprised to see a pair of well-dressed young men with top hats and canes strolling along on the other side of the street. One of them held a handkerchief to his nose, but aside from that, they looked for all the world as if they were taking a Sunday afternoon stroll. Eliza followed the direction of my gaze and snorted.

"Slummers. Here for their afternoon pleasure." Her voice was laden with contempt. One of the gentlemen saw me staring and raised his eyebrows suggestively. I looked quickly away and was relieved when they had passed.

"The pleasure here is cheap," Eliza remarked. "And they can't get it in polite drawing rooms."

I stopped and looked back after them. They had stopped and were talking to a painfully thin girl huddled in a doorway. She had a ragged shawl wrapped around her and nodded at the men with a blank, dead-eyed expression. Then she stood and disappeared with them down a side street.

Eliza shook her head sadly. "Hope they give her a decent sum, at least."

I turned to her. "That was you once, wasn't it?" She flushed, and I added, "I knew that was what happened to you, but it is different seeing it in the flesh."

"Yes," she said quietly. "That would've been me not so long ago. And Beatrice took me away from all that." She bit her lip. "She did that for me. No matter what she done after."

We continued the walk back to our lodgings in silence, but there was no quiet within me. I was enraged by what I had seen. Even though I knew such things happened, it seemed especially monstrous that this could be allowed to exist on the streets of London, only a stone's throw from houses of ease and luxury.

Chapter Twenty-four

A seed had been planted that day at the top of the Monument, and it continued to grow all the next day as I finished up my business in London.

I wrote a letter to Mr. Tripp, informing him that my plans had changed and giving him notice that Eliza and I would be returning to Beulah Lodge shortly. I then included a brief note to Martha, saying how much we were both looking forward to her beef stew.

On our final afternoon in London, I took a stroll with Eliza into Bloomsbury. I had a very specific destination in mind, and as we entered the shop, I smiled at Eliza's puzzled face.

"What we doing here?" she asked.

I indicated the rows of paints, brushes and easels.

"This is where artists come to purchase their supplies," I said. "You could do with a proper sketchbook and pencils."

Eliza waved her hand, dismissively. "I don't need any of that stuff. I ain't Michelangelo."

I stepped closer to her and murmured quietly, "It is usual to buy gifts for your sweetheart, is it not?" Eliza looked at me, her eyes widening. "I would like to give you something to show how much I love you. Think of it as a kind of engagement gift. But of more use to you than a ring would be."

"Engagement? Do you really mean that?" she asked, keeping her voice equally low.

"With all my heart."

Eliza's face creased into an enormous, delighted grin, and it was all I could do to keep myself from flinging my arms around her neck.

"All right," she said. "I suppose in that case…" She gazed around the shop, her face shining with wonder. "But it might take me a while. Will you mind?"

"No, my love. Take all the time you want."

The next morning, we took our leave of Mrs. Dawson, and before long, we were back on a train heading northward.

Eliza's face was positively aglow as the fields and towns flowed past. After a short while, she took out her new sketchbook and pencils and was absorbed in her drawing, her tongue protruding slightly from the corner of her mouth. I sat back in my seat and thought further on the seed that had been planted in my mind at the top of the Monument.

We had just pulled out of Sheffield, and our fellow travellers had left the compartment, leaving Eliza and I alone. As the blackened factory chimneys receded into the distance, I said, "We could, you know."

Eliza looked up from her sketching. "You what?"

"What you said about the urchins of London."

"What did I say about them?"

"You said we couldn't bring them all to Beulah Lodge."

"Did I? Well, that's true enough." She turned back to her paper.

"I don't think so."

Eliza looked up at me again. "What are you talking about?"

"You said that if you had stayed in London, you would be dead by now."

"Reckon I would be."

"And you said Beatrice saved your life by bringing you to Beulah Lodge."

"Yes, she did."

I leaned forward eagerly. "So why don't we do the same? Take girls from off the streets and bring them to Beulah Lodge?"

"Girls from London?"

"Yes. Or from Manchester or Sheffield or anywhere."

"You want to turn Beulah Lodge into a workhouse?" Eliza asked incredulously.

"No, not a workhouse. I mean, sort of, but with kindness. And education."

"What sort of education?"

"We could teach reading and writing, for starters. And then there is so much work to be done in the house and on the estate that it would provide training in all sorts of things. Cooking, housekeeping, gardening, sewing, bookkeeping."

Eliza held up her hand. "You keep saying 'we.'"

"Of course. We would do it together."

"Along with Martha? And Tripp?"

"Martha's heart overflows with kindness. And Tripp, well, I think we must give Mr. Tripp a chance before we presume to say what is in his heart."

"If he don't like it, he can sling his hook. You're the mistress now, after all."

"So you approve of our plan?"

"Our plan, is it?"

"It was you who gave me the idea."

Eliza was silent for a moment, but before long, a smile spread over her face. "I do. I like it very much."

"Good." I leaned forward and risked a brief kiss on her cheek, feeling an excitement for the future that I had not felt in years.

Tripp had engaged a trap to meet us at Thirsk and take us the last leg of the journey to Beulah Lodge. As we rattled along the lanes over the moors, I found my excitement and expectation building. I was longing for the first glimpse of the house, a house that had seemed so unprepossessing when I had first spied it in the rain nearly a year ago but that now held out the promise of hope and change.

As its squat, grey shape came into view over the crest of a hill, my face stretched into a grin. Opposite me, Eliza's face mirrored my feelings, and we beamed at each other.

As the trap pulled into the driveway, I could see two figures waiting for us in front of the house. We came to a stop, and Martha ran forward, smiling broadly. "Oh, ma'am," she exclaimed, as Mr. Tripp stepped forward to offer his hand to me. "We are so pleased to have you back. Although"—her face sobered as if someone had drawn a curtain against the sunlight—"I am sorry to hear that you and your fiancé, that things couldn't—"

"Indeed," I said, sparing her any further embarrassment. "It was most unfortunate but very necessary. It would not have been a happy marriage for either of us."

"Marry in haste, regret at leisure. That's what my old mum used to say," said Martha. She turned to Eliza, who had been directing the driver where to place our bags. "Eliza. I hope you have taken good care of the mistress." She affected a stern gaze, but no one was fooled.

"Course I have. I showed her all the best pubs in town, ain't that right…ma'am?" She stumbled slightly over ma'am, having now acquired the habit of addressing me by my Christian name, but Martha did not seem to notice.

"You han't lost any of your cheek, I see," she said with mock haughtiness.

"And how do you do, Mr. Tripp?" I asked, turning to him.

"Very well, thank you, ma'am," he said stiffly. "My condolences on your…on the ending of your engagement." I thanked him, and then Martha bustled us into the house, insisting that I must be tired and in need of refreshment.

She showed me into the dining room and then gave Eliza instructions to make my room ready for me. I watched Eliza leave to go and make the necessary preparations and felt a stab of misgiving. It would be hard to adjust back to our mistress and servant roles after our sojourn in London.

Seized with a sudden conviction that if I did not establish this now, I would lose the chance forever, I said to Martha, "Actually, I would prefer to take my refreshment in the kitchen, as we did previously."

"Oh, but that was different, ma'am. You're the mistress of Beulah Lodge, and it wouldn't be right."

"It is wasteful to heat an entire room merely for me," I said firmly. "And besides, I would really much rather eat in the kitchen."

"But, ma'am, whatever would people say?"

"What people, Martha?"

"The tradesmen and the people in the village."

"I do not care a fig for what they may say. And in any case, they are used to strange goings-on at Beulah Lodge. I do not intend to disappoint them on that score."

Martha looked doubtful but dutifully led me down to the kitchen and set a place for me at the table. Eliza came down a little while later and looked pleasantly surprised to see me sitting there. She took a seat beside me and surreptitiously squeezed my hand under the table. Mr. Tripp came in shortly afterward. He started at the sight of Eliza and me sitting and eating together at the table and threw a questioning glance at Martha.

"Mistress insisted," Martha said, bending down to the range to check on her rock cakes. Tripp stood for a moment, and I could see a variety of emotions cross his stony, rugged face. Something seemed to win out, and he took his seat on the opposite side of the table.

"As you wish, ma'am," he said. I nodded at him, saying nothing but feeling that this was a significant step forward.

"You've turned Mr. Tripp proper topsy-turvy," Eliza told me later that evening, unpinning my hair for me as I sat at my dressing table.

"What do you mean?" I asked, closing my eyes as Eliza began the soothing motion of brushing my hair out.

"I mean that he ain't got a face like a smacked arse no more. You've softened him up."

"You can tell?"

"Oh, yes. Watching Tripp is like watching the moors. At first glance, all you can see is bleakness, and you think there can't be nothing alive there. But once you get used to reading the signs…" She trailed off as I laughed.

"Poor Tripp," I said. "I hope I have softened him. We all deserve some modicum of happiness."

Eliza finished brushing my hair. Her hands grazed my neck as she arranged my tresses down my back, and I felt a tremor pass through me.

She rested her hands on my shoulders, and our eyes met in the mirror. "You must be tired," she said.

I reached my hands up to hers and then turned to face her. "I am not that tired," I said, my voice thick.

I saw the familiar darkening of Eliza's eyes. She bent to kiss me, and I kissed her back with a ferocity that took me by surprise.

I stood and drew Eliza over to the bed, pulling impatiently at her clothes. We dispensed with them as quickly as we could and lay naked together on the bed.

Eliza reached between my legs, but I was determined that I should touch her first. I caught hold of her wrist and pinned it to the bed. I pushed my free hand against her wetness, and she cried out softly as I entered her. I moved my hand rapidly within her, releasing my hold on her wrist. She gasped and clutched at my shoulders as my rhythm increased, pushing, pushing, pushing until she fell over the edge, her back arching off the bed as her sex shuddered around my fingers.

I stayed resting within her as our breathing returned to normal.

"I've missed this," Eliza said, her dark hair fanned out across the pillow. "Us, being together here."

I withdrew gently from her and laid my head on her breast. "So have I. Which is why I was so insistent."

Eliza laughed. "That's one word for it. Ruth." She said my name thoughtfully, as if she was trying out the sound of it. She rolled over and reached for a folded-up piece of paper on the bedside table. She sat up and handed it to me with a shy smile.

"What's this?" I asked as I opened it up. It was a drawing of me, in three-quarter view, with my chin resting on my hand as my eyes focused off to the side. "Did you draw this in the train?" I asked and Eliza nodded. "You have made me very pretty."

"That's how you look to me," Eliza said. My face warmed with pleasure, and then my eyes drifted down the drawing. At the bottom, in a neat hand, was written, "To my darling Ruth, from your own Eliza." I could see the care and concentration that had gone into every stroke, and my throat tightened.

Eliza leaned forward, her face looking up into mine. "My Ruth," she said with just a hint of a question.

I cupped her face. "Yes," I said. "Yours."

She smiled such a pure smile of joy and happiness that I had to kiss her again. And again. And then this time, when she reached for me, I eased into her touch like a boat settling in its berth.

About the Author

Cathy lives in the UK with her wife and daughter. She writes stories at every opportunity, usually whilst fending off her cat's attempts to contribute. When not writing, she enjoys being outside in all kinds of weather—cycling, walking, and playing sports.

Books Available from Bold Strokes Books

A Convenient Arrangement by Aurora Rey and Jaime Clevenger. Cuffing season has come for lesbians, and for Jess Archer and Cody Dawson, their convenient arrangement becomes anything but. (978-1-63555-818-0)

An Alaskan Wedding by Nance Sparks. The last thing either Andrea or Riley expects is to bump into the one who broke her heart fifteen years ago, but when they meet at the welcome party, their feelings come rushing back. (978-1-63679-053-4)

Beulah Lodge by Cathy Dunnell. It's 1874, and newly engaged Ruth Mallowes is set on marriage and life as a missionary...until she falls in love with the housemaid at Beulah Lodge. (978-1-63679-007-7)

Gia's Gems by Toni Logan. When Lindsey Speyer discovers that popular travel columnist Gia Williams is a complete fake and threatens to expose her, blackmail has never been so sexy. (978-1-63555-917-0)

Holiday Wishes & Mistletoe Kisses by M. Ullrich. Four holidays, four couples, four chances to make their wishes come true. (978-1-63555-760-2)

Love By Proxy by Dena Blake. Tess has a secret crush on her best friend, Sophie, so the last thing she wants is to help Sophie fall in love with someone else, but how can she stand in the way of her happiness? (978-1-63555-973-6)

Loyalty, Love, & Vermouth by Eric Peterson. A comic valentine to a gay man's family of choice, including the ones with cold noses and four paws. (978-1-63555-997-2)

Marry Me by Melissa Brayden. Allison Hale attempts to plan the wedding of the century to a man who could save her family's business, if only she wasn't falling for her wedding planner, Megan Kinkaid. (978-1-63555-932-3)

Pathway to Love by Radclyffe. Courtney Valentine is looking for a woman exactly like Ben—smart, sexy, and not in the market for anything serious. All she has to do is convince Ben that sex-without-strings is the perfect pathway to pleasure. (978-1-63679-110-4)

Sweet Surprise by Jenny Frame. Flora and Mac never thought they'd ever see each other again, but when Mac opens up her barber shop right next to Flora's sweet shop, their connection comes roaring back. (978-1-63679-001-5)

The Edge of Yesterday by CJ Birch. Easton Gray is sent from the future to save humanity from technological disaster. When she's forced to target the woman she's falling in love with, can Easton do what's needed to save humanity? (978-1-63679-025-1)

The Scout and the Scoundrel by Barbara Ann Wright. With unexpected danger surrounding them, Zara and Roni are stuck between duty and survival, with little room for exploring their feelings, especially love. (978-1-63555-978-1)

Bury Me in Shadows by Greg Herren. College student Jake Chapman is forced to spend the summer at his dying grandmother's home and soon finds danger from long-buried family secrets. (978-1-63555-993-4)

Can't Leave Love by Kimberly Cooper Griffin. Sophia and Pru have no intention of falling in love, but sometimes love happens when and where you least expect it. (978-1-636790041-1)

Free Fall at Angel Creek by Julie Tizard. Detective Dee Rawlings and aircraft accident investigator Dr. River Dawson use conflicting methods to find answers when a plane goes missing, while overcoming surprising threats, and discovering an unlikely chance at love. (978-1-63555-884-5)

Love's Compromise by Cass Sellars. For Piper Holthaus and Brook Myers, will professional dreams and past baggage stop two hearts from realizing they are meant for each other? (978-1-63555-942-2)

Not All a Dream by Sophia Kell Hagin. Hester has lost the woman she loved and the world has descended into relentless dark and cold. But giving up will have to wait when she stumbles upon people who help her survive. (978-1-63679-067-1)

Protecting the Lady by Amanda Radley. If Eve Webb had known she'd be protecting royalty, she'd never have taken the job as bodyguard, but as the threat to Lady Katherine's life draws closer, she'll do whatever it takes to save her, and may just lose her heart in the process. (978-1-63679-003-9)

The Secrets of Willowra by Kadyan. A family saga of three women, their homestead called Willowra in the Australian outback, and the secrets that link them all. (978-1-63679-064-0)

Trial by Fire by Carsen Taite. When prosecutor Lennox Roy and public defender Wren Bishop become fierce adversaries in a headline-grabbing arson case, their attraction ignites a passion that leads them both to question their assumptions about the law, the truth, and each other. (978-1-63555-860-9)

Turbulent Waves by Ali Vali. Kai Merlin and Vivien Palmer plan their future together as hostile forces make their own plans to destroy what they have, as well as all those they love. (978-1-63679-011-4)

Unbreakable by Cari Hunter. When Dr. Grace Kendal is forced at gunpoint to help an injured woman, she is dragged into a nightmare where nothing is quite as it seems, and their lives aren't the only ones on the line. (978-1-63555-961-3)

Veterinary Surgeon by Nancy Wheelton. When dangerous drugs are stolen from the veterinary clinic, Mitch investigates and Kay becomes a suspect. As pride and professions clash, love seems impossible. (978-1-63679-043-5)

A Different Man by Andrew L. Huerta. This diverse collection of stories chronicling the challenges of gay life at various ages shines a light on the progress made and the progress still to come. (978-1-63555-977-4)

All That Remains by Sheri Lewis Wohl. Johnnie and Shantel might have to risk their lives—and their love—to stop a werewolf intent on killing. (978-1-63555-949-1)

Beginner's Bet by Fiona Riley. Phenom luxury Realtor Ellison Gamble has everything, except a family to share it with, so when a mix-up brings youthful Katie Crawford into her life, she bets the house on love. (978-1-63555-733-6)

Dangerous Without You by Lexus Grey. Throughout their senior year in high school, Aspen, Remington, Denna, and Raleigh face challenges in life and romance that they never expect. (978-1-63555-947-7)

Desiring More by Raven Sky. In this collection of steamy stories, a rich variety of lovers find themselves desiring more, more from a lover, more from themselves, and more from life. (978-1-63679-037-4)

Jordan's Kiss by Nanisi Barrett D'Arnuck. After losing everything in a fire, Jordan Phelps joins a small lounge band and meets pianist Morgan Sparks, who lights another blaze, this time in Jordan's heart. (978-1-63555-980-4)

Late City Summer by Jeanette Bears. Forced together for her wedding, Emily Stanton and Kate Alessi navigate their lingering passion for one another against the backdrop of New York City and World War II, and a summer romance they left behind. (978-1-63555-968-2)

Love and Lotus Blossoms by Anne Shade. On her path to self-acceptance and true passion, Janesse will risk everything—and possibly everyone—she loves. (978-1-63555-985-9)

Love in the Limelight by Ashley Moore. Marion Hargreaves, the finest actress of her generation, and Jessica Carmichael, the world's biggest pop star, rediscover each other twenty years after an ill-fated affair. (978-1-63679-051-0)

Suspecting Her by Mary P. Burns. Complications ensue when Erin O'Connor falls for top real estate saleswoman Catherine Williams while investigating racism in the real estate industry; the fallout could end their chance at happiness. (978-1-63555-960-6)

Two Winters by Lauren Emily Whalen. A modern YA retelling of Shakespeare's *The Winter's Tale* about birth, death, Catholic school, improv comedy, and the healing nature of time. (978-1-63679-019-0)

Busy Ain't the Half of It by Frederick Smith and Chaz Lamar Cruz. Elijah and Justin seek happily-ever-afters in LA, but are they too busy to notice happiness when it's there? (978-1-63555-944-6)

Calumet by Ali Vali. Jaxon Lavigne and Iris Long had a forbidden small-town romance that didn't last, and the consequences of that love will be uncovered fifteen years later at their high school reunion. (978-1-63555-900-2)

Her Countess to Cherish by Jane Walsh. London Society's material girl realizes there is more to life than diamonds when she falls in love with a non-binary bluestocking. (978-1-63555-902-6)

Hot Days, Heated Nights by Renee Roman. When Cole and Lee meet, instant attraction quickly flares into uncontrollable passion, but their connection might be short lived as Lee's identity is tied to her life in the city. (978-1-63555-888-3)

Never Be the Same by MA Binfield. Casey meets Olivia and sparks fly in this opposites attract romance that proves love can be found in the unlikeliest places. (978-1-63555-938-5)

Quiet Village by Eden Darry. Something not quite human is stalking Collie and her niece, and she'll be forced to work with undercover reporter Emily Lassiter if they want to get out of Hyam alive. (978-1-63555-898-2)

Shaken or Stirred by Georgia Beers. Bar owner Julia Martini and home health aide Savannah McNally attempt to weather the storms brought on by a mysterious blogger trashing the bar, family feuds they knew nothing about, and way too much advice from way too many relatives. (978-1-63555-928-6)

The Fiend in the Fog by Jess Faraday. Can four people on different trajectories work together to save the vulnerable residents of East London from the terrifying fiend in the fog before it's too late? (978-1-63555-514-1)

The Marriage Masquerade by Toni Logan. A no strings attached marriage scheme to inherit a Maui B&B uncovers unexpected attractions and a dark family secret. (978-1-63555-914-9)

Flight SQA016 by Amanda Radley. Fastidious airline passenger Olivia Lewis is used to things being a certain way. When her routine is changed by a new, attractive member of the staff, sparks fly. (978-1-63679-045-9)

Home Is Where the Heart Is by Jenny Frame. Can Archie make the countryside her home and give Ash the fairytale romance she desires? Or will the countryside and small village life all be too much for her? (978-1-63555-922-4)

Moving Forward by PJ Trebelhorn. The last person Shelby Ryan expects to be attracted to is Iris Calhoun, the sister of the man who killed her wife four years and three thousand miles ago. (978-1-63555-953-8)

Poison Pen by Jean Copeland. Debut author Kendra Blake is finally living her best life until a nasty book review and exposed secrets threaten her promising new romance with aspiring journalist Alison Chatterley. (978-1-63555-849-4)

Seasons for Change by KC Richardson. Love, laughter, and trust develop for Shawn and Morgan throughout the changing seasons of Lake Tahoe. (978-1-63555-882-1)

Summer Lovin' by Julie Cannon. Three different women, three exotic locations, one unforgettable summer. What do you think will happen? (978-1-63555-920-0)

Unbridled by D. Jackson Leigh. A visit to a local stable turns into more than riding lessons between a novel writer and an equestrian with a taste for power play. (978-1-63555-847-0)

VIP by Jackie D. In a town where relationships are forged and shattered by perception, sometimes even love can't change who you really are. (978-1-63555-908-8)

Yearning by Gun Brooke. The sleepy town of Dennamore has an irresistible pull on those who've moved away. The mystery Darian Benson and Samantha Pike uncover will change them forever, but the love they find along the way just might be the key to saving themselves. (978-1-63555-757-2)